NMC/RF

'An extraordinary writer'   Clive Barker

'A constant delight of precise images . . . Harrison writes with tremendous panache'   *Independent*

'*Nova Swing* is something different, it is space jazz. Not only state-of-the-art noir SF, but a cunning cryptogram of a novel as well'
                                                            Times Literary Supplement

'There are moments of high science fiction action, beautifully sustained by Harrison'   *Guardian*

'*Nova Swing* is chilling, enigmatic, often darkly funny and beautifully written'   *SFX*

'It reads like mainstream fiction soaked in noir. Coloured by longing and wonder, *Nova Swing* is filled with a humanity that makes it as substantial as it is dazzling'   *Time Out*

NOVA SWING

M. John Harrison

The right of M. John Harrison to be identified as the author of
this work has been asserted by him in accordance with the
Copyright, Designs and Patents Act 1988.

First published in Great Britain in 2006
by Gollancz
An imprint of the Orion Publishing Group
Orion House, 5 Upper St Martin's Lane, London WC2H 9EA
An Hachette UK Company

This edition published in Great Britain in 2013 by Gollancz

1 3 5 7 9 10 8 6 4 2

A CIP catalogue record for this book
is available from the British Library

ISBN 978 0 575 07969 4

Typeset by Deltatype Ltd, Birkenhead, Merseyside
Printed in Great Britain by CPI Group (UK) Ltd,
Croydon, CRO 4YY

The Orion Publishing Group's policy is to use papers
that are natural, renewable and recyclable products and
made from wood grown in sustainable forests. The logging
and manufacturing processes are expected to conform to
the environmental regulations of the country of origin.

www.ambientehotel.wordpress.com
www.orionbooks.co.uk
www.gollancz.co.uk

To Lara, Julian and Dan

'The further into the Zone the nearer to Heaven.'
Boris & Arkady Strugatsky, *Roadside Picnic*

'Nostalgia and science fiction are spookily close.'
A. A. Gill, *Sunday Times*

'Our lives are more like fragmentary dreams than the enactment of conscious selves.'
John Gray, *Straw Dogs*

ONE

The Bar on Straint Street

Vic Serotonin sat in a bar on Straint Street, just outside the aureole of the Saudade event, in conversation with a fat man from another planet who called himself Antoyne. They had been playing dice all night. It was just before dawn, and a brown light, polished but dim at the same time, crept out the street lamps to fill the place.

'I was never in there,' the fat man admitted, meaning the event site, 'but what I think—'

'If this is going to be bullshit, Antoyne,' Serotonin advised him, 'don't even start.'

The fat man looked hurt.

'Have another drink,' Vic said.

The bar was about halfway down Straint, a cluttered, narrowish street of two-storey buildings, along which two out of three had their windows boarded up. Like all the streets in that part of Saudade, Straint was full of cats, especially at dawn and dusk, when they went in and out of the event site. As if in acknowledgement, the bar was called Black Cat White Cat. It featured a zinc counter slightly too high for comfort. A row of bottles which contained liquids of unlikely colours. A few tables. The long window steamed up easily, no one but Antoyne cared. In the morning the bar smelled of last night's garlic. Some mornings it smelled of mould too, as if something had crept out of the event aureole in the dark and, after a few attempts to breathe the air in the bar, died underneath a corner table. Shadow operators hung high up in the

1

join between the walls and the ceiling, like cobwebs. There wasn't much for them to do.

Vic – short for Vico, a name popular on Scienza Nuova where he was born – was in the bar most days. He ate there. He ran his business out of it. He used it as a mail drop, and as a place to check out his clients: but really it was what they called a jump-off joint, positioned well, not too far back from the event site, not so close as to suffer effects. Another advantage it had: Vic was on good terms with the owner, a woman called Liv Hula who never put in a manager but ran it herself day and night. People thought she was the barkeep, that suited her. She wasn't known to complain. She was one of those women who draw in on themselves after their fortieth year, short, thin, with brush-cut grey hair, a couple of smart tattoos on her muscular forearms, an expression as if she was always thinking of something else. She had music in the bar. Her taste ran to the outcaste beats and saltwater dub you heard a few years back.

'Hey,' she told Vic now, 'leave the fat man alone. Everyone's entitled to an opinion.'

Serotonin stared at her. 'I won't even answer that.'

'Bad night, Vic?'

'You should know. You were there.'

She poured him a shot of Black Heart rum, along with whatever the fat man was having. 'I would say you were out there on your own, Vic,' she said. 'Much of the time.' They both laughed. Then she looked over his shoulder at the open door of the bar and said:

'Maybe you got a customer here.'

The woman who stood there was a little too tall to wear the high heels in fashion then. She had long thin hands, and that way of looking both anxious and tranquil a lot of those tourist women have. There was a tentativeness about her. She was elegant and awkward at the same time. If she knew how to wear clothes, perhaps that

2

was a learned thing, or perhaps it was a talent she had never fully brought out in herself. You thought instantly she had lost her way. When she came into the bar that morning, she was wearing a black two-piece with a little fitted jacket and calf-length kick-pleat skirt, under a long, honey-coloured fur coat. She stood there uncertainly in the doorway, with the cold light from Straint Street behind her, and the unflattering light from the window falling across one side of her face, and the first words anyone heard her say were, 'Excuse me, I—'

At the sound of her voice, the shadow operators unfolded themselves and streamed towards her from every corner of the room, to whirl about her head like ghosts, bats, scrap paper, smoke, or old women clasping antique lockets of hair. They recognised privilege when they saw it.

'My dear,' they whispered. 'What beautiful hands.'

'Is there anything we can do—'

'—Can we do anything, dear?'

'What lovely, lovely hands!'

Liv Hula looked amused. 'They never talk like that for me,' she admitted to the woman in the fur coat. Then she had a sudden vision of her own life as hard-won, dug out raw from nothing much even the few times it seemed to swoop or soar.

'You came for Vic, he's over there,' she said.

She always pointed him out. After that she washed her hands of whatever happened. This time Vic was waiting. He was low on work, it was a slow year though you wouldn't guess that from the number of ships clustered in the tourist port. Vic accounted himself intelligent and determined; women, on the other hand, saw him as weak, conflicted, and, reading this as a failed attempt to feminise himself, attractive. He had been caning it for weeks with Fat Antoyne and Liv Hula, but he still looked younger than his age. He stood there with his hands in his pockets, and the woman leaned towards him as if he was the only way she could get her bearings in the room. The closer she approached him the more uncertain she seemed. Like most of them, she wasn't sure how to broach things.

'I want you to take me in there,' she said eventually.

Vic laid his finger on his lips. He could have wished for some statement less bald. 'Not so loud,' he suggested.

'I'm sorry.'

He shrugged and said, 'No problem.'

'We're all friends here,' Liv Hula said.

Vic gave Liv a look, which he then turned into a smile.

The woman smiled too. 'Into the event site,' she said, as if there might be any doubt about it. Her face was smooth and tight across longings Vic didn't quite understand. She looked away from him as she spoke. He should have thought more about that. Instead, he ushered her to a table, where they talked for five minutes in low voices. Nothing was easier, he told her, than what she wanted. Though the risk had to be understood, and you underrated at your peril the seriousness of things in there. He would be a fool not to make that clear. He would be irresponsible, he said. Money changed hands. After a time they got up and left the bar.

'Just another sucker on the teat,' Liv Hula said, loud enough to pause him in the doorway.

Antoyne claimed to have flown navigator with Chinese Ed. He passed the days with his elbows on the bar staring out through the window at the contrails of descending K-ships in the sky above the houses on the other side of Straint Street. To most people it seemed unlikely he flew with anyone, but he could take a message and keep his mouth shut. The only other thing he ever said about himself was:

'No one gives shit about a fat man called Antoyne.'

'You got that right,' Liv Hula often told him.

When Vic had gone, there was a silence in the bar. The shadow

4

operators calmed down and packed themselves back into the ceiling corners so the corners looked familiar again. Antoyne stared at the table in front of him then across at Liv Hula. It seemed as if they'd speak about Vic or the woman but in the end neither of them could think of anything to say. The fat man was angry that Liv Hula had defended him to Vic Serotonin. He drove his chair back suddenly, it made a kind of complaining sound against the wooden floor. He got up and went over to the window, where he wiped the condensation off with the palm of his hand.

'Still dark,' he said.

Liv Hula had to admit that was true.

'Hey,' he said. 'Here's Joe Leone.'

Over the street from Black Cat White Cat it was the usual frontages, busted and askew, buildings which had lost confidence in their structural integrity and which now housed shoestring tailor operations specialising in cosmetics or one-shot cultivars. You couldn't call them 'parlours'. The work they did was too cheap for that. They got a trickle of stuff from the Uncle Zip and Nueva Cut franchises downtown; also they took work from the Shadow Boys, work like Joe Leone. Just now Joe was pulling himself down Straint using the fences and walls to hold himself up. His energy ebbed and flowed. He would fall down, wait for a minute, then struggle up again. It looked like hard work. You could see he was holding something in down there with one hand while he leaned on the fence with the other. The closer he got the more puzzled he looked.

Antoyne made a tube out of his two damp fists and said through it in the voice of a sports commentator at Radio Retro:

'. . . *and will he make it this time?*'

'Be sure to let us know when you join the human race, Antoyne,' Liv Hula said. The fat man shrugged and turned away from the window. 'It's no bet,' he said in his normal voice. 'He never failed yet.'

Joe kept dragging himself down Straint. As he approached, you could see the tailors had done something to his face so it had a crude lion-like cast. It was white and sweated up, but it didn't move properly. They had given it a one-piece look as if it was sculpture, even the long hair swept back and out from his big forehead and cheekbones. Eventually he fell down outside one of the chopshops and stopped moving, and after a couple of minutes two men almost as big as him came out to drag him inside.

Joe started to fight when he was seven.

'Never strike out at the other, son,' his father would explain in a patient way, 'because the other is your self.'

Joe Leone didn't follow that, even at seven years old which everyone agreed was his most intelligent time. He liked to fight. By twelve it was his trade, nothing more or less. He signed with the Shadow Boys. From that time on he lived in one-shot cultivars. He liked the tusks, the sentient tattoos, and the side-lace trousers. Joe had no body of his own. It cost him so much to run those cultivars he would never save up enough to buy himself back. Every day he was in the ring, doing that same old thing. He was getting pretty well messed up. 'I lost count the times I seen my own insides. Hey, what's that? Lose your insides ain't so hard. Losing a fight, that's hard.' And he would laugh and buy you another drink.

Every day they dragged the fucked-up cultivar out the ring, and the next day Joe Leone had been to the tailor on Straint and come out fresh and new and ready to do it all again. It was a tiring life but it was the life he loved. Liv Hula never charged him for a drink. She had a soft spot for him, it was widely acknowledged.

'Those fights, they're cruel and stupid,' she told the fat man now.

He was too smart to contradict that. After a moment, looking for something else to quarrel over, he said, 'You ever do anything before you kept bar?'

She brought out a lifeless smile for him to consider.

6

'One or two things,' she said.

'Then how come I never heard about them?'

'Got me there, Antoyne.'

She waited for him to respond, but now something new on Straint had caught his attention. He wiped the window glass again. He pressed his face up against it. 'Irene's a little late today,' he said.

Liv Hula busied herself suddenly behind the bar.

'Oh yes?'

'A minute or two,' he said.

'What's a minute or two to Irene?'

The fights were a dumb career, that was Liv Hula's opinion. They were a dumb life. Joe Leone's whole ambition was as dumb as his self-presentation until he met Irene: then it got worse. Irene was a Mona who had a good track record working the noncorporate spaceport. She was what you call petite, five three in transparent urethane heels and full of appeal with her flossy blonde hair. Like all those Uncle Zip products she had something organic about her, something real. She watched Joe Leone at the fights and after she smelled his blood she couldn't leave him alone. Every morning when he came home to the tailor's, Irene was there too. Between them they summed up the sex industry and the fight industry. When Joe and Irene were together you couldn't be sure which industry was which. They were a new form of entertainment in themselves.

Irene commenced to hammer at the chopshop door.

'How long you think they'll let her shout before they open up?' fat Antoyne asked. Liv Hula had found a map-shaped stain on the zinc bartop, which she stared at with interest.

'I don't know why you're asking me,' she said

'She's got feelings for him,' said Antoyne, to press his advantage. 'That's undeniable. No one questions that. Jesus,' he added to himself, 'look at those tits.'

He tried to imagine Joe Leone, dead and liquefied while his bones and organs reassembled themselves and Irene gave him the Mona side of her mouth. The joke was, Irene's opinion was no different than Liv Hula's. Every morning she made them fetch her an old wooden chair and put it at the head of Joe's tank, with his faded publicity slogan on it, *Hold the painkillers*. There she sat, ignoring the pink flashing LEDs, which were for show anyway, while the tank proteome slushed around like warm spit, cascades of autocatalysis through a substrate of forty thousand molecular species, flushing every twenty minutes to take off what unwanted product the chemistry couldn't eliminate. She hated the sucking noises it made.

One day you won't get back, she would tell the Lion. One more fight and you're fucked with me. But Joe was an algorithm by now, somewhere off in operator space. He was choosing new tusks from the catalogue, he was getting tuning to his glycolytic systems. He couldn't hear a word.

Oh Joe, I really mean it, she'd say. One more fight.

Liv Hula sometimes watched the rockets too.

Near dawn, you got her and the fat man standing by the window together as two tubby brass-looking freighters lifted from the corporate yard. Then a K-ship exited the military pits on the hard white line from its *f*RAM engine. In the backwash of light a warmer expression came on her face than you would expect. By then the Kefahuchi Tract had begun to fade from the sky, which was tilted like a lid to show one thin eastern arc of pale green, false dawn. Offshore winds would come up soon and, forced along the narrow pipe of Straint Street, churn the low-lying fogs of the event site. That would be the signal for all sorts of people to start the day. Liv Hula and Antoyne the fat man watched the K-ship cut the sky like scissors.

'You ever fly one of those, Antoyne?' she remarked.

He blinked and turned his head away. 'There's no need for that,' he said. 'There's no need for sarcasm like that.'

Just then, Vic Serotonin came back in the bar, walking quickly and looking behind him. He had the air of someone whose morning was already off its proper track. His face was white, with a graze on one cheek leaking beads of blood. He had waded through oily water not long ago it seemed; and his zip-up gabardine jacket had one sleeve half off at the shoulder – as if someone had held on to it while they fell, Liv Hula thought immediately, although she did not know why.

'Jesus, Vic,' she said.

'Get me a drink,' Vic Serotonin said.

He walked halfway across the room as if he was going to drink it at the counter, then changed his mind and sat down suddenly at the nearest table. Once there he didn't seem to know what to do. A few shadow operators detached themselves from the ceiling to examine him; he stared through them. 'Shit,' he kept saying in a quiet, surprised way. After a while his breathing calmed down.

The fat man forgot his hurt feelings as soon as Vic came in. He pulled up a chair and began to tell Vic some story, leaning into it in his enthusiasm so his soft body enveloped the table-edge. His voice was quiet and urgent, but you could hear the odd word, 'entradista', 'hard X-rays', 'Chinese Ed'. Vic stared through him too, then said, 'Shut up or I'll shoot you where you sit.' The fat man looked hopelessly away. He said all he wanted in this bar was a chance, Vic should give him a chance. He was trying not to cry. 'I'm sorry,' Vic said, but he was already thinking about something else, and when Liv Hula brought him his drink, and sat down and said, 'Black Heart, Vic, just the way you like it,' he barely seemed to recognise her.

'Shit,' he said again.

'Where's the woman, Vic?'

'I don't know,' he said.

'Only I don't want to hear you left her there.'

'She cracked and ran. She's in the aureole somewhere. Antoyne, go to the door, tell me if anyone's in the street.'

'All I want is a chance to fit in,' the fat man said.

'For fuck's sake, Antoyne.'

Antoyne said, 'No one understands that.'

Serotonin opened his mouth to say more, then he seemed to forget Antoyne altogether. 'I never saw panic like it,' he said. He shook his head. 'You couldn't even say we'd got inside. It's bad this morning, but it's not that bad.' He finished his drink and held out the glass. Instead of taking it, Liv Hula caught his wrist.

'So how bad is it?' she said. She wouldn't let go until he told her.

'Things are moving about,' he admitted. 'I've seen worse, but usually further in.'

'Where is she, Vic?'

He laughed. It was a laugh he had practised too often. 'I told you,' he said tiredly, 'she's somewhere in the aureole. We never got any further. She runs off between the buildings, I see silk stockings and that fucking fur coat, then I see nothing. She was still calling from somewhere when I gave up,' he said. 'Get me another drink, Liv, or I don't know what I'll do.'

Liv Hula said, 'You didn't go after her, Vic.'

He stared.

'You stayed where it was safe, and shouted a couple times, and then you came home.'

'Vic would never do that,' the fat man said in a blustering way. No one was going to say Vic would do that. 'Hey, Vic. Tell her. You would never do that!' He got up out of his chair. 'I'm going in the street and keep an eye open now, just the way you wanted. You got a wrong idea about Vic Serotonin,' he said to Liv Hula, 'if you think he'd do that.' As soon as he had gone, she went to the bar and poured Vic another Black Heart rum, while Vic rubbed his face with his hands like someone who was very tired and couldn't see his way through life any more. His face had an older look than it had when he left. It was sullen and heavy, and his blue eyes took on a temporary pleading quality which one day would be permanent.

'You don't know what it's like in there,' he told her.

'Of course I don't,' she said. 'Only Vic Serotonin knows that.'

'Streets transposed on one another, everything laid down out of sync one minute to the next. Geography that doesn't work. There isn't a single piece of dependable architecture in the shit of it. You leave the route you know, you're done. Lost dogs barking day and night. Everything struggling to keep afloat.'

She wasn't disposed to let him get away with that.

'You're the professional, Vic,' she reminded him. 'They're the customers. Here's your other drink if you want it.' She leaned her elbows on the bar. 'You're the one has to hold himself together.'

This seemed to amuse him. He took the rum down in one swallow, the colour came back into his face, and they looked at one another in a more friendly way. He wasn't finished with her though. 'Hey Liv,' he said softly after a moment or two, 'what's the difference between what you've seen and what you are? You want to know what it's like in there? The fact is, you spend all those years trying to make something of it. Then guess what, it starts making something of you.'

He got up and went to the door.

'What are you fucking about at, Antoyne?' he called. 'I said "look". I said "take a look".'

The fat man, who had trotted up Straint a little into the predawn wind to clear his head, also to see if he could get a glimpse of Irene the Mona through a chink in the boarded windows of the chop-shop, came in grinning and shivering with the cold. 'Antoyne here can tell us all about it,' Vic Serotonin said. 'Everything he knows.'

'Leave Antoyne alone.'

11

'You ever been in there when everything fell apart, Antoyne?'

'I was never in there, Vic,' Antoyne said hastily. 'I never claimed I was.'

'Everything was just taken away, and you had no idea what established itself in exchange? The air's like uncooked pastry. It's not a smell in there, it's a substrate. In every corner there's a broken telephone nailed to the wall. They're all labelled *Speak* but there's no line out. They ring but no one's ever there.'

Liv Hula gave him a look, then shrugged. To the fat man she explained, 'Vic just so hates to lose a client.'

'Fuck you,' Vic Serotonin said. 'Fuck the two of you.'

He pushed his glass across the counter and walked out.

After Vic Serotonin left silence returned to the bar. It crowded in on itself, so that Liv Hula and the fat man, though they wanted to speak, were hemmed in with their own thoughts. The onshore wind decreased; while the light increased until they could no longer deny it was dawn. The woman washed and dried the glass Vic Serotonin had used, then put it carefully in its place behind the bar. Then she went upstairs to the room above, where she thought about changing her clothes but in the end only stared in a kind of mounting panic at the disordered bed, the blanket chest and the bare white walls.

I ought to move on, she thought. I ought to leave here now.

When she came down again, Antoyne had resumed his place by the window and with his hands on the sill stood watching the payloads lift one after another from the corporate port. He half-turned as if to speak but, receiving no encouragement, turned back again.

Across the street someone opened the chopshop door.

After a brief quiet struggle, Irene the Mona stumbled out. She took an uncertain step or two forward, peering blindly up and down Straint like a drunk assessing heavy traffic, then sat down suddenly on the edge of the sidewalk. The door slammed shut behind her. Her skirt rode up. Antoyne pressed his face closer to the glass. 'Hey,' he whispered to himself. Irene, meanwhile, set her little shiny red urethane vanity case down beside her and began to claw through its contents with one hand. She was still sitting there two or three minutes later, showing all she had, sniffing and wiping her eyes, when the cats came out of the Saudade event site in an alert silent rush.

Who knew how many of those cats there were? Another thing, you never found so much as a tabby among them, every one was either black or white. When they poured out the zone it was like a model of some chaotic mixing flow in which, though every condition is determined, you can never predict the outcome. Soon they filled Straint in both directions, bringing with them the warmth of their bodies, also a close, dusty but not unpleasant smell. Irene struggled upright, but the cats took no more notice than if she had been one of the street lamps.

Irene was born on a planet called Perkin's Rent. She left there tall and bony, with an awkward walk and big feet. When she smiled her gums showed, and she did her hair in lacquered copper waves so tight and complex they could receive the mains hum, the basic radio transmissions of the universe. She had a sweet way of laughing. When she boarded the rocket to leave, she was seventeen. Her suitcase contained a yellow cotton dress with a kind of faux-Deco feel, tampons, and four pairs of high heel shoes. 'I love shoes,' she would explain to you when she was drunk. 'I love shoes.' You got the best of her in those days. She would follow you anywhere for two weeks then follow someone else. She loved a rocket jockey.

Now she stood with tears streaming down her face, watching the Saudade cats flow around her, until Liv Hula waded fastidiously into the stream and fetched her back to the bar, where she sat her down and said:

'What can I get you, honey?'

'He's dead this time,' Irene said in a rush.

'I can't believe that,' Liv Hula said. Immediately she was tidying up inside, planning to stay back inside herself away from the fact of it. But Irene kept repeating in her disorganised way, 'He's dead this time, that's all,' which made it hard to dissociate. Irene took Liv Hula's hand and pressed it to her cheek. It was her opinion, she said, that something makes men unfit for most of life; to which Liv Hula replied, 'I always thought so too.' Then Irene broke into snuffling again and had to fetch out her vanity mirror. 'Especially the best parts,' she said indistinctly.

Later, when Antoyne came and tried to make conversation with her, she gave him the full benefit of her looks. He bought her a drink which settled out the same colours as her skirt, pink and yellow, and which he said they drank on some dumb planet he knew fifty lights down the line.

'I been there, Fat Antoyne,' she told him with a sad smile.

That original Irene, she thought, wasn't good at being on her own. She would sit on the bed one place or another, listening to the rain and trying to hold herself together. On the other hand, she never lacked ambition. The stars of the Halo were like one big neon sign to her. The sign said: All the shoes you can eat. When she bought the Mona package, the tailor promised her hair would always smell of peppermint shampoo. She had gone through the catalogues, and that was what she wanted, and the tailor designed it in. On the Saudade streets it was her big selling point.

'I been there,' she told Antoyne, letting him get the peppermint smell, 'and just now I'm glad to meet someone else who's been there too.'

Antoyne was as encouraged by this as any man. He sat on after she finished the drink, trying to engage her with stories of the places he had seen back when he rode the rockets. But Irene had been to all those places too – and more, Liv Hula thought – and Fat Antoyne had all he was going to get for one cheap cocktail drink.

Liv watched them from a distance, her own thoughts so churned she didn't care how it ended. Eventually even Antoyne could see the way things were. He scraped his chair back and retreated to his place by the window. What time was it? How had the things happened that ended him up here? He looked out on to Straint. 'It's day,' he said. 'Hey,' he grumbled, 'I actually respected the guy. You know?' Meanwhile the stream of cats flowed on like a problem in statistical mechanics, without any apparent slackening or falling away of numbers, until suddenly it turned itself off and Straint was empty again. Across the road at the tailor's they were flushing Joe Leone's proteins down the drain.

At the civilian port, the cruise ships, half-hidden in the mist, towered above the buildings; while along the tall narrow streets a traffic of rickshaw girls and tattoo boys had begun, ferrying the tourists from the New Café Al Aktar to Moneytown, from the Church on the Rock to the Rock Church, while around them their shreds and veils of shadow operators whispered, 'A sight everyone will be sure to see, a discourse of oppositions.' Fur coats were all over Saudade by eight, the colour of honey or horse-chestnut, cut to flow like some much lighter fabric. What sort of money was this? Where did it come from? It was off-planet money. It was corporate money. However cruel the trade that produced them, you could hardly deny the beauty of those coats and their luxurious surfaces.

Shortly after the last cat had vanished into the city, Vic's client returned to the bar.

Where Vic had come back filthy, she came back clean. You wouldn't notice anything new about her, except her shoulders were a little hunched and her face was still. Her hands she thrust into the pockets of her coat. Nothing had been taken away from her: but she held her head more carefully than before, always looking forward as if her neck hurt, or as if she was trying not to notice something happening in the side of her eye. It was hard to read body language like that. She placed herself with care at a table near the window, crossed one leg over the other and asked in a low voice for a drink. After a little while she said, 'I wonder if someone could give that other man the rest of his fee.'

Antoyne sat forward eagerly.

'I can do that,' he offered.

'No you can't,' Liv Hula warned him. To the woman in the fur coat she said, 'Vic's cheap, he left you for dead. You owe him nothing.'

'Still,' the woman said, 'I feel he should have the rest of his money. It's here. And I was fine, really.' She stared ahead of herself. 'A little puzzled, I suppose, at how unpleasant it is.'

Liv Hula threw up her hands.

'Why do they come here?' she asked Fat Antoyne in a loud voice. Before he could say anything, she added, 'They leave the nice safe corporate tour and they end up in this bar here. They always find our Vic.'

'Hey, Vic's OK,' the fat man said.

'Vic's a joke, Antoyne, and so are you.'

Antoyne struggled to his feet and looked as if he was going to challenge that, but in the end he only shrugged. Vic's client gave him a faint, encouraging smile, but then seemed to look past him. Silence drew out a moment or two; then a chair scraped back and Irene the Mona came over to the table where these events were happening. Her little urethane shoes clattered on the wooden floor. She had wiped her tears and done her lipstick. She was over Joe the Lion now. What had she been on, to invest her considerable life-energy that way? Irene had a future in front of her, everyone agreed, and it was a good, light-hearted one. She had her plans, and they were good ones too. Though it was true she would keep Joe in her heart-pocket many years because that was the kind of girl she knew herself to be.

'That sure is a beautiful coat,' she said. She held out her hand.

For a moment, the woman looked nonplussed. Then she shook Irene's hand and said, 'Thank you. It is, isn't it?'

'Very beautiful, and I admire it so,' Irene agreed. She gave a little bob, seemed about to add something, then suddenly went and sat down again and toyed with her glass. 'Don't be hard on him, honey,' she called across to Liv Hula. 'He's nothing but a man, after all.' It was hard to tell which man she meant.

'I feel he should have his money,' appealed the woman in the fur coat. When no one answered she set the cash on the table in front of her, in high-denomination notes. 'Anyway, it's here for him,' she said. She got to her feet in that careful way she had developed. 'If he comes back—' she began. She made her way to the door and stood there for a moment peering up Straint Street towards the event zone, wreathed – silent, heaving and questionable – in its daytime chemical fogs, as if trying to decide what to do. Eventually, she smiled at the other two women; said, 'Thank you anyway;' and walked off back towards the city. They heard her heels go away for what seemed a long time.

'Jesus,' was Liv Hula's comment. 'Hey, Antoyne,' she said, 'you want another drink?'

But the fat man had gone too. He had lost patience with the way they treated him in there. He was just a man trying to fit in, someone who had seen as much as anyone else, more than some. It made him angry they didn't listen.

What the hell, he thought. Nothing keeps.

At least he was out of that bar now, into the morning somewhere he could breathe, heading for Moneytown and the strip mall wonderland running south of Straint, down past the spaceports to the sea. He was narrowing his eyes in the strong light glittering up off the distant water, as if he could discern something which didn't belong there, something he hadn't lost after all. Something, perhaps, you couldn't lose. He was going to look for work. There was always work in the ports.

TWO

The Long Bar at the Café Surf

A couple of evenings after these events a man who resembled Albert Einstein walked into a different kind of bar, off at the money end of Saudade where the aureole, curving across the city like a shaded area on a map, met the sea.

Unlike Liv Hula's joint, the Café Surf had two rooms. These were known respectively as the Long and Short bars, the latter being notable for a strictly drink & run client-base. The man who looked like Einstein went straight through to the Long Bar where he ordered a double Black Heart no ice and stared around with satisfaction at the high-end retro décor of marble pillars, designer blinds, cane tables and polished chrome bar taps. Ancient movie stars laughed out at him from brushed aluminium frames on the walls, exotic beers glittered from the shelves of the cooler: while under a red neon sign the Café Surf two-piece – keyboard and tenor saxophone – ambled its way through the evening's middle set.

All of this was copied faithfully from a minor hologram work, *Live Music Nightly 1989*, by the celebrated tableau artiste Sandra Shen. Like the Long Bar constituency itself – a mix of self-conscious young entertainment executives on release from the corporate enclaves just down the beach in Doko Gin and Kenworthy – this seemed to puzzle and amuse him in equal parts. He had the air, cultivated in middle age, of enjoying the things other people enjoy, so long as he didn't have to take part. He smiled to himself and lit his pipe. Most nights, for perhaps a month, he had sat in the same place. He would pull out a chair, sit down, get up again to put a match carefully into an ashtray on the corner of the bar; sit down again. He did all this with a kind of meticulous politeness, as if he was in someone's front room; or as if, at home, his wife required of him a continual formal acknowledgement of her efforts. He would stare at his pipe. He would begin a conversation with a girl old enough to be his granddaughter, getting out his wallet to show her – and her friend, who wore torn black net tights and industrial shoes – something which looked in the undependable Long Bar light like a business card, which they would admire.

In fact he was not as old as he looked; his wife was dead; and whatever else he seemed to be doing, his attention never wavered from its object.

His name was Aschemann and he was a detective.

Halfway through his first evening there, Aschemann had uncovered a kind of discontinuity in things at the Café Surf. The two-piece, snug under its neon sign on the cramped dais between the Long Bar and the lavatory door, had gained its second wind. It was set-tling to the long haul, drawing down a kind of haunted bebop from the ectoplasmic night air outside – music four centuries old and off another planet. Between numbers there was laughter and shouting; the smell of food grew momentarily stronger, there was a clutter of Giraffe Beer bottles and crumpled serviettes, dark red lipstick on empty glasses, Anaïs-Anaïs scent thick in the air. Yet the tables closest to the musicians were deserted; and in the space between them and the dais, people kept appearing. These people didn't seem to belong in the Long Bar. They were shocked-looking men, white-faced, tall, wearing raincoats; thin shaven-headed boys like camp inmates; women with an eye pulled down at the corner: poor, shabby people, people crippled in small and grotesque ways. They were coming out of the lavatory, to push between the piano

19

and the bar and then wander loose, blinking, looking for a moment both confused and agitated, perhaps by the music, perhaps by the light.

Though they emerged from the lavatory, that was – as Aschemann saw instantly – no guarantee they had ever gone into it. Instead, for a moment, as each of these figures appeared in the orange light, it seemed as if the music itself were squeezing them into existence. As if there was some sort of unformed darkness out there at the back of the Café Surf, where the event site met the sea, and the band was squashing it like a fistful of wet sand into these crude forked shapes. They were lively enough. Once they had oriented themselves, they had drinks at the bar and then, laughing and shouting, wandered out into the lighted street. Thoughtfully, the man who looked like Einstein watched them go.

The next night he brought his assistant along.

'You see?' he asked her.

'I see,' she said. 'But what will you do about it?'

She was a neat, ambitious young woman on a one-month trial from the uniform branch, fluent in three Halo languages, wired for dial-up and with all the usual tailoring. You could tell that from her eyes, which were often unevenly focused; and from the discreet codeflows rippling up the inside of one forearm like smart tattoos. Her experience turned out to be in Sport Crime (the word sport to be interpreted here, Aschemann told himself, as a convenient misnomer for the fights), her speciality the violation of mysostatin blocker protocols in chopshop proteomes. She had failed early on to convey to him either the intricacies or the appeal of this discipline, and it wasn't much use in Site Crime anyway. They stood outside the Café Surf in the warm wind on the beach, looking at the violet breakers, the curious prismatic displays, visible nightly, where the water met the event aureole, and she suggested:

'Do you think they originate in the site?'

Aschemann believed this to be obvious. But he wanted to

encourage her, so he only said in a mild way, 'I've wondered about that myself.' He wasn't comfortable with the possibility. It would mark, he believed, some kind of sea-change. It could only be a marker for change when, without any other help than the music, people came out of the Saudade site who had never gone in.

'Whatever they are,' he said, 'we don't want them out here.'

'I'll call down a team,' his assistant said.

Code flickered along her forearm. Her strange eyes, the same colour as the surf, went out of focus as she dialled up. Her lips moved a little even though she wasn't actually speaking. Aschemann put his hand gently on her arm. 'Not yet,' he cautioned her. His voice collapsed the dial-up. She looked at him vaguely, like someone who has just woken up from a realistic dream.

'I always like to watch a little,' he explained, 'before I do anything.'

There was a note of apology in his voice. Aschemann had a high turnover in assistants because he was fond of advising them, 'The true detective starts in the centre of the maze: the crimes make their way through to him. Never forget, you uncover your own heart at the heart of it.' Another of his favourites, even more puzzling to young men and women conditioned to seek answers, was, 'Uncertainty is all we have. It's our advantage. It's the virtue of the day.'

So now he sat in the Long Bar, in what had become his favourite corner, wondering if he had watched enough.

Just as he decided that he had, something changed his feeling about the place and what might be happening there. The door opened and let in a man he recognised, Antoyne Messner, called by everyone that knew him Fat Antoyne. No one cared about Fat Antoyne. He had a history of low-percentage contraband operations a few lights away in Radio Bay. He had stayed ahead by moving only the lightest stuff – exotic isotopes, cultivars of embargoed local species, tailor packages for the kiddy trade – in a hullshot

Dynaflow HS-SE or -SE2, its cheap navigation tools leaking the illegal daughter-code used to negotiate the complex gravitational attractors and junk-matter flows of the Bay. His rule: make two trips maximum then throw the ship away. The code itself was the risk in that trade. Relax, and it would come down out of the mathematical space and into your head at night. As long as your hygiene was good, the code kept you one step ahead of EMC, but you still had to be a pilot. In consequence the stresses were high. Antoyne didn't do anything at all since he fetched up in Saudade except run errands for Vic Serotonin, and he was therefore widely assumed to be a burn-out.

He pushed his way between the tables and sat awkwardly on one of the chromium stools at the Long Bar. He seemed dispirited. He spent some time trying to order a drink which, when it came, the bartender placed in front of him with exaggerated care, and which settled out quickly into distinct layers of pink and yellow. It was popular, he told the people near him, on Perkin's Rent. No one seemed convinced. Aschemann watched him swallow half of it then went over and said, 'You're a long way from Straint Street.' Then when the fat man stared at him uncertainly:

'Antoyne? Maybe you don't recognise me. Maybe in this light you don't see me as well as you could.'

'I know who you are,' Antoyne said.

Aschemann smiled. 'I would usually find you at Liv Hula's this time of night, caning it with Vic Serotonin.'

'Only I got work now. It's temporary.'

'That's good news, Antoyne!'

The fat man didn't seem to know how to encounter the enthusiasm of this. 'It's temporary work,' he said.

'So how is Vic?'

Fat Antoyne swallowed the other half of his drink and stood up. 'You know,' he said, 'I like the light in here. I always liked a low light to drink by. It's the music I don't like.' He wiped his mouth and gave the band a look which he transferred somehow to Aschemann.

'I was leaving anyway,' he said.

'There's no need for that,' the detective insisted. 'Look, I'll just sit here and have another drink. You should have one, too.' He would be hurt, he implied, if Antoyne went off like that. He pulled up the bar stool next to Antoyne's and took a moment to get comfortable on it. 'You don't mind if I sit,' he said. 'We're both out of place here, surely we can sit together?' He took a matchbook off the barman – it had a tiny hologram of the *Live Music Nightly* sign, which he turned appreciatively this way and that – and then another glass of rum. 'Do you mind if I just fold my coat,' he asked, 'and put it here on the bar?' He held up his drink to the light. He had a habit of smiling around at people to show that he was enjoying the evening the way it had turned out. He tapped his fingers to the music for a minute or two, then concluded, 'Myself, I don't mind this. But what I like is that old New Nuevo Tango.'

The fat man received the news without interest.

'A lot do,' he acknowledged.

Aschemann nodded. 'I heard Vic is taking more risks than he needs to,' he said, as if that was part of the same discussion.

'Vic's OK,' Antoyne said defensively.

'Still, people will get hurt.'

'There's nothing wrong with Vic. Vic Serotonin to my mind never hurt anyone.'

'And yet, you know, he's in and out of the site, like all those people. We can't stop them finding new entrances—' here, Aschemann gave a small chuckle '—sometimes we have our reasons we don't even want to try. But then the next day he's at the Semiramide Club. He's in bed with Paulie DeRaad. Are those kinds of connexions without risk, do you think? For someone in Vic's trade?' After a moment of reflection he added, 'All those travel agents have a reckless streak, Antoyne. The trouble in Vic's life proceeds from that.'

Something new seemed to occur to him. He touched the fat man's forearm suddenly to get his attention.

'Antoyne, has Vic *upset* you in some way?'

Antoyne shrugged.

'I won't give up Vic,' he said, and walked off.

'Vic's giving himself up,' the detective called after him mildly. 'Not just to me. To whatever's in there.'

Antoyne did not reply, but instead pushed his way more energetically between the crowded tables to the door. In the end there was a kind of fat dignity to Antoyne, which remained intact despite his habit of always putting himself at a disadvantage, of appearing to disentitle himself in a society where anyone could be what they wanted. No one understood why Serotonin tolerated him, but maybe that was why. For a moment or two Aschemann considered this. Then he retreated to his favourite corner, where he tried to recoup the rhythm of the Café Surf, taking his time over another glass, drinking in little sips which coated his mouth with the warm rum taste of burnt sugar. He thought about Vic Serotonin, also Paulie DeRaad who, of the two, he liked the least. He thought about the tourist trade, or at least the sector of it which was his professional concern.

While he was thinking, the band squeezed out two or three thin boys in white singlets, earrings and studded leather belts. Aschemann watched closely their struggle through the toilet door and into the sticky prismatic light. They looked, he decided, surprised. They looked incomplete, and surprised to find themselves here. Then the music squeezed out an old woman in a hat and a blue print dress and for a moment all four of them swayed clumsily together as if in time to the music. There was a lacuna, a moment of awry – a moment like falling, which happened between them but spread itself out to everyone else in the bar; and then the Café Surf was itself again. The new customers bought drinks and headed out into the night.

Aschemann stood at the door and watched them go. The next night he had some of them arrested.

The way this came about was unforeseen. Three women and one man were picked up two miles from the Café Surf, in the back lot of another bar, where they were apparently trying to have sex with one another. There was some sense they didn't know how to progress with this but were willing to learn. Aschemann, who got notice of the event from the uniform branch, contacted his assistant and had her go down there. 'Take them to a holding cell,' he told her. 'I can't go myself.' He had other things to do – he was out on the edge of the noncorporate port investigating a long-running series of crimes against women – but it seemed pointless to waste the opportunity. 'Don't interrogate them,' he ordered. 'Strictly, there is nothing wrong with trying to have sex in the back lot of a bar, otherwise we would all be in prison. Just settle them in and then you can go home. Oh, and one other thing.'

'What's that?'

'Make sure no one hurts them.'

She was back on to him perhaps an hour later. Things were fine, she said. It was like handling refugees. Though they were curiously pliable, they were slow to give names. They smelled a little. They didn't seem to be from an alien species. They didn't seem to be hungry. They were not chipped, she said, by any method the holding cell diagnostics understood, neither were any of the usual markers encoded into their DNA; she could therefore assign them no point of origin in the Halo.

'What do they look like to you?' Aschemann asked her.

'They look like idiots,' she said.

When she last saw them, that was how they looked. It was perhaps two after midnight. They stood all night like that, puzzledly, in the centre of the cell, talking to one another infrequently in their slow, gluey voices; and in the morning they were gone.

*

'There's no explanation for it,' she said.

Her skin ran with data. It was like a pore-bleed. Nervousness or anger was causing her to clench and unclench one fist, as if by pumping the forearm muscles she could pump the mathematics too. He wondered if she had been taught that, or if it was just a mannerism. 'Look at the nanocamera record! We had saturating coverage. There was never a moment those people were specifically and exactly *not there*. In some lights there still seems to be a trace of them, even now. And even after the holding cell was empty, it turned out they had been seen in other parts of the station.' She stared at her arm as if it had let her down. 'What can have happened? There was never a moment they weren't there. They just seemed to evaporate.

'There's no explanation,' she concluded again.

Aschemann scratched his head. 'Higher up they might want one,' he decided. 'But we don't have to provide it right now.' And then, trying to help her, 'This isn't anything anyone could have predicted.'

Next, she wanted them to raid the Café Surf.

'Not yet,' he said. 'But it's a nice day. Let's visit by all means.'

She stared at him. 'What?'

'It would make a change for you to drive,' he told her, and gave his usual driver the day off. Twenty minutes later she was stuck with him. He sat in the front passenger seat with his arms folded, smiling around comfortably as the pink Cadillac convertible slipped down from his office, between the Moneytown palms and white designer duplexes of Maricachel Hill, to the Corniche. It had rained early, but mid-morning sun was etching the last traces of humidity off the surface of the air. He loved to be driven, and he was proud of the car. After a few minutes he told her. 'You see? You feel better already. Take your time.'

She gave him a look from the side of her eye.

'Oh ho,' Aschemann said. 'Now I'm irritating you.'

'I can't believe you're so undisturbed. I can't believe you're not angry.'

'I'm angry,' he said, 'but not with you.'

He allowed her to absorb that; then, to change the subject, began telling her about the killings at the noncorporate port. Called to the scene of the original crime some years before, he had discovered two lines of a poem tattooed in the armpit of the victim: *Send me a neon heart/Unarmed with a walk like a girl.* 'She was a Mona from five lights down the Beach. The usual juvenile in box-fresh urethane shoes. This tattoo was unique,' he said, 'in that it was not smart. It was just ink, driven into the skin by some antique process. Forensic investigation later proved it to have been made after the heart stopped beating, in the style of an artist now dead but popular a year or two before.'

'Is that possible?' his assistant wanted to know.

Aschemann, who had been trying to light his pipe, threw another spent match out of the Cadillac. 'Look around you,' he advised her. 'In the middle of the city we're less than two miles from the event aureole. No one is certain what happened in there. Anything is possible. What if crimes are motiveless now, whipped off the crest of events like spray, with no more cause than that?'

'A surprisingly poetic idea,' she said. 'But the murders?'

The man who looked like Einstein smiled to himself. 'Maybe I'll tell you more later, when you learn to ask better questions.'

'I think we're here.'

The Long Bar at the Café Surf was full of fractured sunlight and bright air. Sand blew across the floor from the open door; the staff were sleepy and vague. Someone's toddler crawled about between the cane tables wearing only a T-shirt bearing the legend SURF NOIR. Meanings – all incongruous – splashed off this like drops of water, as the dead metaphors trapped inside the live one collided and reverberated endlessly and elastically, taking up new positions relative to one another. SURF NOIR, which is a whole new existence; which is a 'world' implied in two words, dispelled in an instant; which is foam on the appalling multitextual sea we drift on. 'Which is probably,' Aschemann noted, 'the name of an aftershave.'

He beamed down at the toddler, which burst into tears. 'Show us the toilets,' he heard his assistant demanding at the bar.

They skirted the dais and went through the doorway. Thereafter the floors were checkerboard black and white linoleum, the walls papered red and enlivened at intervals with reproductions of the poster art of Ancient Earth. There was a smell of urine, but that was artificial. Smart grafitti made the usual promises and demands – size, weight, preferred metabolic disorder. 'A toilet is a toilet,' Aschemann concluded shortly, 'though these could be less contemporary. Nothing is here.'

She looked at him in surprise.

'You're wrong.'

'Suddenly I'm the assistant,' he complained.

'I can feel something.' She tilted her head as if listening. 'No. The *code* can feel something. We should get an operator in here.'

'I don't work with an operator.'

'But—'

'That's all now,' he insisted. 'We go outside.'

She shrugged. 'Apparently this door is never closed.'

A condemned pier awaited them out back. Rusty cast-iron pillars, forty feet high, marched out towards the distant water, the wet sand dimpled and weedy around their bases. Reflected sea-light flickered and wheeled across the rotten boards above. Somewhere between the pillars, the event aureole began. There would be no firm distinction. One moment you would be here, the next you would be the other side. No warning, only a tangle of rusty wire which fell to powder at your touch. The Café Surf, you saw immediately, backed straight into the darkening greenish volume of it. You could hear the water lapping tentatively far out. You could hear other sounds less easy to describe, which to Aschemann sounded like children reciting something in a playground. The air was cold and soft. He bent down and squeezed some of the wet sand into a lump which he brought near his face.

'What do you think?' he heard his assistant say.

'I wonder they were allowed to build here,' he answered. 'I wonder there isn't more wire. I wonder if I ought to close them down now and not proceed any further with this farce.' It was his responsibility after all. He dropped the handful of sand at her feet, where it fell apart easily and without a sound. 'How far would you go in?' he asked her in return.

'Into the site?'

'I'm interested to know.'

Even as they stood looking at one another, a wave passed through them. It went through Aschemann like a drop in temperature, and he saw for an instant the beach behind the Café Surf tipped ten degrees off the horizontal; and, falling softly through the air into the water, snow. A metal taste in his mouth – very quick, it was a memory of something – then snow, or something like it, whirled between the pillars, and through it he saw a row of houses fallen into disuse stretching away beneath the pier. Then a room, with more snow falling into it on some live thing he couldn't make out, he was close in and trying to back away, its head tilted to one side in the coy manner of a child asking a question. Human, or perhaps not.

At the height of the wave, anyway, that was what he saw. An upper room papered with faded roses, open to the air. Something that might have been a child. But it was soon gone, and just as suddenly he found himself sitting down in the damp sand, listening, for what he didn't know, while his assistant bent over him to ask:

'Are you all right? What did you see?'

'Snow!' he said, looking up at her in a kind of desperation. He gripped her arm but, imagining he could feel the data running through it under the skin, let go again immediately. 'You saw something too? Can you confirm that? Snow on houses? I—'

But she had seen something else altogether.

'I was in the bottom of a narrow valley, very warm. Mosses grew on everything.' She found herself standing in front of a building full of disused turbines. 'It was a turbine hall, very old,' she said, 'by a river. It went back into darkness with arched windows either side. Great annular shapes. Spindles absolutely crimson with rust, laminated like choux pastry. Chalk marks. 6II/600rpm.' This made her shiver. 'They had put chalk marks on many surfaces,' she said. The building was open to the sky. That was the only particular she would agree, a building open to the sky. 'You looked up through the roof and saw the valley side going up and away to limestone knolls thick with vegetation. Light fell through at sharp angles on to the machinery. But it was very damp. Very humid—'

Aschemann tried to get up.

'I don't feel well. Can you help me?'

They stumbled along the beach and sat in his car.

'Do you want a drink?' he offered. He laughed shakily. 'I would feel safer if I had a drink.' She began to laugh too, but neither of them wanted to go back into the bar.

'It's only the aureole,' she said.

Neither of them said anything else for five minutes. Then Aschemann went on to dial-up, with a request for increased surveillance on Vic Serotonin. 'Well, do what you can, then,' she heard him instruct whoever was at the other end. 'What? No.' He cut them off suddenly. 'Always a problem,' he complained. 'The fact is,' he admitted to her, 'it may have been a mistake to go so easy on Fat Antoyne. He is the link between this and Vic.'

'You can always pick him up again.'

Instead of answering, Aschemann stared across at the Café Surf. 'I feel braver now,' he said. 'How about you?'

She shrugged. She wasn't sure.

'If you're better now,' he said, 'go back to the office.' He patted her arm. 'Take this beautiful car, I'm feeling generous.'

'What will you do?'

He got out of the Cadillac.

'Drink a glass of rum,' he said. 'Perhaps two.'

She drove along the Corniche and back up the hill. The traffic was good until midtown, where the streets were packed with rickshaws. On her own she seemed less animated. If Aschemann had been able to observe her expression he would have described it as 'inturned'. But how useful a description was that? When she was alone, she knew, she was herself. When she was alone, she did only the things she did. She was a policewoman driving carefully. She was a policewoman glancing at her forearm datableed, then up at the street again. She was a policewoman consulting the driving mirror before she waved on a sweaty rickshaw girl in electric-blue lycra. She left Aschemann's car in the parking garage and went and sat quietly in his office and waited to feel calm. Thin from lack of appreciation, Aschemann's shadow operators crept out of the corners and took up their customary forms, whispering, 'Is there any way we can help? Is there anything we can help with, dear?' They knew her. They liked her. She always tried to find them something to do. She had them adjust the slatted blinds so that the light fell across her face in precise lines of black and white. She had them bring her up to date. After a moment or two she asked them:

'Why is he the way he is?'

'All we know, dear,' the shadow operators said, 'is you don't make the kind of sacrifices that man has made, not without suffering.'

'Oh no, dear.'

'He's a saint, that man.'

'Can you get me his records?'

Aschemann waited out the afternoon in the Café Surf. The colour was back in his face. He ate a dish of falafel. He watched possessively the scraps of sunshine move across the floor, change shape, fade to a kind of eggy yellow, like a painting of sunshine, then vanish. The tide came up the sand outside, bringing a reflective violet light all its own. With that arrived the first customers of the evening, who began to talk and laugh – quietly at first, then with more animation.

By seven every table was taken and they were three deep at the bar. The place was rammed. Seven-thirty, the neon sign went on. Then the two-piece arrived, and after a gin rickey for its nerves rolled right over everyone. The keyboard guy – twenty years old, blond spiked hair and sly, mobile mouth – wore a plaid drape suit. He was a clown and a thief. He was a geek genius. Everything he played that evening, the audience understood, would be a joke at the expense of some other tune, some other musician, some other kind of music. They were delighted. They were complicit. Every so often even the saxophonist – an older man, the muscles round his mouth tightened into two deep grooves by years in the job – would stop playing and listen: it was as if he'd heard someone this good once before but now forgot who or when or where. Then, putting these speculations behind him, he would pull sharply on his cigarette, glance down at the saxophone, and pick things up a little. Rhythms flicked and ripped, tangled and separated. They tore into *Parking Orbit, Entradista* and *New Venusport South.* Things slipped a little toward the sentimental side with *Moonlight in Moneytown*; then came right back on track, to rising cheers and whistles, in the genuinely awesome hard bop autopsy and deconstructed chamame beats of *Gravity Wave.*

At the height of the wave, five men in evening wear were squeezed from the Café Surf lavatory; then two dock-boys with dyed brush-cuts and steel-toed boots, arm in arm with an emaciated blonde who kept wiping her nose on her pliable white forearm.

Aschemann leaned forward tensely in his seat.

They looked half-formed, sticky, fresh from the chrysalis. Half an hour in the music dried them out. Soon they were straggling aimlessly along the Corniche together, singing, linking arms, running suddenly for no reason. The detective followed, observing their amazement at the moth-haunted cones of light beneath the Corniche lamps. They were awed by everything. They visited another bar, called The Breakaway Station, and from there found their way down to the beach where the blonde danced off on her own to trip and fall laughing in the thick sand while her new friends clung together in the wind at the edge of the sea. Then all eight of them turned inland and trudged solemnly up Maricachel in the warm scented darkness until they found themselves, as perhaps they had always intended, in Carmody.

Aschemann had the quarter pumped with nanodevices which, drifting like clouds of milt in the neon light, could detect two molecules of human pheromone in a kilometre cube of air, filter the DNA out of a Friday night, illuminate each casual exchange of fluids in wavebands from far infra-red to near ultraviolet. The results of this expensive, operator-rich technique were streamed to him as simultaneous separate edits of the data, which he built into composites and profiles at will. Even so he lost his quarry almost immediately among the bars and transsexual brothels, the streets that stank of perspiration, oil products and lemon grass.

Midtown they still clung together in a group. Then the men, quiet and greedy, peeled off one by one. They had a poor hold on things but they knew what they liked. Fried food, sex, hard drugs, smart tattoos, tank parlours, any kind of music from chamame to rockit dub. One minute they were still distinguishable, gawking up at buildings like black & gold cigarette packs against the sky: the next they had entered an alley, climbed a flight of stairs, paid cash to get processed through some pocked security door. They had merged somehow with the life around them. They were gone. Aschemann had a sense of them fading away in front of him. The hardware felt it too.

The blonde was the last to go. Where her friends had appetites, she had a sense of herself. She was puzzled by her own drives. She stood in her short white sleeveless satin dinner frock at the intersection of Montefiore and Bone, smiling at a lull in the traffic. She took off one shoe and rubbed her foot. She took off the other shoe and held them both in her hand. She looked one way, then the other, then back again, smiling expectantly each time as if she would suddenly see something new. But it had all stopped happening. The street remained empty, the neon blinked on and off. The smile faded. Aschemann looked away briefly and when he turned back she was gone.

'Can you confirm that?' he asked his team.

They could. Even so, he expected to look up and see her in the middle distance, trudging purposefully towards the next bar.

Something about the blonde reminded Aschemann of his wife – her sense of expectation, something, he didn't entirely know what. He remained in Carmody another hour, hoping the nano-device operation would produce results. Things didn't work out that way; and although he could easily have returned to the Café Surf to collect a fresh group of suspects, in the end an impulse made him hail a rickshaw and take it down to Suicide Point, where his wife had lived.

By then it was nearly dawn. Along the concrete service road between her house and the beach, Point kids stood about in loose groups waiting for customers. One or two of them glanced up briefly at the rickshaw bowling past, trailing its coloured smoke of junk holographic ads, then away again. They all had small heads and blank faces. Sand blew round Aschemann's shoes as he stood on his wife's doorstep and raised his hand to knock. Before he could complete the gesture he heard his own voice say clearly, 'What are you doing?'

He didn't have to knock. He had the key. He could go in any

time, nevertheless he went back and sat in the rickshaw and explained to the rickshaw girl:

'My wife's dead.'

'It's a problem we'll all have.'

'I forgot for a moment,' he said.

He felt embarrassed. The rickshaw girl, who had clambered out of the shafts and was rubbing down her legs with a pertex towel, seemed willing to forgive him. 'Hey, I'm called Annie,' she said. 'Just like the rest of them, I guess. I mean, I know you didn't ask.' Like all those Annies she had opted for the extreme package. She was tailored up as big as a pony – with eighteen inches on Aschemann even when she stooped – and her damp candy-coloured lycra exuded a not-dissimilar reassuring smell. *Café electrique* and a malfunction of her onboard testosterone patch caused her to stamp about restlessly in a fog of her own perspiration. 'Maybe you ought to go somewhere else?' she suggested. 'Your wife being dead and all? This time of night I'll take you anywhere.'

Aschemann said he would like to go back to Carmody.

He made a vague gesture towards the sea, which could be heard sucking meditatively at the sand behind the house. 'It's nicer in the day,' he said. 'Really I just come here to think.'

'Most people visit the chopshop and get a cultivar,' the rickshaw girl observed. 'They get back the person they love that way.' She reinserted herself between the shafts, turned her vehicle round and faced it up the hill. 'No one has to lose anyone now,' she said. 'I wonder why you don't do that, the way everyone does.'

Aschemann often wondered too.

'She lived here on her own,' he said. 'She retreated.' He wasn't sure how to expand on this. 'With her it was drink, fuddled political principles, old emotional entanglements. Help only confused her.'

Two or three times a week she had wanted to talk about their lives together, to find out what the weather was like where he was, discuss the view from her window or his. 'You see that boat out in the Bay? Do you see it too? The blue one? What sort of boat is that?' Then she would encourage him: 'Come over! I'll get the Black Heart rum you like so much.' He always said yes. But in the end he rarely had the courage or energy to make the visit, because if he did she would soon sigh and say, 'We had such times together, before you took up with that whore from Carmody.'

'At Christmas,' he told the rickshaw girl, as the rickshaw slipped along between the ragmop palms and peeling pastel-coloured beach houses either side of Suntory Boulevard, 'I bought her a perfume she liked called Ashes of Roses.' The rest of the time he had tried to stay away. 'I was no longer in a position to look after her, yet she wouldn't look after herself. Because of this I felt not only guilt but an increasing sense of irritation.'

'Ashes of Roses!' the rickshaw girl said. 'No shit.'

Thinking he heard voices back on the access road, he turned to look out the rear window. Sand was blowing across the concrete in the purple light. No one was there, not even the Point kids.

'Go back!' he said. Then: 'I'm sorry.'

The rickshaw girl shrugged.

'Hey,' she said. 'I don't care where you go.'

THREE

The Liquid Moderne

After what had happened with his latest client, Vic Serotonin slept a lot. He slept as if he was dead, without any dreams. You spend time on the Saudade site, you don't dream. But you wake up feeling like hell and it gets worse all your life, just something else to look forward to as Vic always said. The exertion of not dreaming drove you to a sweat.

Vic's home was a coldwater walk-up in South End which he inherited, along with his entrée into the business, from a retired entradista and tour guide called Bonaventure. He had two rooms and a shower. He never cooked or ate there, though there was an induction stove and the place always smelled of old food. It smelled of old clothes, too, old tenancies, years of dust; but it was close enough to the event aureole, which was his professional requirement. Vic slept on a bed, he sat in a chair, he shaved in a mirror; like anyone else he bought all those things at a repro franchise at the end of the road, the day he moved in. He kept his zip-up gabardine jackets and Inga Malink artisan shirts in a wardrobe from Earth, rose veneer over boxwood circa 1932AD, that far away, that long ago. Out one window he had a good view of a bridge; out the other it was a segment of the noncorporate spaceport, primarily weeds and chainlink fence.

Late one afternoon he got up, looked in his mirror and thought:

'Jesus, Vic.'

Whatever happened had made him look fifty years old. He still had the taste you get in your mouth after you've been in there recently, and he was still seeing the client run away from him in the weird elongated dawn light. There was something in her panic, there was something in the way she ran: he couldn't remember what it was, but at least he wasn't angry any more.

Among the litter in the apartment Vic kept a Bakelite telephone with cloth-covered cables and a bell that rang. Everyone had one that year; Vic's was as cheap as everything else he owned. Just after he finished shaving, the bell rang and he got a call from a broker named Paulie DeRaad, which he was expecting. The call was short, and it prompted Vic to open a drawer from which he took out two objects wrapped in rag. One was a gun. The other was harder to describe – Vic sat by the window in the fading light, unwrapping it thoughtfully. It was about eighteen inches long, and as the rag came off it seemed to move. That was an illusion. Low-angle light, in particular, would glance across the object's surface so that for just a moment it seem to flex in your hands. It was half bone, half metal, or perhaps both at the same time; or perhaps neither.

He had no idea what it was. When he found it, two weeks before, it had been an animal, a one-off thing no one but him would ever see, white, hairless, larger than a dog, first moving away up a slope of rubble somewhere in the event site, then back towards him as if it had changed its mind and become curious about what Vic was. It had huge human eyes. How it turned from an animal into the type of object he finally picked up, manufactured out of this wafery artificial substance which in some lights looked like titanium and in others bone, he didn't know. He didn't want to know.

'Hey,' he said into the telephone, 'yeah, I got it. It's still here.'

He listened for a moment. 'Why would I let that happen?' he asked. Then he said OK and hung up. He wrapped the item in its rag and left the building with it. 'I don't do this for love,' he complained on his way downstairs, as if he was still talking to

Paulie DeRaad. DeRaad, one-time vacuum commando, facilitator and all-round Earth Military Contracts factotum, ran a joint he called the Semiramide Club, the visible part of extensive holdings in which EMC subsidiaries were implicated to the hilt. Wait-and-see was Paulie's working pattern, safety first his motto; and in this case, he said, he preferred Vic to meet with one of his operators, who would check things out and only make the buy if the goods were good.

Vic wasn't sure who he liked least, Paulie or his operators. Nevertheless he went down through Moneytown to the ocean, and not long after he left home found himself at the Suicide Point end of the Corniche, waiting in the half-dark of a one-room cinderblock structure which might once have been a bar, or a place where you bought cheap finance with predictable consequences, but which now, anyway, had peeling walls, boarded windows, a signature of disuse. Advertisements for legal services flickered softly round the heads of the Point kids in gun-punk outfits who stood talking between the ragmop palms outside.

Vic waited inside, listening carefully, for some minutes. It seemed a long while before anything happened. Then the palm trees were agitated by a cold breeze, and silvery rain poured down at an angle through the blue light on the beach. The Point kids shouted and ran about in the rain for a minute or two; then they were gone. As if he had been waiting for this, Vic took out the package and held it in one hand; he took out his gun and held it in the other. The room smelled of standing water, electricity, darkness.

Vic stood there watching the weather until he heard a soft voice which sounded as if it originated both inside and outside the building.

The voice said, 'Hello, Vic.'

'You want to come in out the rain,' Vic advised.

'That's funny, Vic.'

'Even so. I'm not here to talk to the climate.'

The voice said, 'I'll send someone.'

Vic shrugged as if it had asked him for something he didn't intend to give. 'The wrong thing happens here,' he warned, 'and I'll shoot the goods. You should be aware of that.'

Another laugh.

When Paulie DeRaad's operator came in, it came as one of the Point kids, male, maybe ten years old, wearing the usual tawdry Point notion of gun-punk chic, a sun-faded gabardine coat buttoned up tight to the neck and falling away unbelted from there to just below the knee. The kid walked in under his own power, then began to shake violently and fell against the wall. 'How come you do this to me?' he asked, in a puzzled voice. 'I never even saw you before.' He coughed, wiped the back of one wrist across his mouth and tried to make eye contact with Vic Serotonin, who turned determinedly away. After a minute or two Vic heard a sigh. The light flickered outside. The kid stopped making an effort and slid down the wall.

'Turn around now, Vic,' the operator said.

Vic licked his lips.

'I promise you it's safe to turn around now.'

Vic turned around. 'You look like my mother,' he said. He had no idea why his mother came into his mind, only that he was no longer certain what sex the Point kid was. It stood quite still and calm. Vic thought that if it ever did choose to move, to walk or run or anything understandable like that, it would be as graceful as a dancer. Its face seemed bigger. Its eyes too – they made too much contact with you. There was a kind of morning glow in that face, the unsexed unknowable personality of the Shadow Boy inside, an optimism so bare no one could look at it long.

'This is how it is,' Vic said. 'I put Paulie's goods on the floor between us, and you do whatever it is you do, and I shoot both of you if anything happens I don't like.'

'You should try and relax more,' the operator recommended.

40

It smiled disconcertingly until Vic set the artefact on the floor, then a kind of music came out of its throat, three or four thin, pure tones, less like a voice than a musical instrument: to which the item lit up faintly in response, glowing through the cloth Vic had wrapped it in. 'This is very real,' the Shadow Boy said, as if it was describing the artefact for someone else. 'This is very beautiful stuff.' In a single seamless movement it knelt down, leaned forward and made a circle with its arms, a curiously childlike sheltering gesture which embraced somewhat more space than the artefact occupied. Next, electromagnetic vomit issued from its mouth. Thousands of motes like violet neon tapioca slowly dripped on to the goods. 'I just want to see what we've got here,' the Shadow Boy said, 'before we go any further.' Dazzle from the interfacing operation blew back into its face, temporarily erasing the features. The walls of the room lit up then darkened again. Vic saw graffiti, he saw chipped plaster, exposed rebar.

He said, 'I'm not happy with this.'

There was complete silence in the place. Intelligence had left the eyes of the kneeling figure, and was now concentrated in the thick honey drip of light, the exchange of code.

'This is going too far,' Vic said. 'I'm not happy with this.'

A faint voice answered him. It was Paulie DeRaad's voice, piped in live from the Semiramide Club on a nanofraction of the operator's bandwidth. 'Hey, Vic,' it said, 'I won't need you any more tonight. The money's in your account.'

'Fuck you, Paulie,' Vic promised, 'if it isn't,' and he backed out warily, holding his gun out in front of him in both hands in a gesture less aggressive than imploring. Light continued to flicker and buzz from the doorway for some minutes, as the operator detached itself stage by stage, interface by interface. Eventually there was a kind of muffled sigh, almost of relief, and everything went dark.

By then, Vic Serotonin, heading east again, had crossed the lagoon bridge into the tourist port, where he entered a bar called

The World of Today. He had them bring him a bottle of Black Heart to take out; then changed his mind, sat down in one of the booths and ordered a meal. While he was eating he dialled up his account. As soon as he saw how much the sale of the artefact had grossed him, he pushed his plate away. He had lost his appetite.

'I'll take the bottle after all,' he told the barman.

Vic knew he wouldn't keep his luck. Money like that, his experience told him, has luck of its own. Money like that doesn't care about you, you should never get involved with money like that. Less than ten steps out of The World of Today he was kerb-crawled by a pink Cadillac convertible digitally revisioned to co-ordinate with the streamline moderne revival popular just then in some Saudade circles. He was as familiar with this car as any other travel agent. It belonged to Lens Aschemann, known to Vic as a high-up in Site Crime; a man who resembled the older Albert Einstein, whose mild manners and unwearying persistence were a legend from the very beginnings of artefact policing in Saudade. Aschemann had seen them come and go, from Emil Bonaventure onwards. He took the pipe out of his mouth and smiled.

'Hey, Vic,' he called, 'is that you?'

Vic stopped.

The Cadillac stopped too. 'You know it's me,' Vic said.

'Vic, get in, we'll drive.'

'I don't think so.'

'It's a pity to waste this beautiful car.'

Vic, who expected Aschemann to come with a team, was trying to look everywhere at once, up and down the street, back into the bar, inside the car. The street was empty. It was coming on to rain again, just enough to lacquer the sidewalk. Aschemann's driver proved to be a woman who gave Vic a smile like salt, which Vic returned. Her face was lighted from complex angles in two or three different registers, by the dashboard, the neon, the splashout from The World of Today doorway: but he could see she had good tailoring

42

and blonde hair cropped down to nothing much. She switched the engine off, got out of the car and came quickly round the trunk towards him. She was substantially taller than Aschemann, which you would expect, and built. Some kind of datableed ran oriental-looking ideograms down the inside of her arm.

'We asked you to get in the car,' she said.

Vic made a very small motion of one shoulder. This seemed to be as far as it could go at that time. They regarded one another frankly until the passenger door of the Cadillac swung open. Lens Aschemann bustled on to the sidewalk, breathing heavily and fussing with his raincoat.

'Wait!' he ordered his assistant. 'I'm afraid of what you'll do.'

He patted her arm. 'Calm down,' he told her. Then, to Vic, 'We can talk here.'

'I thought that would prove possible,' Vic Serotonin said.

'In this bar if you want, or just here on the pavement,' the detective assured him. 'We can talk. Sit in the car,' he urged his assistant. 'Go on. Really, it's fine. You can do that, because Vic would never be a problem to us. Vic, convince her you would never be a problem!'

Vic smiled.

'You're safe with me,' he told the woman.

'Vic, she could swallow you with a glass of water. Behave! You should see what they did to her reflexes.'

'I know I'd be impressed.'

The woman lifted one side of her mouth at Vic and went back round to the driver door. 'You're like dogs, you young people,' Aschemann called after her. 'I wonder you live until you're thirty.' He put his arm round Vic's shoulders. 'I know I'm getting old, Vic. I dreamed a mandala last night. It was simple, very simple. Just four or five concentric circles, quite compulsive to watch. They were silver in colour.'

'That's very interesting,' Vic said.

Aschemann looked hurt. 'Vic, you've got a moment to listen to me. The mandala, it's a sign you're changing for the better, as a human being. You're accepting a good orderly move from one big room of your life to the next.'

'Is that what they say?'

'It is. So I'm pleased with my progress. Maybe I'll retire happy.'

Serotonin held the Black Heart bottle up to the light.

'I must be doing well too,' he said. 'I've seen something like that at the bottom of every one of these.'

Aschemann gave a short laugh.

'You're too clever for me. But look!' He used the stem of his pipe to indicate the Kefahuchi Tract, which lay draped across the night sky of Saudade like a string of bad jewels. 'I used to dream of that,' he said with a shudder. 'Night after night, when I was young. You can't get change less ordered. Look at it, so raw and meaningless! The wrong physics, they say, loose in the universe. Do you understand that? I don't.' He tapped Vic's forearm, as if he thought Vic hadn't got the point, or as if he wasn't entirely sure he had Vic's attention. 'Now it's loose down here too. We have no idea what goes on in the event site. But whatever comes out,' he said, '*I* have to deal with the consequences.'

Vic couldn't think how to answer, so he said nothing.

This only seemed to confirm whatever the detective was thinking, because he shook his head, turned his back, and got into the Cadillac where he sat fussing with his raincoat and pipe. 'Do me a favour, Vic,' he asked in a remote voice, 'and shut this door for me.' When Vic had done that, he went on, 'You're a tour operator, that's fine. Unless you force it under my nose I can't be bothered with a little traffic of that kind.' He shrugged. 'Under normal circumstances, get in bed with Paulie DeRaad and that's your loss too. It's between you and him; why should I be interested? But whatever you and Paulie are up to at the Café Surf is new.'

Vic had never heard of the Café Surf.

'I don't know what you're talking about,' he said.

'Vic, if you're smuggling out some new kind of artefact it will be the end of you, I promise.'

'I never heard of this place!' Vic said.

But Aschemann had already turned to his driver and was saying something Serotonin couldn't hear. She replied, and they laughed together. They were a weird pair. Her eyes refocused for a moment, becoming flat, reflective and mysterious in the rain-wet light; the datastream pulsed energetically up and down her arm. She gave Vic a last smile, a louche, amused salute as if to say she would see him again soon. Then she fired up the engine and let it draw the Cadillac slowly from the kerb.

'Hey, Vic?' Aschemann called over his shoulder as the car moved off. 'Give my love to Emil Bonaventure next time you see him. Say hello to Emil for me!'

'Well then, what do you think?' Aschemann asked his assistant.

They sat in the warm faux-leather smell of the car, streetlight flickering regularly across their faces. Her hands rested on the wheel. Her feet rested on the pedals. She had a purposive manner, Aschemann had already noted, with anything like that.

'You know him better than I do,' she said at length.

'It's clever of you to see that. Is there more?'

'If anything he seemed surprised.'

'That's our Vic,' the detective said, 'always surprised.'

'I don't know what you mean by that.' She looked ahead at the empty street. Aschemann gave her time to say more if she wanted to, then smiled to himself. After a moment he made a business of extracting a match from his Café Surf matchbook; pulled open the ashtray, which released a stale smell; and put the match in there without lighting it.

'You know he could have hurt you,' he said.

It was her turn to smile. 'You shouldn't worry about me,' she assured him. A career in Sport Crime, she said, gave you access to chops the civilian tailors never saw. That was just one of the professional benefits it conferred.

'Go by Rosedale Avenue,' Aschemann ordered.

All the streets in that part of town were overlooked. The interstellar cruise ships towered over everything – PanGalactic's *Jayne Anne Phillips*, the Fourmyle *Ceres*, the Beths/Hirston *Pro Ana* and half a dozen more, their enormous hulls scoured to matt-grey by re-entry fires, ablated to a wafer by the unpredictable gamma-ray storms of Radio Bay. Every planetfall they made, another layer of paint was burned off them; you could tell how far into the tour they were by the effect of burnished metal glowing through the faint reds and blues of their corporate livery. While deep in the engine rooms, particle jockeys in lead suits scratched their heads and tried to reconcile three different kinds of physics – each with its own set of 'unimpeachable' boundary conditions – so they could take off again without the customers experiencing G.

Aschemann stared out at the great hulls, shifting relative to one another like trees in a wood with the motion of the car.

'All our troubles come from up there,' he said.

'I thought they all came from the site.'

This went too far, perhaps, because he changed the subject. 'I looked in at the Semiramide last night. Who do I see there but Vic's friend Fat Antoyne, drinking that foul stuff he likes. There was a Mona on his arm.'

'There's your connection,' she said.

To her it was bankable: Serotonin to Antoyne, DeRaad to Antoyne, Antoyne to the Café Surf. But Aschemann only shrugged. 'Perhaps it means something,' he agreed, 'perhaps it doesn't. Stop a moment.'

Something had caught his eye, a movement, a shadow, at the chainlink fence of the tourist port. It was gone next time he looked. It could have been a figure climbing in or climbing out.

'Go on,' he said. 'Nothing is there.' He had no faith in the tourist port fences. 'Or any fence for that matter,' he told his assistant. The ports attracted outlaws and psychic cripples, but that wasn't why he disliked them. They were just another connection with the undependable, the random, the exterior. The Cadillac turned ponderously north, then down towards the sea, where ragmop palms bent compliantly, showing the napes of their necks to the offshore wind. The rain had stopped. Aschemann was silent for some time. The assistant glanced sideways at him and eventually, as if he was answering something she had said, he murmured:

'Vic Serotonin's no threat to anyone but himself. But perhaps it's time we had a proper talk with Paulie.'

Serotonin stood in the rain after they had gone. A rickshaw shushed past, trailing softly coloured butterflies. Two doors down from The World of Today, light poured out of the display window of an Uncle Zip franchise, exciting everything it fell on with the promise of immanence and instant transformation. He spent a minute or two on the sidewalk, staring at its open catalogues – emblems, brands and smart tattoos, loss-leader holograms offering to mod you with the qualities of the great men and women of the past: the genius of Michael Jackson, the looks of Albert Einstein, the nourishing spiritual intelligence of Paul Coelho – wondering if now was the time to make some changes to his self-presentation then leave for another planet. He didn't want Paulie DeRaad in his life. He didn't want Aschemann and the Saudade artefact police there either. Possession of an item from the event site would net him ten to life: he couldn't at that moment recall what he'd get for selling it on through a Shadow Boy.

As if to keep the event site at arm's length in this, the latter part of his life, Emil Bonaventure had retired hurt to the third floor of a small house in GlobeTown, a triangle of quiet, narrow, picturesque streets gentrified by their proximity to the port. There, in the shadow of the big interstellar ships, he was looked after by a woman who called herself his daughter. She mopped up after the deep fevers, the days of hallucinations, the wasting fits and other legacies of Bonaventure's time in the Saudade site. Her loyalty was fierce, if indistinct. Otherwise she kept herself to herself, in rooms of her own on the ground floor; and her behaviour was such that, for all anyone knew, he might really have been her father.

'I did a stupid thing, Emil,' Vic was forced to admit, after the woman let him in and he climbed the stairs to the third floor. He described what had happened; also Paulie DeRaad's part in it, and Paulie DeRaad's operator's part. Meanwhile, he added, Lens Aschemann was on to some other scam of Paulie's, right the other side of Saudade at some bar no one had ever heard of; and he had Vic in the frame for that too.

'You're in a worse condition than me,' Bonaventure said, 'if this is the way you're going now.'

'Tell me something I don't know,' Vic said.

He offered Bonaventure the bottle, which he had sneaked upstairs hidden under his jacket. Bonaventure took it and stared greedily at the label. Sometimes his vision was as bad as his memory: it wasn't a physiological problem. 'Is this Black Heart?' he said.

'I overpaid if it isn't,' Vic said.

'Want some advice?'

'No.'

Bonaventure shrugged and let himself fall back against his pillows, holding the bottle in a defeated way as if it was too heavy to drink from. He was in his sixtieth year, but he looked older, a long, disjointed man with white hair like a crest which in profile accentuated the weight and hook of his nose. Eventually he got the bottle to his mouth and left it there for some time. While this was going on, Vic looked round the room at the bare floorboards and clean linen; then he said, 'Jesus, Emil. That was for both of us.'

'I can't seem to get enough to drink,' Bonaventure said. 'Don't ever pick up anything in there, Vic,' he begged suddenly, as if he had brought the subject up himself. He gazed at Vic sidelong, the whites of his eyes yellowing in the lamplight. 'Promise me you won't?'

Vic smiled. 'It's a little late for that, Emil. Besides, you brought stuff out by the truckload.'

'Things were different then,' Bonaventure said, looking away.

He was so frail you could see the drink on its way into him, percolating from vein to vein. His hair was the colour of cigarette ash, and the white stubble in the lines of his face never seemed to get any longer. He didn't leave the house now. He rarely left the bed. On a good day his eyes were a bright blue, still amused, but on a day like this they looked boiled. All his energy went into a Parkinsonian shake, a buzz of low-grade fever, a kind of continuous electrical discharge under his skin which gave it the colour of heavy metal poisoning. On a day like this even his bedclothes seemed to be infected. He looked like a bag of rags. He tried to say something more, but in the end could only repeat:

'Things were different.'

'I wanted to talk to you about that,' Vic said carefully. 'Something's happening in there.'

The old man shrugged. 'Something's always happening in there,' he said. Then, with a logic typical of his generation: 'That's how you know you aren't out here.' He gave Vic a moment to process this. 'Take my advice,' he went on, 'don't be like the kids who think they have it all mapped out.'

'Which kids are those, Emil?'

Bonaventure chose to ignore him. 'They never heard of contingency,' he said, 'that's the fact of it.' He stared at the label of the Black Heart bottle as if he was trying to remember how to read. 'These kids,' he asked himself, 'what are they? Entradista Lite. They think there's a career structure in that business! They've got a map they bought from Uncle Zip, and a Chambers pistol they'll never shoot. Good thing, because that gun's a particle jockey's nightmare.'

'Hey, Emil,' Vic said. 'Give me the bottle.'

'They dress for the tourist trade. They talk like bad poets. They never say anything about themselves but at the same time they can't bear you not to know who they are.'

'Who are you talking about, Emil?'

'They never get lost in there, Vic: they never risk anything.'

'Are you talking about me?' Vic Serotonin said.

He tried to describe what had happened to him in the aureole the last time he was there, but it already seemed like some event in another world, and maybe that was what it was. It was a clear but meaningless event from some other world, already folded over itself, and – worse – over other memories of his. The client ran away from him across a pile of partly overgrown rubble, her fur coat open to the spitting rain. At the same time the artefact he had sold to Paulie DeRaad was zigzagging down the slope towards him like an animal whose curiosity had got the better of it. It was a deer or a pony, or perhaps a large dog – lurching but graceful, a hairless animal with cartoon human eyes. Then he was back in Liv Hula's bar and threatening to shoot Antoyne the fat man for having a history. 'The site's expanding,' he tried to explain to Emil Bonaventure: 'We're in for some movement there, Emil, and none of us knows what to do.' By that Vic meant himself, because who else did he know? No one stupid enough to go in there on a daily basis. That was why he needed Bonaventure's view of it, but to ask directly would feel like giving something away.

'It's on the move again,' he said, 'for the first time since your day.' The boundaries were newly elastic; at the same time, something was changing deep inside, and everything that happened to Vic in there felt as if it represented something else. 'It's like a metaphor, Emil,' he thought of saying. But he was still in awe of Bonaventure's generation, and of Bonaventure's generation's definitions, so in the end all that came out was, 'I think things are taking a whole turn for the worse.'

The old man didn't want to know. He only lifted the bottle to his mouth again, then let it fall on to the bed and stared into himself instead, his face stubbled, leaden, collapsed. 'It was a long time ago,' he said. 'Everyone had his own ideas.'

'You remember more than that, Emil. Don't pretend you don't.'

Bonaventure shook his head. 'In those days, everyone had his own ideas,' he repeated. Then he seemed to relent, and asked Vic, 'Were you ever at the Triangle? Were you ever in that deep?' When he saw Vic had no idea what he meant, he shrugged. 'Because for a while Atmo Fuga thought that was the centre of it all. He was there once and it was all shoes. The air was perfectly still but full of old shoes, floating around one another as if they'd been lifted up on a strong wind. As if shoes had a gravity of their own. He said they exhibited something that looked like flocking behaviour. Filthy old shoes, cracked and wrinkled, soles hanging off. He saw other stuff too. It was Atmo's belief the Triangle was at the centre of it.' He shrugged. 'But if you were never there—'

'I've been further in than anyone I know,' Vic was able to state, 'and I never saw anything like shoes.'

Bonaventure couldn't seem to grasp this. Perhaps he didn't want to. He blinked and bit his lip, and it seemed to Vic he was refusing some basic understanding – something about the world he knew well but wouldn't share because he preferred to be in denial. He stared over Vic's shoulder for a moment, weak tears coming to his eyes. 'None of these kids know anything,' he appealed to the room at large, as if there was someone other than Vic he could talk to. 'It's all show with them.'

'You *are* talking about me,' Vic said. Despite his good intentions he felt his face contract and harden. 'Well then fuck you, old man.' He pulled out the Chambers gun and dropped it on the bed where it lay against Bonaventure's frail form defined by the bedclothes, its magazine a matt-black roil of particles held in suspension by some kind of magnetic field. 'I'm forty years old, so fuck you.'

Bonaventure winced away from the gun. He curled up and threw one arm across his eyes.

'Don't leave me, Atmo!' he cried. 'Not here!'

'You're fucked with me,' Vic Serotonin said. 'Why should I keep coming here, for you to insult me?' He regretted that immediately. He picked his gun up again and secured it. 'I'm sorry, Emil,' he said. He laid his hand on the old man's shoulder. 'Hey, if only you'd help sometimes,' he said. 'Just help out.'

'You've got a low startle point,' Bonaventure said finally.

Vic laughed. 'It's how I survive,' he said. 'Come on, finish the rum. No one buys Black Heart to keep it for tomorrow!'

After he had calmed the old man down, and got him to sleep, he hid the empty bottle with several others under the bed and made his way downstairs; where Bonaventure's daughter reminded him quietly:

'He sold you a business, Vic. That doesn't make him your father.'

'Does it make him yours?' Vic asked her.

She shrugged. 'Say what you like to me,' she said. 'You're not so clever as to make a difference.'

She was a black-haired woman, with wide blunt hips, who blushed up quickly under her olive skin. Whatever Vic thought, she had made her way here across the Halo, planet to planet, starting out two years old in the crook of Emil Bonaventure's arm. He named her Edith, no one knew why, and though she did not resemble him at all, was always careful not to drop her. That was almost forty years ago. She had no idea where they started from, or why, but she could still remember the endless stubby Dynaflow freighters, noncorporate rocket ports, afternoons in sawdust bars, Monas and barkeeps exclaiming over her, filling her with bad bar food and milk blued by the effort of keeping itself milk in the face of where it found itself. In return she filled the vacuum for them, the day they saw her and maybe even thereafter, as a cheap blurred smiling memory they could keep until whatever they'd been denying caught up with them at last.

In those days Edith was both pretty and talented. She had clever feet. She learned to play the accordion early, dance on a table while she squeezed. Her energy was endless, especially for any kind of public appearance.

'You can say what you like, Vic Serotonin, but we were nation-wide. Emil the entradista and his Accordion Kid.'

'I never heard of you,' Vic said.

Some days when he said that it would make her laugh. Today it made her think of being eleven years old.

'Hey, make yourself at home,' she said. 'Do you want a drink? Or was the rum enough?' When Vic looked away she said, 'You think I didn't notice? You shouldn't encourage him to drink.' That was a caution he'd heard before, so he was surprised to find her standing in close to him suddenly, saying:

'If I gave you his book, Vic, would you leave him alone?'

'Don't joke, Edith,' Vic said.

When Emil Bonaventure arrived in Saudade thirty years ago, every-one was writing on paper.

It was one of those things. They loved paper suddenly. The nos-talgia shops were full of it, all colours of cream and white, blank or with feint lines, or small pale-grey squares, shining softly from the lighted windows which were like religious cubicles or niches. There was every kind of notebook in there, paper between covers you could hardly believe, from wood bark to imitation grey fur to holographic pictures from the narratives of Ancient Earth reli-gious figures, with their fingers and their bovine eyes uplifted, who smiled and raised a cross as you turned the book in your hands in the retro shop light.

As artificial as the textures of the paper itself – an Uncle Zip product franchised out of some chopshop on another planet – these notebooks came in all sizes, fastened any way you could think, with clasps, hasps, magnets, combination locks or bits of hairy string you wrapped around and did up in a beautiful knot. Some were fastened in more contemporary ways, so you could see a little flicker in the air near the edge of the pages – if you're the wrong person don't get your fingers near those!

Everyone was buying these books because it was cute to write your thoughts in them – thoughts, a shopping list, those kinds of things.

People wrote, 'Who do I want to be today?'

They wrote diaries.

Everyone suddenly loved paper, no one could say why, and soon they'd love something else. But it was more practical for some than others. Emil Bonaventure kept the habit where others kicked it, and wrote everything down until the day he went into the Saudade site for the last time. He didn't trust his memory by then. He'd been in there once too often. The stuff he had to remember was complex – directions, bearings, instructions to himself. It was data. It was clues. It was everything you daren't forget in that trade. It was everything he couldn't trust to an operator. Work with the Shadow Boys, Emil used to say, you don't trust any kind of algorithm. Even the tame ones. Among the data he also wrote descriptions about his achievements, of which he had done more than one. He wrote observations, like: 'It's always snowing in Sector 7. Whatever time of year it is outside, whatever time of year it is inside.' He had the whole site divided up, Sector this, Sector that. In those days, whatever he said now, the entradistas had to believe in facts; they had to believe they knew things no one else knew.

Emil wrote it all down in that water-stained letter – as if he had to convince himself of something – in a kind of slanting disordered scribble which did not reflect his personality. Then he hid the book. He was as cagey as all those entradistas, and when Vic Serotonin bought the goodwill to Emil's business, the book was not included.

'It's no joke, Vic. You remind him of too many things. If I gave you the book would you leave him alone?'

'I wouldn't stop coming here,' Vic said.

She stepped in closer, so he was just in the warmth of her. 'Oh no?' she taunted. Serotonin tried to kiss her, but she was too quick for him. 'Vic, if you got that book we'd never see you again. Anyway, it would be the death of you. It was as good as the death of him.

'Come here, Vic,' she said. 'And look at this.'

Two or three little child-star costumes with short stiff faux-satin skirts a ferocious emerald-green. Pairs of black patent leather shoes with straps and taps, in ascending sizes. Accordions, and parts of them. Some of the accordions she had played until they broke or got too small, some she bought later in life because she liked them. They were all colours, electric-blue, through the same savage green as the outfits, to a kind of resonant maroon, all under a high-lacquer finish with metal emblems of rocket ships, shooting stars, snowy mountains. Each keyboard grin exposed rare ivories adopted from alien animals. The small shoes now made her cry, Edith was forced to admit. Wherever she lived she laid out these keepsakes on shelves, or in breakfront cabinets whose glass doors were etched with exotic scenes from Ancient Earth. Today she had something new to show him.

'I performed in this on Pumal Verde.' Folded into yellowed tissue, it looked like some kind of marching band uniform, and actually she couldn't remember wearing it. 'I was fourteen years old.' She buried her face in the bolero jacket, caught odours she didn't recognise. 'You would have liked me then. I was so innocent, Vic. You want to smell it too?'

'That's unjust to me,' said Vic, who didn't like her tone.

Edith smiled benignly to herself and decided to look at the skirt next. As she unfolded it something dropped out on to the floor. 'Hey, Vic,' she said. 'What's this?'

It was an old notebook with a leather cover.

'Jesus,' Vic Serotonin said.

He was reaching for it when something fell over loudly in the old man's room upstairs. Vic looked at the ceiling despite himself, which allowed Edith to sweep the book quickly from under his hand. Their eyes met.

'Emil's awake, Vic,' she said. 'You should go see if he needs help.'

'I'll want to talk about this,' he warned her over his shoulder as he left the room.

Edith watched him go. He would always care for the old man. As for Edith, the Accordion Kid still played to packed audiences in her head, its pipeclay face Uncle Zipped to a perfect Shirley Temple, one instrument following another – bigger and more expensive, with more chromium and japanned rare wood – each year as she played herself clear across the Halo into adolescence and a career in the New Nuevo Tango; always trying to look after Emil because he did such a job of looking after her, packing in a kind of comfortable guilt until now it was a permanent situation, because Emil would never be able to look after either of them again. Close her eyes and the accordion danced, and she felt like a cultivar – a succession of perfect little-girl bodies in shiny skirts with kick-up net petticoats, white socks and round-toed patent leather sandals.

She followed Vic Serotonin up the stairs, thinking of these scenes.

Emil Bonaventure's CV was this: he started out indentured to some arm of Earth Military Contracts – in his case on a project known only by the number '121', which he never talked about. After that he brawled and drank and fucked his way across the Halo with his baby daughter in tow until he wound up in the Saudade site and she wound up an adult. That stopped him in his tracks. It got his attention. As a young man he was like any of those people. He had a lot of appetites but until he got to Saudade he had no idea who he was. All those years later Vic found him lying half out of bed in this upper room at the edge of the tourist port. A damp sheet was tangled round his white old upper body, which had bruises in all stages and colours from similar falls and incidents. His face was pushed into the wall by his own weight. 'Help me, Edith,' he said.

'I'm Vic,' Vic said.

'Come on, help him!' said Edith.

Between them they wrestled him back into bed, then she said, 'I'll let you two brave entradistas talk.' She went to the window, and stared out of it across the port where rain was falling through the halogen lights.

'Vic,' Bonaventure whispered, as soon as she had moved away, 'come here. Sit down. I thought about the things you said.'

'What things were they, Emil?'

'Listen Vic, everybody I ever took in there, I took them on a promise of more than they could have—'

'They want to go, Emil. It's what they want.'

'No, listen!' He clutched Vic's arm. 'I knew that. I knew that every time. There's something in there, but it's nothing. They always see that in the end. They see you've fooled them.'

'Where's this leading, Emil? Is it leading to the same old shit?'

Bonaventure shook his head tiredly.

'I just want to know where you've been, Vic. I want to know what locations we have in common.'

'You want to compare dicks,' Vic said.

'Because you must have been in Sector 7 and seen that immense white thing like a face, hanging over the roofs—'

'Give it up, Emil.'

But Bonaventure refused to be saved. 'Listen to me!' he

demanded. 'Just for once!' Whatever decaying memory had hold of him was pulling him down. His generation all had the same need to rehearse, compare adventures, keep alive the things that terrified them in there. Vic could feel his whole old body trembling with it. 'After that the houses are piles of bricks, this fucking utter wasteland of bricks. There's an echo every time a tile falls, and the face watches you—' He saw Vic's expression, and the tension went out of him suddenly. He sighed. 'Why am I bothering?' he asked. He shrugged. 'If you haven't seen that,' he said, 'what *have* you seen? Nothing.'

'Here it comes again,' Vic predicted.

'He only wants to talk, Vic,' Edith said tiredly from the window.

'Stick to the safe edge,' Bonaventure advised the world in general, Vic in particular. He said, 'Be a tourist like the rest of them.'

Vic threw up his hands. 'I can go anywhere and have a better time than this.' He appealed to Bonaventure's daughter, 'I could have a better time than this at the Semiramide Club.' Edith shrugged. She gave him a direct look – If you go, the look suggested, don't come back – and resumed examining the street outside as if it was full of things which, though they didn't interest her much, were more interesting than Vic.

'Jesus!' Serotonin said. He had a sudden image of Paulie DeRaad's Shadow Boy, and the face of its doomed proxy lighted by the splashback from whatever operation had gone on at Suicide Point. 'No one gives a fuck about the things *I* have to deal with,' he complained. He got up to leave.

'I'm sorry,' Bonaventure said. 'Vic, it's a big place. Maybe we just saw different parts of it.'

Vic said from the doorway, 'I don't think so.'

'I can't dream, Vic!' Bonaventure called. 'I can't dream!'

'You knew it would come to that,' Vic said. He didn't know how to help. 'You always knew it would come to that.'

'Wait till it happens to you, Vic.'

'Hush,' Vic said absently. 'Hush up, old guy.'

Edith Bonaventure found him downstairs, coldly ripping pages out of the old man's notebook.

'I thought I hid that again,' she said unconcernedly.

'There's nothing written in it.'

'Isn't there? It mustn't be the right one then.'

'You already knew it wasn't,' Vic said.

She acknowledged this with a smile 'Even the ones he's written in aren't necessarily the right one,' she said. 'Emil wrote a lot of stuff in his time. Do you want a drink?'

Serotonin dropped the notebook on the floor and yawned. 'I ought to go,' he said. She brought him the drink anyway, and stood in front of him while he swallowed it. 'What *is* that?' he said.

'You finished the good stuff,' she reminded him.

Serotonin wiped his mouth. He looked round the room, with its shelves full of little-girl memorabilia; he couldn't resolve into one image the Edith he knew and the Edith who kept those things. He set down his glass and pulled her in close until she was compelled to sit on his knee. 'Does he need money?' he asked her. Edith looked away and smiled. She pulled Vic's head down and made him kiss the nape of her neck.

'We always need money,' she said. 'Mm. That's nice.'

After he had gone, she lay on the sofa thinking about him. Serotonin reminded her of all the men she met on her way across the Halo. Everyone she encountered in those days was trying to live out some dream already irretrievable when they were sixteen.

If she was fair she had to include herself in that. On Pumal Verde, for instance, she got bagged on Dr Thirsty's, hallucinating for eleven hours straight a huge white bird flapping slowly and ecstatically through vacuum. Her boyfriend of the time said, 'Edith, that bird is *your life*, and you'd be wise to follow where it leads.' He didn't do much with his own life, only joined EMC like the rest, and was made pilot of some kind of fighter craft which necessitated him being rebuilt by the military tailor so that wires came out his mouth and into the controls. They were supposed to have damped out the gag reflex, but sometimes he felt the wires in there like a mass of sinewy fibrous stuff he couldn't swallow. If he panicked, or let his concentration slip, he heard his mother's voice in the cockpit, calm and firm, telling him to do things. It was hard to disobey. She said not to be frightened. Not to be angry. She said, concentrate now and get this part right. Then everyone will be saved. That was mostly the end of him as far as Edith was concerned.

Towards dawn she went back upstairs to see to the old man.

He was still awake, staring ahead of himself as if he was spectating at some event no one else could see; but he must have known she was there, because he took her hand and said, 'The worst things we ever brought out of there, we called them "daughters". Bring out a daughter and you had nothing but trouble. A daughter would change shape on you. It wasn't alive, it wasn't technology either: no one knew what it did, no one knew what it was for.'

Edith squeezed his hand.

'You told me that already,' she said.

He chuckled. 'It was me who started calling them that. Whatever you brought out, it had better not be a daughter.'

'You told me that a hundred times before.'

He chuckled again, and she squeezed his hand again, and after a while he went to sleep.

She stayed with him. Every so often she looked round the room, at the painted wainscoting a warm cream colour under the low-wattage lights, the old bed piled up with coloured pillows, bits of mismatched cloth she liked, or thought the old man might like. We saw worse places than this, she thought. There was a flare from the rocket field, then another; they lighted her strong profile and cast its shadow on the wall.

FOUR

At the Club Semiramide

Liv Hula opened her bar in the late mornings. However she caned it the previous night she could never sleep more than two or three hours, but after that would wake suddenly from dreams of being sucked down, listen in a daze but hear nothing except the usual sounds from Straint Street outside – a rickshaw rumbling and bumping downhill into Saudade on the uneven pavement; a woman singing. Or she would have dreams of some other planet, from which she always woke thinking, 'Where was that? I had a better time there.' These minute, crisp little visions of her past not connecting one with another, or to here and now, she would look round at the room with its clean bare white walls, then get up suddenly and kick last night's clothes around the floor.

It was easier to be downstairs. Sweep, push tables about, wash glasses, breathe the stale air, splash cold water on your face from the bar sink. You unlocked the door, daylight poured in on the slant and the shadow operators flickered about in it for a minute or two like reef fish before retreating to their corners. At about the same time Liv Hula retreated behind the bar. She always stood in the same place. Polished the zinc with her elbows, moved the cash drawer in and out. By now her feet fit a dip in the springy floorboards. She didn't want to remember how many years she spent behind the bar in Black Cat White Cat.

Check stock, order food, watch the chopshop traffic, watch the light swing slowly round the room, and by early afternoon she would have her first customer. She was glad to see anyone. Usually it would be Fat Antoyne, but Fat Antoyne hadn't been in since Joe Leone died. Or if it wasn't Antoyne it would be Vic Serotonin the travel agent, who at that hour hardly looked better than Liv herself.

Today it wasn't either of them.

When Vic Serotonin did arrive, it was with that preoccupied air of his – hands in pockets, shoulders in a permanent shrug, needy eyes fixed away from everything – as if he was thinking so hard about his life he didn't know what part of the city it was going on in. He leaned on the bar and said:

'Rum.'

'Hi, Vic,' Liv Hula said. 'Nice to see you.'

After a pause she said in a fair imitation of Serotonin's voice, '"Nice to see *you*, Liv."'

'Cut it out,' said Vic Serotonin.

'When you pay your tab I will,' she said sweetly. 'Black Heart over ice? Well, how did I know that?' She let him drink it – standing a little back from the bar with something between satisfaction and amusement in her eyes – then said, 'Your client's back, Vic.'

Vic looked round and saw the client had been sitting there all the time on one of the window stools, staring out the misty glass into the street. Her face was tilted so the light fell evenly across it and, without disclosing anything, gave it a milky, transparent look. A cup of hot chocolate was in front of her. She didn't seem to be drinking from it. The moment Vic saw her he was aware of other images spinning off her, too quick to really see. He had images of running, then a board fence green with lichen in the rain. An abandoned street from a wrong angle.

Generally Vic would walk away from anything difficult. Clients came to him, he looked them over; he knew a time-waster.

'I don't want to see you here again,' he said.

He walked quietly up behind her where she sat on the stool and put his mouth near her neck and said, 'I don't want to see you here again.' He was startled by his own intensity. She stared at him for a moment, as if she was trying to understand something in a foreign language. Then she got to her feet and began to fumble in her bag, out of which eventually she took a business card. She said:

'This is where I live. I wish you would help me. If you change your mind, I still feel as if I want to go in there.'

'That's the problem,' Vic said.

'I'm sorry?'

Vic said, 'I know my mind. You don't know yours.' He stood in the doorway and watched her walk away down Straint. This time she was dressed in a black tulip skirt to mid-calf. Over that was a little silver fur peplum jacket with lightly padded shoulders; the jacket came with a matching pillbox hat. She hailed a rickshaw and got in it.

'She wishes you would help her, Vic,' Liv Hula called from behind the bar. Vic told her he would like another drink.

On the card the woman had given him was an address in Hot Walls, which Vic recalled as tall old-fashioned townhouses on the wrong side of being corporate, run down twenty years ago when the current generation of executives traded up into the purpose-built complexes of Doko Gin. He wished he hadn't said anything to her at all, because that made a connection between them.

'Why would a tourist have an address on Hot Walls?' he asked Liv Hula.

'I'd ask how she got your *name*, Vic.'

'That too.'

Liv watched him tear the card up and toss the pieces on the bar. Later, though, he collected them together and put them in his pocket.

Vic got another call from Paulie DeRaad.

DeRaad seemed irritated. At the same time he was dissociated and vague. He wanted to talk about the artefact he had bought, he said. He said he was puzzled. He said he wasn't sure what he had. But each time Vic asked him what was wrong, his attention seemed to be somewhere else. 'Is something going on where you are, Paulie?' Vic asked him. 'Because you should attend to it if there is, especially when you don't have anything to say to me.'

'Hey, be polite, Vic,' Paulie advised him. Eventually, he said Vic should come over to his club, the Semiramide. That would be the best way of doing it, he thought. There was something Vic should see; he could see it for himself.

'I've got other things to do,' Vic said.

'You haven't got things more important than this,' DeRaad said. 'Hey, Vic, I'll send someone to pick you up, save you any trouble.'

'There's no need for that,' Vic said.

The Semiramide lay midtown like a cruise ship at dock, placed to attract a mix of tourists and local players, class and income to be decided by Paulie himself. When Vic got there, six-thirty p.m., he found an ongoing situation. It was empty but for the customary DeRaad footsoldiers, a dozen contract gun-kiddies sitting round the back tables excitedly comparing weapons and throwing dice. Some of the furniture was tipped over and a couple of charred holes in the walls indicated someone had let go recently with a reaction pistol. Paulie's people seemed less connected than usual.

'Paulie won't be happy you go in there,' one of the gun-punks informed Vic when he tried to get in the office.

'The fuck he won't,' Vic said, looking down at her.

The punk's name was Alice Nylon, she was eight years old and wore a blue plastic rainslicker buttoned up to the neck. *Café electrique* rotted Alice's front teeth before she was seven, giving her an interesting speech defect. She enjoyed cookery, aquacise sessions at the local pool, and in her spare time was studying to do her own accountancy. 'Vic,' she told him, 'you *would not believe* the raid

64

we had. No, really! Right here at the Semiramide Club.' She shook her head in disbelief, slowly from side to side. 'Those losers from Site Crime, all over us like a cheap holo of the Kefahuchi Tract. That guy who looks like Albert Einstein? We had to be tuff, Paulie said, and not do what comes naturally. We had to keep a tight rein.'

'I wish I'd seen that, Alice,' Vic said politely.

Alice shrugged. She was a professional. It was nothing to her.

'We would of iced them, Vic, but what do you do?' She gave him her tired, raddled little smile. 'So maybe it would best if you waited here? For Paulie?'

Vic said OK and went over to one of the tables.

'Hey, Vic,' Alice called after him. 'This morning I cooked brownies on my own!'

Vic hated the Semiramide.

As a storefront it was an insult to the intelligence.

It wasn't much of a joint either.

The instant you walked in you knew Paulie DeRaad made his money elsewhere. There were forty tables, each to seat four, in a circular high-ceiling space originally the premises of a predictable alien technology scam calling itself FUGA-Orthogen. (This scam founded itself on the ownership of three mining machines parked above some unknown gamma-emitter in Radio Bay. At best guess they'd been there one million years already, and no one knew how to operate them. 'What those jockeys were going to dig up was also a little unclear,' Paulie used to say with a faint smile. 'So we had to let them go.') When he moved in he had the walls calcimined white and illuminated with selected UV frequencies. Paulie liked high-end light because it reminded him of his glory days. Holograms floated about, advertising product; Monas floated about, taking commissions for the back room where people could be more comfortable. Paulie's customers could eat, they could play dice a little. He had a band so they could listen to music. Paulie's only major proviso, they should dress well: his was a weakness, he completely acknowledged, for the glitterati.

Vic bought a drink.

To pass the time, he pieced together the visiting card his ex-client had left him when he threw her out of Black Cat White Cat. It puzzled him that a tourist would keep an apartment in Saudade – a Hot Walls address was too genteel to be cheap, not gentrified enough to be corporate.

It was seven by then, and the joint was beginning to fill, mainly with couples who would get a cocktail before they went on elsewhere. Seven-ten, Vic was surprised to see Antoyne Messner walk into the Semiramide and head for the tables at the back. 'Antoyne!' he called, but though the fat man acknowledged him with a nod, he didn't come over. Instead, he sat down with the gun-punks and they all threw dice together. 'Well, fuck you, Fat Antoyne,' Vic said to himself. Just then the office door opened, and Paulie DeRaad's voice was heard calling:

'Hey, Vic! You incompetent fuckhead! Where are you?'

Paulie DeRaad was younger than Vic Serotonin. He had a sharp nose, a shock of white-blond hair that went back in the famous 'widow's peak' of his service years, highlights of which sometimes played as holograms in the main room of the Semiramide Club.

Paulie was at Cor Caroli, fourteen years old. Later he was one of the three people who got out alive from *El Rayo X* after its orbital collision with the Nastic heavy cruiser *Touching the Void*. Since then he had been wiry and intense and bunched-up, and when he became excited the skin of his face would seem to get thinner and shinier and the blood would seem to lie too close to the surface. This was a legacy of radiation burns, and a general ablative thinning of his skin which he didn't have repaired and wore like a badge. Paulie never stopped. He liked everything. He wanted everything. That, at least, was the first impression he gave you: behind that, you sensed almost immediately, his plan was to stay alive and prosper.

'You want to take a look at this?' Paulie asked Vic.

He meant his office, which was in worse condition than his club. The air smelled of ionisation and char, the furniture was strewn about. There had been some kind of fight in there. It was a small room for that. Worse for Paulie, though, Aschemann's team had brought in equipment that went through his shadow operators as if they were a wooden filing cabinet. So now they were in the ceiling corners, folded up so tight across themselves it would take days to get them down again. They were in shock. They felt violated. They had nothing left to disclose. Paulie looked bad too. He was sweating, and his face had gone a hard, meaty colour.

'Do you know anything about this?'

Vic said he didn't.

'Well, fuck, Vic, you ought to.'

Vic went and found a chair, which he tipped the right way up so he could sit down. This gesture allowed Paulie DeRaad to sit down too, and wipe his face. 'Some new kind of artefact is coming out the site,' he said, 'this is Aschemann's story. He has us in the frame for it.' He put his fingers in his mouth then took them out again and stared at them. 'Look in my mouth, Vic, tell me if my gums are bleeding.'

'Fuck off, Paulie.'

DeRaad laughed. 'I nearly got you, though, Vic. You were halfway out the seat.' He was calming down, looking amused. He was enjoying his life again. He said, 'You know this joint they call the Café Surf?'

'I never heard of it,' Vic said.

'Hey, you can talk to me, Vic, I'm your friend.'

If Vic was worried about nanocam coverage, he said, there was no need. Site Crime's equipment was a disgrace. It was ten years old. It was insanely expensive to run. Ninety per cent of the time it was out of service. Paulie had EMC cover anyway, he implied. 'You're invisible, you go anywhere with me.' Vic, who until that moment hadn't been remotely worried, stared at him, then shrugged.

'Is that why you brought me here?'

Paulie stopped looking amused.

'No,' he said. 'There's something I want you to see.' He got to his feet. 'Well, come on,' he said. 'Do you think I keep it here?'

'I wouldn't know, Paulie.'

DeRaad called for his rickshaw girl. He winked at Vic. 'We're not going far, but why should we walk?' The evening had turned chilly. Marine airs swept through midtown, condensing out on the street furniture, the rickshaw shafts. You could hear service work going on in the military yards. Every so often a K-ship fired up and went for the parking orbit at Mach 40, capturing everything from Straint to the Corniche in its brutal torch glare, varnishing the side of Paulie DeRaad's sharp face so that for a second you had the illusion you could see right down into the musculature. Paulie hung out the rickshaw. He loved all of that military stuff. 'Look at the fucker, Vic! Just look at it!' You had to smile at Paulie, a bottle-rocket going off could put him in a good mood.

'Hey,' he told the rickshaw girl, who was running up hard into her shafts, 'you needn't kill yourself over this.'

'I ain't got but the one pace, Paulie.'

'Your funeral, kid,' he advised her. 'It's just down here,' he said to Vic Serotonin.

Paulie had bolt-holes all over Saudade. This one was a bleak single room off Voigt Street in the noncorprorate hinterland, no different from the rest except Paulie kept a military cot there, which he always made up himself; along with a few things he valued from his vacuum commando days. He also ran some of his communications through it, via the various FTL uplinkers and orbital routers which made him nationwide. As soon as he opened the door, a foul smell came out. It was like shit, urine and standing water.

'Jesus, Paulie,' Vic said.

Paulie told him he didn't know anything yet. Along with the smell, there was a kind of bubbling sound. Lying on Paulie's cot, partly out of its clothes, was the entity that called itself 'the Weather'. Last time Vic saw it, they were at Suicide Point together. Somehow it had choked on Vic's artefact, and the two of them were glued together at some level no one but another Shadow Boy could understand. A wedding had taken place. Whatever tied the knot had also wed them to the proxy. They were all three stuck with one another – although, to judge by the Point kid's unfortunate condition, not for long. He looked frightened and ill. He had tried to undress himself and get under the blanket, for comfort as much as warmth. His shorts were half-down, his skin a fishy white under the low-wattage illumination. Every so often he convulsed, his mouth gaped open and he threw up what looked like cold tapioca.

'So what's this, Vic?' Paulie DeRaad wanted to know.

The kid heard Paulie's voice. It sat up trembling and looked from one to the other of them. It caught Vic's eye. It recognised him. He could see the operator far down inside, and the Point kid, and in there with them both the artefact, still white and unknown, some animal-like thing running towards Vic across the event site. There was no way to avoid the directness of this: something wrong was happening. Wherever Vic and Paulie situated themselves in the room they couldn't hide from it. They still caught flashes of the Shadow Boy's unhomely charm. For a moment the foul air would be full of rain falling through sunlight, the smell of the sea. Between moans from the proxy and bursts of code like music, they heard its voice.

'Am I here?' it appealed to Paulie. 'I can't seem to see myself.'

'This happened two or three days afterwards,' Paulie said to Vic. 'I can't pass this off on my buyer. I can't use it for myself, even if I knew what it was. This ain't good business, Vic.'

'I see that,' Vic said. 'Can we get out of here?'

The Point kid laughed. 'No one gets out of here,' it whispered, in three separate voices at once.

'I'm revolted,' Paulie DeRaad said.

He locked the kid back in and the rickshaw returned them to the Semiramide, where the evening had warmed up a little. The air was thick with music and talk. The tables were full. Monas wafted between them on four-inch urethane heels, reeking mainly of peppermint or vanilla essence, though some had chosen cinnamon when they bought the package. Images from EMC actions at Cor Caroli and Motel Splendido were showering across the walls, along with footage of Paulie DeRaad's old ship, the *Hellflower*, going up in a silent flat-plane blast after it took a hit from some top-end Nastic asset. Vic and Paulie sat down in the office again, and Paulie had Alice Nylon shut the door to keep the noise out. They got drinks, and Paulie said, 'You see the direction I'm thinking. I have to ask, Vic: did you bring something bad from in there?'

'Everything in there's bad,' Vic said. 'You know the risks.'

'I'm the buyer,' Paulie reminded him. 'You're the one with the professional skills.' He seemed to be having trouble with his swallow reflex. Also, his hands had a tremor which was new to Vic Serotonin. 'You take the risks,' said Paulie. 'Not me. What if I caught something from that thing?'

'Well, then, you would begin to feel bad. But you look fine to me, Paulie.'

'I ain't fine,' Paulie said. 'I got a temperature ever since this started. I don't care about my food. You bring a Mona in, I even forget she's there for a moment or two. I get vague. What sort of life is that?'

'One thing,' Vic advised, 'you should shoot it.'

Paulie stared.

'I tried that right away. But it reassembles itself, Vic. White lights rolling together from all over the floor. Eeriest fucking thing you ever saw, crying and whining the whole time.' He added, as Vic got up to leave, 'By the way, I got your boy Antoyne working for me now, that's OK with you.'

Eleven p.m., too late to go anywhere, too early to go home. Vic was puzzled by everything he had seen and heard. He thought about going to visit Emil and Edith Bonaventure. He thought about going home to bed. In the end he didn't do either of those things. On his way out he stopped at the table where Fat Antoyne Messner sat. Antoyne, who was wearing a brand new royal blue drape suit over a yellow shirt, had been joined by one of the club Monas. At close quarters this vision turned out to be Joe Leone's ex-squeeze, Irene. Irene was leaning in close so Antoyne could see deep into the promise of her hot-ochre Mexican-style blouse. She had her fingers on his wrist as if she was taking his pulse, and they were both drinking those pink and yellow drinks he liked.

'Hi, Irene,' Vic said, 'Fat Antoyne! Nice suit!'

He had to shout to be heard over the crowd. 'Why don't I sit down with you?' he suggested. When they looked at each other then back at Vic and didn't answer, Vic made a *What can you do?* gesture, as if the general noise levels were causing him to mishear what everyone said, and sat down anyway. He ordered drinks.

'So: everyone works for Paulie now?'

'It's temporary, Vic,' Fat Antoyne replied quickly, as if he had been expecting that question.

'It's work,' Irene corrected him, at the same time giving Vic a look. 'Everyone has to work,' she said. 'I don't care how direct I am when I say that.'

Naturally, a person with Antoyne's skills sought port work, shipyard work, Irene went on to explain; but the civilian yards weren't doing as well as anyone thought. 'He looked everywhere, and evidently I found him this opportunity instead.' Things were tough all over, she reminded Vic, and in a shortening labour market you couldn't always have your first choice: luckily Paulie DeRaad was there to fill the gap. She had always found Paulie to be a fair employer, also he was known for good pay. Vic could see how well it was working out, she said, by the new sharp way Antoyne could afford to dress.

Vic agreed he probably could.

'I didn't have no real place there,' Antoyne said suddenly, meaning Liv Hula's bar. As he saw it, that was the problem. 'All I wanted was a chance to fit in, Vic.'

'Still,' Vic said, 'don't you miss those nights we caned it with Liv?'

'Another benefit is, here they just call me by my name. Which I prefer that. Not "Fat Antoyne" like in some other joints.'

'It's great you lost weight,' Vic said.

To Irene, with her honed Mona instincts for the feeling nature of life, Vic Serotonin had the face of someone who walked around the town a lot on his own. When he finished his drink and said goodbye to them both, and added courteously to Irene, 'Be sure and have a nice night,' she felt all the things Vic didn't know about himself quiver in her own nerves. She watched him make his way through the Semiramide crowd, passing a moment with Alice Nylon on the door, and told herself sadly, 'I knew a million men like him.' With his black hair and sad hard eyes, he looked like the New Nuevo Tango itself, she had to allow. But he had no idea about other people, and less than no idea about himself. She couldn't express it any other way. A man who walked around a lot on his own and despite that knew himself less well than others knew him. She put her hand over Fat Antoyne's.

'Vic Serotonin,' she said, 'will learn too late about the realness of the world, and how none of us is put here in it long.'

Fat Antoyne shrugged. 'We don't need to think about him.'

This was his signal they should return to the conversation they were having before Vic interrupted them. It was the same conversation they had every night since Joe Leone died, the mythology of which was: they would soon leave Saudade and travel the Halo again, but this time together. Which was surely, as Irene pointed out, the simplest and most direct of gestures, since travel had by definition brought them both here and together in the first place. 'I've washed so many planets out of my hair, why not this one?' she said. 'Joe would want it for me,' she said. 'I know he would!' Her eyes were reckless and bright. 'Oh, Antoyne, wouldn't it be so nice?' Antoyne, less certain, was anyway pleased she said it. Each time they had this talk, he felt bound to warn Irene she could find more rewarding travel companions than himself – and better men, though he had had his day, that was certain. In response, he would always hear her say:

'Never talk yourself down, Antoyne!'

If he talked himself down, she warned him, a man wasn't for her. She counted herself fortunate, she said, to meet Antoyne the awful night Joe died. She was known for her belief that life was follow your heart and never talk yourself down. The future was bright for both of them now, and sad men like Vic would never find that out.

Unaware of these harsh judgments, Vic Serotonin made his way down through Moneytown to the Corniche. Half an hour's walk brought him to the shadows underneath an abandoned pier, where he stood looking out across the sand. The tide was neither in nor out. The sea had a light in it, as if something was happening just over the horizon. Where it fizzed and fumed at the perimeter of the event site, the surf was a violet colour, and gave off faint odours of oxidants and aftershave like an empty dance hall.

Vic had a familiarity with venues of this kind. He had instincts of his own about any place caught halfway between the event site and the city. But this one told him nothing, except he would not try to run anything across the line here. It didn't strike Vic as a good way in. It didn't strike him as a good way out. He smoked a cigarette. He looked and listened. Behind him, rickshaw girls stamped and panted in the crushed oystershell parking lot of the Café Surf, wasting their breath on the cool night air. Customers hurried towards the bar, laughing and batting out at the ads which fluttered in their hair. Every time someone opened the door, music spilled out. It wasn't Vic's kind of music, but he went inside anyway.

When he left an hour later, he was none the wiser. Fake Sandra Shen décor. Standing room only. Overflowing ashtrays, tables littered with screwed-up napkins, half-empty plates and Giraffe Beer bottles. The smell of steam from the kitchen. And under the red neon sign, *Live Music Nightly*, a cheap two-piece to grind out endless bebop remixes of last year's sentimental tunes. You couldn't even get near the toilet for the stream of people coming out. Vic leaned on the bar, listening to the band and shaking his head; then he turned on his heel suddenly and pushed his way to the door. If something was happening there, he didn't know what it was.

He took a rickshaw back into the city and made the girl stop outside the uptown police bureau at the intersection of Uniment and Poe, where Lens Aschemann maintained an office. Past midnight, and damp winds chased wastepaper across the deserted pavement. A single second-floor window remained illuminated. Broken silhouettes came and went against the blind. It wasn't hard to picture Aschemann up there, drinking rum while he methodically pasted Vic into the frame for some scheme Vic didn't even know about. What had Site Crime stumbled over at the Café Surf? Paulie DeRaad's EMC connexions, maybe, running an artefact-related operation of their own. But then why put Vic Serotonin in the frame for Paulie's lack of discrimination?

'Hey,' the rickshaw girl reminded him, 'you pay a horse to run.'

'So run,' Vic told her.

'You know I got to towel down if I stand around too long. People just don't *get* that.'

'I'm sorry,' said Vic.

'Life's too short to be sorry, hon.'

Vic paid her off on the edge of a weed-grown lot a few streets away from his rooms in South End, then took the roundabout route home. No one followed him, yet when he got into the hall of his building he couldn't convince himself he was alone. A package had been left for him. When he opened it, he found a small leather-bound book, on the cover of which was a line-drawing of a hand holding some flowers. Though the flowers were all on the same stem, and the same shape, they were of different colours. For a moment, he thought that Edith Bonaventure had found her father's diary and brought it to him. But the handwriting wasn't Emil's, and the first sentence Vic read began, 'Am I confused when I remember, or try to, the time before my childhood?' Serotonin stared at this in exasperation, then ran upstairs to his room, where, instead of putting on the light, he stood by the window in the dark and looked down into the street. Ten or twenty yards away on the opposite side, someone looked back at him. It was the woman from Liv Hula's bar, her face blanched by the vapour lamps, framed by the collar of her fur coat. By the time he had forced the window up and shouted, she was gone.

Some hours later, across the city, the man who resembled Einstein let himself into his dead wife's bungalow by the sea.

The front door, swollen with salt moisture, must be lifted as you opened it; sometimes it stuck anyway. Sand feathered across the linoleum in the hall. Rather than switch on the lights, Aschemann paused and allowed his eyes to adjust to the faint sea-glimmer limning every surface. He made his way carefully to the kitchen, where he wiped the window and regarded the ocean. 'How are you?' his wife's voice said to him. 'You see that ship out there?' It was the kitchen of an empty house, empty cupboards, empty shelves, dust and sand in a thin gritty layer on everything. Aschemann ran warm water from the faucet, catching it in his cupped hands to splash his face. Then he went back down the hall and took off his raincoat.

While he was doing that his wife's voice said, 'Can you see the same ship as me, those lights to the right of the Point?'

In life she had constantly asked him similar questions, whether he was standing next to her or lying in bed with some other woman halfway across the city. She had, somehow, never trusted her own eyes.

'I see the ship,' he reassured her. 'It's only a ship. Go to bed now.'

Comforted by this fragment of an exchange the rest of which lay at some inaccessible level of memory, he sat down in the lounge, unbuttoned the collar of his shirt, and dialled up his assistant, to whom he said, 'I hope you have something good for me. Because we aren't doing so well since the other day.' He knew this was ambiguous. Let it stand, he thought.

After the raid on the Semiramide Club, they had argued in the car. 'I don't like to have shots fired,' he had informed her. 'Now I'll have to apologise to Paulie.'

'Paulie is a violent creep.'

'Still. Shots fired is not my way. Find nothing and set light to a wall, is that a day's work? Threaten some children! The problem with DeRaad will always be the same. He's never quite intelligent enough for his own good, and never quite stupid enough for ours. That's Paulie.' He touched her arm. 'And drive slower,' he said. 'I don't want to lose this nice car. I don't want to hurt someone.' She stared ahead, and, if anything, accelerated a little. Moneytown was all round them with rickshaws and pedestrians, the Cadillac embedded in early evening traffic one minute, prised free the next. Stop, start, stop, start: it made Aschemann feel ill.

'They aren't children,' she said.

'You're angry, I can understand that.'

The Semiramide raid had left him none the wiser. He had

expected nothing less – who, after all, would store a proscribed arte-fact in the back room of a dance club? Not even Paulie DeRaad. Since then, without quite knowing why, Aschemann had returned repeatedly to the Café Surf, telling himself, Everything proceeds from there. To watch is best when you have no theory. He tracked his bebop golems into the night, observed their lateral slide and vanishment into the hustle of things in central Saudade. It was like a card trick. One in ten lasted a little longer, going as far, perhaps, as to negotiate for a room. 'That must mean something,' he told his assistant now. 'Ten per cent of them are more than ordinarily restless. They want something. Are they even artefacts as we know them?'

All this, she responded, served only to confirm what he already knew. Aschemann shrugged. 'So it's three in the morning,' he said, 'and I don't understand why you waste your time talking to an old man like me.'

'Vic Serotonin walked into the Café Surf tonight, half an hour after you walked out. I've been trying to reach you since.'

FIVE

Ninety Per Cent Neon

'Ah,' Aschemann said.

'I can't report to you when you disconnect.'

'I suppose not.'

'You disconnect and wander about on your own,' she complained. When it became clear he wasn't going to answer that, she said, 'We got a little coverage. Would you like to see it now?'

Aschemann said he would.

The house lurched, then vanished from around him. He was looking down a nanocam feed, at jumpy visuals of people in some crowded space. His assistant's voice came in across the top of that, its hollow, reverberant qualities an artefact of the transmission process. She seemed closer, but not quite in the room with him. 'Is this all right?' she said. 'Only they're routing it down some kind of low-priority EMC pipe. Ours are all down.'

'The pipe's fine. The material itself is poor.'

'They had some technical problems with that, too.'

It wasn't anything like being there. The image stream wavered, held, dropped suddenly into greyscale while slow bars of black rolled queasily down Aschemann's field of view. You could be the most experienced user, you would still throw up in the end. But there, quite visible, was Vic Serotonin, perhaps eight feet away from Aschemann, propping up the Long Bar at the Café Surf with his gabardine jacket open and his hat pushed to the back of his head, while the people around him conversed jerkily or ran fast-forward as if they lived in another world. 'It looks as if he was waiting for someone,' Aschemann said, shaking his head irritably as if to dislodge something, while his eyes focused and refocused on a spot in the empty room. People often sought to clarify an incoming image this way. You would catch them squinting or banging their temple above one eye, it was a common reaction, which never worked.

'Do you have the same view as me?' the assistant said in an excited voice. 'From about waist height? And there's a woman in a red dress to the right of the bar?'

'That's the view I have.'

'There he is. Do you see him? He said he never heard of the Café Surf, but there he is! This is exactly what we need!'

Aschemann wasn't so sure. He asked her to close the pipe, and when his vision had returned to normal said, 'All I see is a man having a drink in a bar. If that was illegal we would all be in the orbital correction facility. Where did Vic go after he left?'

'They don't know.'

'That's helpful.'

'If you watch the whole thing, the fault gets out of hand about two hundred and eighty seconds in, and they disconnect everything to fix it.'

Aschemann thanked her for the pictures. 'Go home now,' he recommended. 'Get some sleep. We have a lot to think about here.' He rubbed his eyes and looked around the room his wife had died in. He would be there until morning, sprawled in a stained yellow armchair and surrounded by her things. He would hear her voice, asking him what day it was, offering him a drink. He spent more time in that house than he would admit to his assistant; and missed his wife more than he would admit to himself.

Something in the Café Surf footage had caught Aschemann's attention, but he couldn't say what it was. Then, the evening of the next day, as he sat at the Long Bar listening to the two-piece, a young woman took the stool next to his and ordered a cocktail called 'Ninety Per Cent Neon'. She was a Mona, so he thought at first, a Monroe look-alike in a red wrap-bodice evening dress and matching stilt-heel shoes.

'I've seen you here,' Aschemann said.

She leaned towards him when he spoke. Asked him for a match, upper body bent forward a little from the waist, head tilted back so that the dress offered her up wrapped in silk, jazz, light from the *Live Music Nightly* sign. She needed only a brushed aluminium frame to complete the image of being something both remembered and unreal. He'd seen that dress in the nanocam pictures of Vic Serotonin. More importantly, perhaps, he'd seen it fourteen days ago, when she stumbled out of the toilet at the Café Surf disoriented by the neon light and music as if she was new in the world. She still had an unformed, labile air. Her smile was cautious, but the dress was ready to promise anything.

'I'm here a lot,' she said. 'I like the band. Do you like them?'

He took a moment to light his pipe. He swallowed a little rum. 'They're as guilty as ever,' he said.

'Guilty?'

'Under his dexterity, this pianist hides neither intellect nor heart, only compulsion. If no one else is available he will play against himself; and then against the self thus created, and then against the self after that, until all fixed notion of self has leaked away into the slippage and he can relax for a second in the sharp light and cigarette smoke like someone caught fleetingly in an ancient black and white photograph. Do you see?'

'It's only music, though,' she said.

'Perhaps,' Aschemann agreed. For the detective, he thought, nothing is ever only itself. He offered to buy her another cocktail, but all she did was look at him vaguely as if she hadn't heard, so he went on:

'The older man has come to a different understanding of things, one which to his friend would seem bland and self-evident. He believes that it is only because no music is possible that any music at all is possible.' Here, Aschemann smiled briefly at his own cleverness. 'As a result,' he finished, 'the universe now remakes itself for him continually, out of two or three invariable rules and an obsolete musical instrument called the saxophone.'

'But guilty? Is that enough to make them guilty?'

The detective shrugged. 'Complicit, then. It's only a way of putting it. Myself, I prefer the New Nuevo Tango. There's more heart.'

She stared at him, got down off the stool, laughed in a nervous way which revealed the flecks of lipstick on her white teeth. He caught briefly the smell of her, strong, warm, a little unwashed, a little cheap; in some way reassuring.

'Goodbye,' she said. 'Maybe I'll see you again.'

Aschemann watched her leave, then finished his drink and shadowed her unhurriedly into the warm air and black heart of the city. He could smell the guilt and excitement that came up out of the street gratings to meet her. He could smell her excitement at being alive there, in Saudade among the sights. Did she know he was behind her? He wasn't sure how she saw the world, but she hadn't forgotten him. He was certain of that, but he wasn't certain how dangerous she might be. He followed her to a coldwater walk-up behind the bottled-milk dairy at Tiger Shore, running up the last few metal risers of the outside staircase to catch her and lay his hand on her warm shoulder. His footsteps rang and scraped, she fumbled with the door. Dropped the key. Picked it up.

'Wait,' he ordered. 'Police. Don't go in without me.'

She stared at him in despair; then over his shoulder, less as if there was someone there than at the city itself. 'Please!' she said. 'I don't know what I've done wrong.'

'Neither do I.'

Whatever happened next, he wanted to make sure he was there.

It was bare: grey board floor, bare bulb, a single bentwood chair. On the wall opposite the window, the shadow of the slatted blind fell across a poster with the logo *Surf Noir*. 'Hey,' she said. 'I know: why don't you sit here—?' When she bent forward from the waist to undo his raincoat, the red dress presented her breasts to him in a flickering light. She knelt, and he could hear her breathing. It was placid, rather catarrhal. Later she lifted the hem of the dress and positioned herself astride him. So close, he saw that her gait, the shadows round her eyes, the foundation caked in the downy hairs by the corners of her mouth, had conspired beneath the Café Surf neon to make her seem older than she was. She whispered when he came, 'There. There now.' She had been a month in the same dress. She was a victim, but of what? He wasn't sure. He had no idea what she was. How had he smelled her excitement yet failed to smell his own? He felt weakened by it.

'Where do you sleep?' he said puzzledly. 'There's no bed in here.'

This idea let in a moment of confusion. It was very brief. But when he shook his head to clear it and turned to pay her, she was standing in the corner motionless with panic, facing the angle between the walls. She had learned enough to know what the city wanted but no more. New clothes were scattered across the floor, clean but disordered, as if she had tried to wear them but wasn't sure how. She had collected objects too, some coloured feathers on a stick, an unopened bottle of 'Ninety Per Cent Neon.' She started to fade as he watched, but he was out on the iron stairway long before the process was complete. He returned to the Long Bar, where he drank until he stopped shaking. Resting in the music and light he thought: does it matter who she was, when every night here the world is somehow touched? Guilt made him report to his assistant:

'I think I begin to see what's happening.'

*

Two days later, hands in pockets at the end of an afternoon spent with his friend the bottle, Vic Serotonin lounged in the doorway of Liv Hula's bar watching the cats flow back into the event site. He had been waiting there five minutes and Straint was still thick with them.

'Pay that tab any time,' Liv Hula reminded him from behind the zinc counter.

'Sure,' Vic said.

He stood there a minute or two more without saying anything then turned up his collar and left.

Liv Hula rubbed at a stain on the counter. She threw the rag into the sink. 'Always good to see you, Vic,' she said quietly to herself. 'Come again soon.' She went upstairs and turned on Radio Retro, but they were just then announcing the evening's fights, and that only made her think of Joe Leone.

Outside it was Saudade.

At one end you got the tall black and gold business towers and tourist hotels, with the lights coming on in them in angular cyphers; at the other, the pastels of the Corniche dimming in a sunset of impure hot pinks and greens. Between them the sea; and the horizon somewhere past the tremendous roll of the surf, like a crease in a piece of paper the colour of doves. Onshore winds, persistent as a hand on your arm, came up the streets from the front, picking up in transit the rich smells of seafood and low-end mixed drinks. The hotels were emptying, the bars were filling up, surf noir basslines were bumping out of every open door.

Vic Serotonin passed all this, his shoulders in a permanent shrug.

Vic was puzzled. He had a leather-bound diary in one pocket and a Chambers gun in the other.

He walked down Straint to its intersection with the top end of Neutrino, where two rickshaw girls and their clients were already in a traffic altercation, then turned left on to Cahuenga, which brought him eventually to Hot Walls. After that, he was five minutes finding the right door. It was one of those tall narrow townhouses, six floors split into apartments. Vic rang the bell. There was a long wait, during which he rang the bell a couple of times more. Then an uncertain voice said:

'Who's there?'

'Remember me?' Vic said. 'You want to see me. You want me to help you.'

'Come in, Mr Serotonin.'

He ran up the stairs two at a time.

Her diary had unsettled Vic, but he was unable to stop reading it. 'I fear the unknown,' she had written, 'but the fear of the known is *so much* worse.'

There were pages of this kind of thing. You got a list of expenses – a rickshaw downtown, meals at upscale venues like Els and Encientum, underwear from Uoest, clever books from Parker & Bright. Then a description of the fights – naphtha flares casting a kind of anti-illumination over the arena, burnt cinnamon smells, the cultivars strutting about, all tusks and tattoos, 'their erect cocks the size of horses', the sudden flash of an eight-inch spur then something slick and ropey levered out and steaming in the shadows. 'There's a moral dimension here no one seems aware of,' was her conclusion about the fights. That was fine. It barely scratched the surface, but it was more than understandable. It was the travelogue you'd expect. But then she was off again:

'The known is slicked on to everything like a kind of grease. You would do anything to avoid the things you already know.'

It made her hard to place. She seemed like someone who had spent time in Saudade; then like someone who hadn't. But if she belonged somewhere else, no clues were left where that might be. You got the impression of a woman who'd depended on privilege one planet past what she could handle, and who had inevitably become lost in space. Other than eat and shop and take rides around town, she stayed home and got tense. She loved her apartment, she said, but her relationship with the city was partial, unconstructive. Despite that, she didn't just catch a ship out of there, which is what any tourist would have done.

'Am I meant to live this way?' she asked herself. 'Is it the same for all these other creatures? Is that how they see things here?' Speaking as one of those creatures, Vic would like to know too.

But answers weren't forthcoming, and the diary's language was empty because its true object – her own anxiety – would always remain both present and unstated: so that every observation suggested more than it could ever contain. As a result even the physical object sometimes seemed packed and decodable. Pressed to the nose, its pages gave out the scents of midtown: coffee, perfume, polished wood. Then, very faintly, human sex. Vic couldn't imagine that. The words rose from among these smells as if they were sensations too: 'I dream entirely in tiny mad paintings. A man seems to be spewing up a snake. Someone else is helping him. The roof of their house is on fire. They recoil from one another yet seem entwined, bent in the shapes of a body language which no longer has any meaning.

'Is this what will happen to me inside the site? Am I dreaming what it is like? I don't want to go in but I must.' There being no attempt to explain this combination of need and paralysis, Vic was forced back repeatedly on to the entry which had first caught his eye. 'Am I confused when I remember, or try to, the time before I was born?' Then, as if this weren't enough:

'The vast craneflies, *libellulinae* and locusts which somehow filled my life then were emblematic. They were alien species, icons of difference; as tentative and fearful as they were frightening. They were usually trying to speak, through the woman I knew as The Girl Beneath the Dragonfly. She was translating for them, caught up, electrified, pushed out of herself, taken over, by their need. She had no life of her own. She was a radio, a retro radio. She lay on the sodden black ash. She was myself. They stood over her, trembling. They were trying to explain through her how badly things had gone wrong. How they had been blown here by circumstances they could not control. How they didn't mean to be here. In a sense they were my parents, but they had never been meant to be here, in the world as we knew it then.

'Insect,' she concluded, 'is an anagram of incest.'

Even for a childhood on another planet it seemed extreme.

At least he had learned her name, written repeatedly across the first two or three pages in a hand which, formless at first, soon became practised and fluent. It was Kielar. 'Mrs Elizabeth Kielar,' she had written again and again, like a girl trying out future identities from the safety of some expensive New Venusberg school. 'Elizabeth Kielar. Mrs *Kielar.*' Vic would never use it, but it was a name. She stood looking at him uncertainly from her doorway. The fur coat Irene had so admired was loosely slung over an oyster satin slip, which encouraged the hallway light to pool up blue shadows behind her thin collarbones.

'I'm sorry,' she said. 'I—'

'In the end,' Vic said, 'sorry's never enough.'

He pushed past her and into the apartment. It was seven or eight rooms one after the other, the connecting doors open so you could see the length of it. A bank of identical windows ran all the way down on the left, lighting it like a single artfully divided space, a restaurant or a gallery. Vic could feel her standing behind him, pulling the coat closed across her breasts, watching him with that continuous bland puzzlement of hers. She smelled of Anaïs-Anaïs, and also some expensive flowered soap.

'You knew that,' he insisted, without looking back, 'but until now you've never had to acknowledge it.' He held up the diary. 'Why give this to me?'

She shut the door quietly behind her.

'You're angry,' she said. 'I don't know why you're so angry.'

'I can't work with uncertainties on this side.'

'Would you like to have a drink?' This idea seemed to restore her. 'I was asleep when you knocked,' she said. 'Please come in and have a drink.'

'I want to know what you think I can give you,' Vic said.

'It didn't work because you were so angry. I was more afraid of you than that place.'

'Maybe that's how it seems to you now,' Vic said.

In the end though, what could he do but shrug? He followed her down the curious linear apartment, accepted a drink, sat at one end of a sofa with a green chenille cover thrown over it and watched while she arranged herself at the other, in the corner as far away from him as she could get. She drew up her knees. She allowed the fur coat to fall loosely around her, and watched Vic in return. Vic made a pantomime of placing her diary carefully on a small table, which was perhaps his way of saying that was over now, he'd just leave that alone. There was a single narrow glass vase on the same table. In the mornings the light would fall harshly across it, tangle the transparent shadow of the vase in the shadows of the window frame. 'Is that the drink you like?' she asked him. 'Is that the way you prefer it?'

After a moment he said:

'When you walked into Liv Hula's bar, I thought you were a tourist. That was a mistake. It put both of us in danger.'

'Mr Serotonin, I—'

'Look at me,' Vic urged. 'Listen. I'm telling you this. In there, the most unreliable people are the ones looking for something. Their lives were too difficult to solve. Now they hope something good will happen to them, but they've been hoping for too long and that's what makes them dangerous. You never know what will happen to them in there. They thought they wanted to find something – it would have been easier to stay this side of things.' It was his standard speech to women like that. He usually gave it in a corner of Liv Hula's bar, or a suite at one of the tourist hotels.

He swallowed his drink. He leaned forward.

'Do you understand?' he said.

She shivered and pulled the coat back round her suddenly. 'You're angry because you're afraid of everything,' she said.

Vic shrugged and smiled.

'It's good we can agree,' he said politely.

At this, she pursed her lips and turned her head away from him so that the long tendons of her neck stood out. Vic could see the tension in them. Her skin was a little darker than he remembered. 'This morning,' she said quietly, 'I sat here for an hour without moving. I ache. I'm waiting for something to happen, and I don't even know what part of my life it will approach from.' She turned back to him suddenly and asked, 'Have you ever lost your way?' Her eyes, a curious colour between green and brown, were so wide and direct he couldn't look into them for fear of disappointing her in some obscure fashion.

'Would I know?' he said.

'People lose their way as an act of defence. Then they panic and decide they have to find it again.'

She got up from the sofa and stood in front of him smiling. 'Come and look,' she said. 'Come over here with me and look out of the window.' When he didn't respond, she walked over to stare out anyway. 'I won't wait for you,' she said. Then:

'Look!'

Outside it was Saudade, rooftops and streets stretching away in the soft rain and dark. Lines of lights. Cabs and pedestrians flickering under the neon, adstreams like migrations of pastel moths. Distant cries came up; laughter. Past all that, past the tourist port and the military pits, out at the limits of vision, you could see something – a whitish, roiling strip like surf, the boundary of the event site, a stationary vapour of uncertain physics. Beautiful but very strange. Above it, the Kefahuchi Tract had stretched itself across the yielding black sky like the generative principle of some old cosmology. Vic Serotonin stood next to Mrs Kielar. He frowned briefly as if he had seen something out there he wanted to be certain of. Finally, he looked down at her.

'It's quiet tonight,' he said.

She smiled to herself. 'Is it?' she said. 'Why did you come here?'

'I don't know.'

'Tell yourself that if you like. It won't help.'

The fur coat had fallen open again. City light splashed behind the narrow collarbones, and where the edge of the satin slip lay across it, her skin was the colour of balsamic cream. An unexpected warmth came up from her. The moment he became aware of that, she knew. She gave a low laugh and moved a step or two away from him. 'You never had to see me again. What do you care about some tourist? It wasn't the diary. It was me.' By then Vic had her by the shoulders, which were small and rounded.

'What's this?' he said. 'What's happening?' and began kissing her.

His mouth safely on hers, she backed towards the sofa and pulled him down. Vic worked the coat off and tugged the slip up round her waist, felt the heat of her on his face; caught broken glimpses, through his own excitement, of the light on her skin. She was one of those women who writhe and push a lot. Some internal struggle with themselves – as urgent as their own narrow bones, skin over muscle – causes them to sweat immediately they touch your clothes. Everything is in their way. You don't know if they want you or not, but something won't stop in them. She bit Vic's arm. One foot pushed and kicked impatiently at the coat as she placed herself, then she had him in her.

'Christ,' Vic said.

'You like this,' she said. 'You like it.' She made a small agitated noise, as if she liked it too. She smiled at the ceiling for a moment, then drew up her legs and began to say yes, in a determined yet meditative voice, in time to Vic's thrusts: 'Yes. Yes. Yes. Yes. Yes,' until he came.

'How you wanted to do that!' she said.

Vic, as puzzled as he'd ever been in his life, tried to roll away from her and sit up. She only wrapped her legs round him and held him by the shoulders until he couldn't avoid her eyes.

'Will you take me into the site, Mr Serotonin?'

He stared at her, shook his head. Pulled himself away. 'It's Vic,' he said thickly – then, sitting on the edge of the sofa staring at the window and talking to himself as much as her, 'I'm Vic.' He felt used. He didn't know what he felt. He sat there for half an hour with his back to her in a defensive curve. Neither of them said anything, then he turned round and had her again. Facing away to present herself, she whispered, 'You have no idea who you are.'

When Vic woke it was still night, and he was alone.

He toured the long apartment looking for her. White wainscoting and layers of ethnic rugs gave way to shoulder-height marble tiling over large black and white linoleum squares; then green silk wallpaper and dark wooden floorboards worn unevenly but polished to a high shine. Objects were everywhere – feathers from a dead alien, musical instruments casting angular shadows, three sketches of someone else's ancestors in thin, black-japanned frames. Ceramics from some culture no one knew the name of, a thousand lights down the Beach, a million years down the drain. Everything changed, room to room, except the row of windows, and through these the city light fell cleanly, downshifting colours, accentuating the museum values of the space, emptying everything out. He felt glad of the slight chill on his skin. It reminded him he was alive.

'Mrs Kielar?' he called. There she was, crouched on a window seat naked, legs drawn up, twisted from the waist so she could look out. Her sharp, vulnerable elbows on the windowsill supported her upper body; her hands were clasped in front of her face. She rocked a little, to and fro. Vic touched her.

'Mrs Kielar?' No response. It was the body language of someone waiting for the worst to happen. 'I ache,' she had said to him, 'I ache.'

'I'll take you in there,' he offered. 'Soon.'

Across the city, the man who looked like Einstein sucked with satisfaction on his empty pipe and nodded to himself. 'For once this technology worked,' he told his assistant. 'We have him now.'

He nodded to himself again. 'We have Vic now,' he said.

'I don't see why,' his assistant said.

It was nearly dawn, and she was hungry. They had been sitting in Aschemann's office for ten hours while a pick-up detail from surveillance mothered the obsolete nanocams Vic Serotonin had brought unwittingly into Mrs Kielar's apartment to join the house dust, the aerosols of perspiration and warm breath, the tiny drifting flakes of Elizabeth Kielar's delicate cream-coloured skin which already floated there. In the end the usual series of transmission faults had corrupted the image stream, freezing it on Mrs Kielar in her strained attitude by the window while the travel agent, naked, bent over her solicitously, his mouth open to repeat something, a curiously inappropriate point of reflected light in one eye making him look like an untrustworthy dog.

'Drive me home,' Aschemann said, 'and perhaps I'll tell you.'

Once they were in the car, though, he changed his mind and started to talk about his wife instead. Why, the assistant couldn't tell. He insisted they have the top down while they drove. He looked tired, cheerful, a little frailer than usual, his white hair disarranged by the rush of cold morning air into the Cadillac. When she suggested they find a place to eat breakfast, he made an irritable gesture.

'My wife,' he said, 'was an agoraphobe. You didn't know that.'

When the assistant failed to respond, instead running through her repertoire of calm practical actions – glancing into the driving mirror, changing gear, slowing to allow a group of cultivars to stagger across the road in front of the Cadillac, drunk, bagged, bleeding out happily from their injuries in the ring – he said, 'This will be useful for you to know. You should listen to this if you want to understand the meaning of the Neon Heart murders.'

'I can listen and drive,' she pointed out.

'So you say.'

There was a silence. Then he went on:

'There are kinds of agoraphobes to whom even a knock on the door is too much of the outside world. Someone else must answer it for them. Yet as soon as you step into their houses they become monsters.'

In his wife's rooms, he said, every inch of floor and furniture space had been filled up with objects, so that you didn't quite know how to get from the door to the sofa. 'Once you had got there you couldn't move about, except with extreme caution. All quick movement was damped by this labyrinth—' here, he laughed ' – where there was even a code, three or four quick pulls on the cord, to get the lavatory light to go on. It's less, you see, that they are uncomfortable in public than that they only feel in control on their own ground.'

He seemed to expect a response to this, but she couldn't think of one. Eventually, she said, 'Poor woman. Where would you like to eat?'

Aschemann folded his arms and stared ahead.

'Is that all you can say? "Poor woman"? Problems like hers are so easy to cure, no one should have them. Is that what you believe?'

'I thought you might want to eat.'

'Agoraphobia is an aggressively territorial strategy: refusal to go out forces the outside to come in, to where it's manageable. On the agoraphobe's ground you walk through the agoraphobe's maze.'

'I don't see,' she said, 'what this has to do with the murders.'

'Well, you have no patience.'

Other crimes had come and gone for him, Aschemann said, but the murders continued. 'They continue to this day.' He said this with a kind of bitter satisfaction. Each one published new lines of the verse, with nothing to connect the victims but their shaven armpit and Carmody-style tattoo. 'And, of course,' as Aschemann reminded her, 'the investigation itself.' He had long ago forbidden the detective branch to work the case. Track record as well as seniority had allowed him to do that, sheer weight of cases solved, paperwork successfully filed. Word went out that it was Aschemann's crime. He can keep it, was most people's opinion.

'And so?'

'Stop here,' Aschemann ordered 'We can have a nice breakfast here.' They swept into the kerb outside E Pellici.

A notorious cholesterol venue halfway down Neutrino, Pellici's offered Deco walls and *Café electrique*. More important, Aschemann said, you could hear the food smoking in the animal fat. At that time of the morning Pellici's was full of rickshaw girls in pink and black lycra gorging themselves on simple carbs. They stood awkwardly up to the counter, unable to use the seating, ducking their heads needlessly, embarrassed to be among people of ordinary size. Aschemann smiled around at them, one or two smiled back. Once he was eating he seemed to forget both his wife and the murders. Grateful for this, the assistant brought up the subject of Vic Serotonin again.

'Our so-important Vic,' Aschemann said, recovering his humour with his blood sugar. 'Oh, Vic,' he chided, as if Serotonin were sitting across the table from him, 'Vic, Vic, Vic.' He made a dismissive gesture. 'As well as rather ordinary sex, Vic has a conspiracy with this woman Kielar, we can prove it. So now there's a site crime. We can pick him up, have a talk with him.'

'I don't see how that helps.'

'We'll put it to him this way: why should Vic go about his business unconstrained when we don't get what we want?'

'You could have done this any time.'

Aschemann shrugged. He gave her a smile which suggested that though she was right, she had missed an important point which he would illuminate for her out of pure generosity of heart.

'Vic was nothing,' he said, 'now he's something.'

He lit his pipe and sat back. 'Eat your food,' he recommended, 'before it gets cold.' He watched her encouragingly for a moment, nodding his head and smiling at every forkful she put in her mouth, then said, 'All this time, people like me have been wrong. We've been afraid of the site for the wrong reasons.' The assistant wouldn't be tempted by this. She looked firmly down at her plate. 'For sixty years we've tried to control what came out of there – new code, new kinds of artefacts we thought might get loose, all that alien stuff, we can't predict its behaviour, or even in many cases say what it is.

'We never considered it might be two-way traffic.'

She stopped eating in surprise and looked at him.

'Nothing goes in,' she said.

Aschemann smiled and nodded. 'Very good answer,' he said. 'You're sure of that, are you?' He passed her a hot towel. 'Use this to wipe your lips.'

Next evening, Vic Serotonin went to the fights.

He wasn't keen on them himself. You can claim, and people do, that every fight is different: but it is a difference that works itself out within sameness, so that when you've seen one fight you've truly seen them all. That was Vic's view. But he felt so nervous about guiding Mrs Kielar into the site again that he thought he'd better have one more try at getting Emil Bonaventure's journal – his hope being that, against the odds, it might feature a more robust description, a more dependable map of the site than any

Vic had concocted. His hope was it might give him an edge. So he dialled up Edith Bonaventure and invited her down to Preter Coeur with him.

'Because I know you love to go,' he told her.

'I wish I could, Vic,' Edith said. 'But Emil, you know, he's bad. That man is so ill for all his sins! Also I was going to wash my hair. Goodbye now, and enjoy.' And she closed the connection.

Vic sighed and re-established it. 'You need a night out, Edith,' he tried.

'Besides which,' Edith said, as if the conversation between them had never broken off, 'since Joe the Lion died I lost my previous intense interest.' She laughed coarsely. 'Name me a girl didn't,' she suggested in a low voice, as if she was talking to someone Vic couldn't see. Crammed into the cheap public pipe, her voice gained a sardonic echo. Behind it he could hear accordion music, New Nuevo Tango music deconstructing its own mannered precision to the raw absurdity of the tango life: Edith herself, Vic bet, recorded in her glory days. Thirteen years old and already a hologram in her own right.

'Hey, I'm sorry, Vic, but you know how it is.'

This time it was Vic who broke the connection. 'Fair enough,' he acknowledged. 'I guess you know what you want.'

Edith got right back to him. 'Maybe I'll come,' she said.

Fights were held all over, you could see one on any street corner after six; but the place they called Preter Coeur was Saudade's premier venue. Rank with pollutants and the native flora that throve on them, it spread, cavernous and vaulted, a waste of covered pits and roofed concrete expanses, across several acres backed up against the event aureole, at the end of a line extended from Cahuenga Boulevard. By day the rain blew between the support pillars of its many unwalled sections, through oblique bars of sunlight which fell upon bodies – the lost, the sleeping, the befuddled, the dead. It had been a military shipyard of some kind, before EMC moved to their present location. Now it sprang back to life at dusk every day, as big as a city quarter, in business for itself, self-governed, self-policed, self-made, a sprawl of food stalls, flop houses, flea markets, bookmakers, makeshift chopshops and tattoo booths around each ring, trawled by every kind of cultivar and fetch. The voices of the Radio Retro announcers, piped out the very air by sophisticated entrained-wave techniques, shouted the odds. Monas worked the rickshaw lines in giggling groups. Sexually aroused New Men staggered by, bagged on Night Train and looking for a quiet corner in which to jack off. All this under a mixed il-lumination of naphtha flame or blank interrogatory halogen glare, and everything in between. In Preter Coeur the shadow of a pillar fell on you with all the weight of the pillar itself; the next moment you were losing your sense of balance in the unpredictable jump and turn of smoky flickers like shoaling fish. Adstreams floated everywhere, their unbearable lightness of being – their simple promise – catching you up: until the crown of butterflies round your head morphed into a crown of thorns and you found you had surrendered your intimate data to some twink-farmer forty blocks away on Pierpoint Street.

Through this flow of light and smoke and people events, which you could describe every instant of yet never predict its next state, the fighters moved with studied, looming, fuck-off grace, speech reduced by careful tuning of their inboard hormonal patches to the amused, confident, inarticulate growl of those who are invin-cible at what they do, and will never be less than what they are, and will always be more than you. The light fell on their strutting cockerel-legs, clawed and brazen-scaled. It showed you suddenly the weird articulations at knee and hip, the vast perpetually erect cock bursting from the leather britches, the second thumb a brass spur too, the spangles of live tattoo and treasure map like riding lights across the blackened torso ripe with scabs and scars. A day old, if that, and already mythological, already dead.

Tourists loved it. If you could look down at night from five or six hundred feet in the air, you'd see every rickshaw in Saudade converging there like T-cells rushing to the site of infection, to be drawn in under the sign *Uncle Zip's Preter Coeur*.

Edith Bonaventure loved it too.

'Oh Vic,' she said, 'look at it all! Look at the lights!' Her customary tough manner was softened with delight, and every passing fighter captured her heart. 'Look at the monster cock on that!'

'None of them is alive like us,' Vic said. This surprised him as being true. 'They're confections.'

'Oh ho,' laughed Edith. 'Do I hear envy? Do I hear you jealous? Vic, I believe I do!' But Vic felt less envy than a sort of generous puzzlement. How would you chop carrots, with your dick always in the way? Get in and out the bath? It was true, he thought, that despite their vitality – which streamed out into the air like the life force you would expect of a horse or other large animal – the fighters were less than real, an in-the-end pointless looping of their personal dreams into parity with some sort of public idea of what a fighter ought to resemble. 'Dreams' was, anyway, the wrong word to use here, Vic thought. Dreams were by-numbers. They were cheap. They had been Uncle Zipped, like everything else in the Halo. No one except a Mona would be seen dead in possession of a dream these days. Edith, however, broad of hip and wearing her best grown-up clothes, a lively one herself since age thirteen, wouldn't have this. They were out for an evening's entertainment, she ruled, not a political debate. She clung to his arm, her eyes bright, which made him feel good in a distant way.

'You're excited,' he said.

This netted him a sidelong look, both mysterious and pragmatic

'You can tell, can you?' said Edith. After which they were engulfed in a smell like cinnamon and adrenalin, a molecular adstream which, bypassing the neocortex and heading straight for the brainstem, caused her to scream in delight.

'I want to bet! I want to bet!'

It was a night of solid bouts, technically predictable but with plenty of live action drama. The smell of haemoglobin layered itself over the ring thick as country mist, laced with chemical signatures specific to each fighter and traditionally borrowed from the flavours of Ancient Earth alcopops – Two Dogs, JopaLume, Decoda, Yellow Fever and that great old standard made popular by Joe the Lion himself, Alcola. Edith was loving it. Her first two fighters had won, in three-and-a-half minutes and four; the third wasn't doing so well but she hadn't noticed yet. While her mood remained good, Vic said, 'Have you seen any sign of that diary? Emil's old diary?'

Edith stared distractedly at him, naphtha light flaring across her small features. Then she said:

'Jesus, Vic, I don't know. What do you care?'

'I'm going into the site.'

'Vic, you go into the site every week. It's your career.'

In the ring her latest favourite had slipped on a coil of his own lower bowel, which was the end of him for that evening. He seemed delighted with his injuries. The crowd gave up a good-humoured jeer as his handler dragged him into the blue shadows the other side of the ring, upon which Edith shook her head as if clearing it and gave Vic an intent look. 'Did you bring me here to get Emil's book? Is that why you asked me out?' She laughed. 'Jesus, Vic, you didn't need to spend your money! I could have told you no at home, a quiet night in, just you and me until Emil fell out of bed or threw up, or choked in his sleep, which he does a lot now.' She shook her head slowly in disbelief. 'Vic,' she said, 'you're a loser.'

'Look,' Vic said, 'I—'

'You lost a good fuck you could have had tonight.'

'Edith—'

98

She walked quickly off into the crowd. He caught sight of her once more then she was gone. It was always hard to see in Preter Coeur. That change in the light at the corner of your eye, you never knew if it was a shadow or a Shadow Boy, some gangster algorithm with its sense of humour puckered in the kiss of profit. Vic Serotonin shrugged. He couldn't blame Edith. Edith was focused; she understood her own needs, perhaps to a degree no one else could. She would be back in her own time. Meanwhile he bought a fight card, from which he gathered that he knew one of the contestants in the next bout, a Straint Street boy whose chops originated a couple of doors down from Liv Hula's bar. On paper this boy was quick, and looked like a bet. Twenty minutes later, three fights behind in the attempt to salvage his dignity, Vic felt a tug on his sleeve, looked down: there was Paulie DeRaad's lieutenant Alice Nylon, in her little plastic rainslicker and red Wellington boots.

'Hey, Alice,' Vic said. 'You here to change my luck?'

Alice had backed herself up with two or three of Paulie's soldiers, their faces contorted for Serotonin's benefit into expressions of juvenile threat. She craned her neck to see what was going on in the ring, winced. 'So where's your money in this sad affair, Vic?' she wanted to know; and, when he told her, shook her head, indicating professional disbelief. 'Looks like we got here too late to save you from yourself,' she said. Vic, meanwhile, made a gun of his fingers and aimed it at the kiddies.

'Don't do anything stupid,' he warned them.

Alice sighed. 'Paulie says to come with us,' she informed him not unsympathetically. 'He ain't in such a good mood today.'

Not too far away in the crowd, Irene the Mona watched these events with a certain amusement. Her eyes were intent. Her intuitions were sharp. In the undependable light of Preter Coeur her face looked older, and anyone who knew the original Irene – style-refugee from a planet few ever thought to tour – would have recognised her, installed there like a tectonic structure beneath the more obvious curves and planes of the Mona package. It was that Irene, perhaps, who noted how Edith Bonaventure flounced off into the crowd, only to be replaced immediately by Alice Nylon, as if those two were the single bald choice in Vic's world, the splitting point on a lonely man's journey. It was that Irene, perhaps, who thought to herself, It's easier to get into that stream than out of it, my girl; while to Fat Antoyne Messner she observed:

'Things will always catch up with Vic Serotonin.'

'I got to agree with that.'

At Preter Coeur he would agree with most things Irene said. He was a man of sluggish temperament, she felt bound to admit: but the fights made him put his arm around her, and buy cheap things. The fights made him want to have sex. What she liked most about sex with Fat Antoyne was how unpractised and tentative he was – how unprofessional. She could press his head to her breast after he came and he was still sprawled there panting and saying, 'I'm sorry,' and reassure him, 'Shush, shush, I like any kind of fucking. I'm made that way.' Being with Antoyne in those circumstances caused her heart to swell up warm, so that she had dreams of being one of the alpha females of Ancient Earth.

She watched Alice Nylon lead Vic away, and clutching Fat Antoyne's arm, said:

'Hey, you know, maybe Vic would help us.'

'I ain't asking Vic,' said Fat Antoyne.

'Well then we'll just have to find the money another way,' she told him. 'Maybe we could sell something?'

'I haven't got anything.'

'Everyone's got something they can sell, pet. Oh Antoyne, we'll soon be so happy and successful! But real. Wherever we go we'll stay very real and good, and make all the best decisions out there in those million stars. *I heart love!* we'll say. *I heart my life because it's so real up there on TV!*' While she counselled herself quite rightly: We will have to get him Zipped first. He can buy a package makes him look razor and quick with those hands, but sensitive too; and underneath he'll still be the Antoyne I know and love. He will always be Antoyne to me, who comes too quick and doesn't understand I can forgive that because I seen it all.

SIX

Tanked on C-Street

An hour later, when Alice Nylon and her punks delivered Vic to the back office of the Semiramide Club, Paulie DeRaad was sprawled in the same chair Vic had last seen him in, as if during the intervening period he hadn't moved at all, only got sick. Alice believed he had sat there for at least a day. She brought him drinks from the bar, she said, but he didn't seem as interested as usual; in fact he didn't seem interested at all. 'He's not himself, you know?' she said to Vic. 'Generally, you fetch him a Night Train, he'll put it down in one and crush the can that way he has against the side of his head, it's all one fluid move? Well, today he don't drink nothing. Then he wakes up suddenly and asks for you.'

'How did he put that?'

'Well, he says, you know, bring that fucking fucker Vic to me,' Alice recalled. 'Then he's like this again. I mean,' she offered, 'take a look.'

Paulie's legs were straight out in front of him, his head thrown back as if the chair had a headrest, which it did not but was just an ordinary uncomfortable moulded chair. His whole body was in a rigid condition. Where it wasn't the bluish colour of milk, his skin had a heavy-metal tinge particularly evident where it was ablated around his cheeks and forehead. His eyes were closed, though somehow you gained the impression they might flicker open any moment. It was hard to tell how sick Paulie was, and Paulie himself didn't help with this. He was smiling as happily as a girl. Some of those smiles were surprising, they were surprisingly sexy. It was as if Paulie wanted to share something. Sometimes he wanted to share it so much that he was practically winking. Vic Serotonin didn't care to know what it was. These weren't real smiles, he could tell: they were what you got when there was nothing left to smile for.

'Fuck it, Paulie,' Vic said.

'He wakes up sometimes, we don't understand what he says.'

Vic went to the office door, which he opened a crack. When he looked out into the Semiramide Club it was smoke, music and alcohol fumes, business as usual; no one was looking back in. He shut the door again. 'Does anyone else know about this? Any of his EMC connexions?' Alice didn't think they did. 'Let's keep it that way then,' Vic recommended. 'Those assholes don't need to know, we can agree on that?' As far as she was concerned, Alice said, they could. 'Good,' said Vic. When he turned back to Paulie, he found Paulie had woken up and got out of the chair and was standing right in Vic's personal space, his face – pumped up with blood under the skin so it was bright red – thrust forward, his blue eyes open as wide as they would go.

'*What have you done to me, you fuck?*' he screamed.

Vic felt the hair go up on the back of his neck. 'Jesus, Paulie,' he said, 'I don't know.' Before he could add anything to that, Paulie had pushed him aside and was kneeling down in front of Alice Nylon.

'Are you my pretty little girl?' he said.

'I am,' said Alice.

'Then give me your best smile!' Paulie cajoled her. 'There! You see? You feel better already!'

He stood up again and began to lurch restlessly about the room, walking from the hips with his knees stiff. He seemed to get interested in things, then he would stop and stare at the wall and do nothing. After he had been walking around like this for a while, examining the bits and pieces he kept in the office as if trying to understand who he was, he stopped in front of a hologram of himself with the other guys who came out alive from the wreck of the old *El Rayo X*. They looked a little sunburned but they were all grinning broadly, still in the bottom half of their vacuum suits, giving the thumbs-up with one hand and brandishing various kinds of guns and tools with the other. 'Who are these people?' Paulie asked Vic, but when Vic told him he didn't answer. The blood had leached out of his face again. Vic looked at Alice, who shrugged.

'He ain't the Paulie we know.'

Faintly, from the Semiramide Club outside, came the sound of laughter and applause. The entertainment had started in on their second set with the moderne classic *Jordan V-10*. Vic Serotonin thought a moment.

'Is there another way out?' he said.

'Door at the back there exits in an alley.'

'Fetch his rickshaw girl,' Vic told her. 'Don't talk to anyone else.'

When Alice had gone he went through Paulie's clothes until he found the key to the room where Paulie kept the artefact Vic had sold him. This would be an unsettling process for anyone, but Paulie stood compliantly throughout, his head tilted up slightly so he could face the hologram of himself. His eyes were closed again. A few minutes later the rickshaw girl ducked in through the back door.

'This is Annie,' Alice said, coming in behind her.

'Oh boy, you don't look good,' the Annie told Paulie. Between the three of them they manhandled DeRaad out of there; it took further effort to get him into the rickshaw. Alice Nylon sat on Vic's knee. Vic sat crushed in next to Paulie and tried to work out what sort of situation he was in. He wished he had handled Edith Bonaventure a little better, because perhaps her father's book would have told him more about Paulie's condition. He wondered if he was about to make another mistake.

'I can't believe this is Paulie DeRaad,' the rickshaw girl said after a mile or two. 'I mean, is he dead?'

'Turn left into Voigt,' Vic told her.

'Hey, forget I asked.'

'Are we there yet?' said Alice.

Nothing much had changed in the room off Voigt Street. The smell was still bad. Paulie, who had woken up again as soon as they got close, caught it from twenty yards away. His head went up and his nostrils dilated. He stood passively enough on the steps outside, while Vic struggled with the door and the rickshaw girl clopped away into the night of the noncorporate hinterland, but you could tell he was interested.

If Paulie was interested, so was the boy inside. When they got in the room, he had dragged himself off the bed and pressed himself into a corner. He was naked. He watched them with a soft smile while his hands made shy, pushing motions in Paulie's direction. Paulie smiled too. The boy's whole body shivered once, from head to foot: under the filth it had a clear, waxy look, and it had contracted in on itself a little as if something had been used up inside. 'I don't want you,' he said in that three-toned voice which sounded more like electronica chords than anything human. A few bright motes trickled out of one eye. Suddenly he made a break for the door, but Paulie reached out and caught his upper arm. The force of the boy's lunge swung them both around. 'Hey,' Paulie said, as if to himself, 'naughty, naughty.' They tottered for a moment, clutching at one another, then fell on the bed where they lay winded and face to face. Paulie got a wide gentle smile on his lips and laid his cheek close to the boy's; he whispered something. The boy looked up at the ceiling emptily at first, then he started smiling too.

Vic had no idea what was happening.

'We've got to stop this!' he said

Alice didn't think there was any need. 'Paulie won't hurt him now,' she said. 'Look. They're friends.'

'That's what I'm afraid of,' Vic said.

The situation remained like that for perhaps two minutes, then the boy's face got a light in it exactly as if someone had switched on a lamp inside his skull. His mouth opened slowly and light poured out over the room and all over Paulie DeRaad, as bright and fierce as the radiation that took his skin off all those years ago. It was a light you could hear. It had organ values. It issued from the boy's mouth but reflected so instantly off the walls that it seemed to come from everywhere else too. Vic and Alice covered their eyes but they could still see the light unabated, and they thought they could feel heat though no heat was there. Then it had passed, and the room was quiet and dark again, and the boy on the bed was just a Point kid lying confused and naked in his own filth and tangled clothes. Paulie DeRaad lay next to him with his eyes staring open, screaming at his old friend Vic:

'You fuck! You fuck!'

'Paulie, I—'

'It's daughter-code, Vic. You fucking unprofessional fuck, you brought me a daughter and I'm walking around dead!'

He wasn't walking around at all. Paulie was lying there on his back immobile except for some of his face, mostly the eyes and mouth. His eyes were popped out with the effort of holding something at bay. His jaw was clenched so hard his voice sounded as if it came down a bad datapipe from some location in the parking orbit. You could hear his teeth crack. His hands plucked at his clothes. 'This isn't me,' he said. 'Am I me?' He laughed suddenly. It was the distinctive DeRaad laugh, they heard it from Cor Caroli to Motel Splendido, wherever there were difficult times to be had. 'Hey! Vic! Like the old days!' This thought seemed to relax him. He sighed and turned to face the boy; code began to pour out the boy's mouth like cold tapioca. Vic and Alice pulled them apart. The boy convulsed, rolled away, curled up in a foetal position, held a murmured conversation with himself in three different voices. By then Paulie DeRaad was unconscious again. He had managed to get some of his clothes off and his bare arms had the same waxy pliable look as the boy's.

'This was such a fucking mistake,' Vic said. 'We should take him back to the club.'

Alice shook her head.

'Leave it with me,' she said. 'He needs to be in his own place now. I don't want the Semiramide crowd to know about this.'

'I can't tell what you're thinking, Alice.'

Alice smiled vaguely. 'I'll take care of him for now,' she said. Her eyes were inturned and he realised that she had dialled someone up. Just because Alice was eight didn't mean she was bad help: the contrary was true, or she wouldn't be Paulie DeRaad's best little girl. She was already on it. She was making arrangements. 'Yeah,' she said, 'ten minutes, Map Boy. Back of Voigt. By the way, a rickshaw won't do it. Hey, don't try to fuck me with that. And don't come in,' here she gave a flat little chuckle, 'unless you ain't got enough problems of your own. Yeah, yeah, fuck off, I heard it all before.' She joked a little more with Map Boy, then her eyes refocused and she said, 'You still here, Vic? To be honest I don't need you around now.' Serotonin shrugged and went to the door. He was halfway out when she called:

'You'd better know how to sort this out, Vic.'

It was two a.m. by then, and he felt peripheral to everything, especially Paulie. DeRaad always thought of Vic as one of his con-temporaries. Though nothing could be further from the case, there being ten years in it as far as Vic knew, Vic had always understood this as a compliment he might one day deserve – as though in Paulie's book you could be elected to a generation particularly favoured by craziness and poor judgment. At the beginning of their relationship Vic had been flattered, but for some years now he had no intention of ending up like Paulie or any of Paulie's friends. It complicated his position that he found himself responsible for a bad turn in Paulie's life.

The streets were deserted, and a thin salty mist in the air would be rain by morning. Vic stood undecided for a minute at the corner of Voigt and Altavista; then, rather than go back to the Semiramide Club, turned up his coat collar and took himself off to Straint Street and Liv Hula's bar; where he found Liv herself yawning on one side of the zinc counter, while, from the other, Mrs Elizabeth Kielar made halting conversation.

At about the same time, in his office across the city, Lens Aschemann, a man who bore an unmistakable resemblance to the aged Einstein, was informing his assistant:

'Just from its surface you know when water is deep. As a child you learn to interpret the colour, the movement, the way the light plays on it.' Hard orange street light played on Aschemann's surfaces; while his shadow operators, unused and unloved, moved uncomfortably in the corners of the room. 'We have a species need,' he went on, 'to make estimates like that. By implying everything that isn't there – not just in the case itself but in the world the case seems to have some relation to – crime awakes in the detective a similar need.

'Do you understand? No. Well then think about it, while I go see my friend Emil Bonaventure.'

'I'll drive you,' the assistant offered.

'A man can't visit his old friend without bringing the police along?' Aschemann asked. He waved his hand dismissively. 'Take the night off,' he instructed. 'Go home, wash your hair.'

She studied him as if she had never seen him before.

'Oh, now I offended you again. So go to a bar, whatever: I can give you a list of nice ones, only don't get caught trying to have sex in the back lot.'

'Thanks for that advice of yours,' she said.

This amused him. 'We're getting to know one another now,' he acknowledged. He offered her the keys to the Cadillac. After the Semiramide Club raid, he had forbidden her to return there, or to the Café Surf, alone.

As soon as he left, she had the shadow operators open a pipe to his records. Unnerved by the inappropriateness of this, they fussed around, whispering, 'Is there anything else we can bring you, dear?' while she sprawled in Aschemann's leather chair and stared into space like someone in the early stages of arousal, her lips moving gently as the raw data cascaded down the inside of her arm. There was an item about the death of his wife. She kept returning to it because although it seemed to hold the key to him, she had no idea how to turn it in the lock. 'Are you sure you're comfortable?' the shadow operators asked. 'It looks such an awkward way to sit.'

'I'll be fine,' she said. Later, she drove Aschemann's Cadillac down to the Corniche and parked facing out to sea.

It was a quiet night, with low cloud and a crack of greenish light just above the horizon. Onshore breezes whipped up the sand around the ragmop palms, hissed over the bodywork of the car. She walked down the access road to the bungalow where Aschemann's wife had lived. It was damper down there. Inside, the bungalow had a stale smell, not quite food or people. She stood in the kitchen, in the passageway, in the single reception room, in the cobalt dark and the shush of the sea, with her eyes closed, waiting for Aschemann and his wife to assemble themselves in front of her. Nothing like that happened. They were absent and dead respectively: they would never self-disclose. She would have to find them, in the old furniture, the stale carpets. She decided to begin with the bundles of letters piled in the fake bureau.

'To be as happy as this,' the detective had written to his wife just after they met, 'to be this open to someone else, is something I never expected.' It was a prophetic failure of nerve. He never settled. He was unfaithful from the moment they married, in tourist hotels during the afternoon and the back lots of bars at night. She forgave him over the years but he could never forgive himself; suddenly you found him telling her, 'Part of me has lost patience with both of us. It wants to fall back into life. In the end, one person always gives more than the other and is disappointed.' He had left her because she couldn't defend herself against him, but this only made him as miserable as she was. 'Late afternoon it rained,' he wrote, from an apartment on Third Street. 'I felt completely lonely and upset without you. For a second all I wanted was to be at home, among the things I knew, as if this life I have here was just some visit I had made without you.' Her name was Prima, but for reasons the assistant couldn't make out, he often called her Utz or Utzie. Dear Utz. Hello, Utzie. After they separated, he stopped writing about himself and wrote to her about the city instead. He wrote to her about ordinary things. He wrote to her about his job. To catch the criminal, he said, you had to go down inside: that's where you would find him.

Throughout the correspondence, if that was what it could be called, he had favoured a flimsy, almost transparent paper, light blue, prefolded so that it could be made into its own envelope. The earliest letters, full of endearments and graphic descriptions of the sex they had (as if by reliving it, perhaps, he could prove to himself he was there), were brittle but intact; while the later ones, though cruel, fell apart at the folds, as if they had been handled every day since.

Why had he chosen to write letters to her, when they lived in the same city, the same house? Had Prima ever answered them? It was impossible to know. 'I'm increasingly shortsighted,' he had written, three days before her death, 'yet my dreams are as compactly constructed as advertisements.'

Aschemann's assistant re-read all the letters, then stood at the window. Outside the bungalow it was the sound of waves on the beach, the smells of salt and marram, a blowing mist, all condensing into one substance like a block of smoky plastic. Nevertheless, she seemed to hear something out there: a cry or a laugh. As she trudged back to the car, a group of kids emerged from the darkness, hunched up in their shiny gun-punk rainwear, exchanging casual murmurs, jostling one another, eyeing her frankly. 'Try me out,' she invited them, her smile so accommodating that they slipped away into the mist shaking their heads. 'You see?' she whispered. On the way home, she looked in the driving mirror, she looked in the wing mirrors, she shifted gears with care: a policewoman, practical and calm but never still. She wondered why she understood neither Aschemann nor his wife, who, aware of their disaster from the outset, had encouraged it to roll over them anyway. She wondered if only half of her was there.

Aschemann always described as equivocal his relationship with Edith Bonaventure. 'What he means,' Edith would say, 'I don't like him.' Aschemann and her father were friends and sparring partners from the very first days of artefact policing in Saudade. Almost as soon as Emil arrived on-planet, touching down at the noncorporate port with a Halo tan and a would-be accordion-star daughter, Aschemann was arresting him. 'Those were the good old days,' Bonaventure always reminded Edith, as if at thirteen years old she hadn't been mature enough to appreciate them for herself. 'Things weren't so serious.'

Even at thirteen Edith had had her doubts about that; but was never less than loyal. 'I don't like a man who arrests my father,' she told Aschemann now. 'On any grounds.'

The detective sat on a wooden chair in her room, smiling round at the holograms and trophies, the costumes pinned on the wall with their pretty skirts fanned out as if she was still in them. Accordions like old dogs, wind broken, teeth bared in rippling tango smiles, eyed him savagely from the shelves and glass-front cabinets. 'Still,' she said, offering the Black Heart, 'have a drink before you go up.

Vic Serotonin brought us this, just the other day.' Aschemann, who had seen nanocam footage of Edith and Vic's ringside disagreement at Preter Coeur, didn't believe her; but it wasn't displeasing to have Vic's name come up so soon in the conversation.

'That Vic,' he said with a smile. He shook his head, as if the travel agent's character was a burden they could share.

Edith regarded him equably.

'Vic's generous to his old friend, just like you.'

'Everyone loves Emil,' Aschemann said. 'That's what you get for being famous in your day.' He took a drink. 'This is good rum of Vic's,' he congratulated her.

'Have some more.'

'I'm fine.'

'After another glass perhaps you'll be brave enough to cuff Emil. He's upstairs like always. A little weaker today, he'll be no trouble.'

Aschemann would not be distracted.

'A pity Vic is caught up in something bad,' he offered.

'We're all caught up in something bad.'

'Vic opened a door, I don't even know if he meant to. New sorts of artefacts are coming out of it.'

Edith made a spoiled face. 'What's new about new?'

'They walk about,' Aschemann was surprised to hear himself say, 'as if they own the place.'

Edith was still thinking about new. Everything presented as new in those days; as a result, the argument went, nothing was. She had seen that written on a wall. Her philosophy: you had your time at being new.

'Maybe they do,' she said.

'Another thing: Paulie DeRaad gets involved, suddenly we can't find Paulie. Our equipment doesn't see him. It's good equipment, perhaps a little old, but someone has talked to it in a language we can't afford. Perhaps this is a military language. Perhaps his friends from EMC will soon be asking questions we don't know how to answer.' After all, Aschemann decided, he'd have another drink. While he was pouring it for himself, he said, 'I daren't let Vic go into the site again until I know what's happening. Edith, what you know you should tell me, because this isn't just a little tourism. It isn't just a little thrill for the offworld girl with time on her hands.'

Several expressions passed across Edith's face, complex, but with contempt as their keynote feature.

'You would know all about that,' she accused.

She took Aschemann's glass out of his hand, emptied it back into the bottle and put the bottle away. 'My father is upstairs,' she said. 'Remember him?'

'I was hoping he would help me.'

'How can he? He gave up long ago. You and Vic are all he has, but when he sees you, you make it worse—' Edith stopped suddenly. She stared up at the musical instruments in their presentation cases, like someone confronting all over again the boundary conditions of her life. Then she said tiredly, 'I won't give Vic up, forget it.'

Aschemann had expected nothing else.

'Let's go and see Emil,' he suggested, as if it was a new idea.

Bonaventure slept half upright against the head of the bed. The pillows had slipped out from behind him so that his emaciated trunk made a slumped S shape against the whitewashed wall. He was staring vaguely into the furthest corner of the room. At the left side of his mouth the upper lip had drawn back off his teeth, but this expression seemed to have little to do with anything he might be thinking. When he saw Aschemann, his eyes lit up.

'Hi, Vic!' he said.

'I'm not Vic,' Aschemann said.

The animation faded from Emil's face. 'So arrest me,' he said faintly. After that he appeared to fall asleep.

'Is this something new?' Aschemann asked Edith.

'No,' she said shortly. 'It's just the same old thing, Lens: your friend's dying.' He had cancers they couldn't describe, let alone cure. Everything ran wild inside of him, as if his body was trying to be something else but had no plan: his organs switched on and off at random, his bones didn't make platelets any more. The latest thing, Edith told Aschemann, was some hybrid virus which self-assembled in his cells from three or four kinds of RNA and a manufactured gene no one could identify. 'That's nothing in itself,' she said. 'The worst thing is he still can't dream. I'm going to leave you with him. I get enough of him all day, it's a relief someone comes to visit.'

'I don't like to see him like this,' Aschemann said.

He sat on the hard chair by the bed for a while, but nothing happened. 'I need to talk to you, Emil,' he said. 'There's a problem with the site.' Then, 'You could help me with this, it doesn't matter we're on opposite sides. I worked out something none of us knew.' Bonaventure moved restlessly in his sleep. 'Don't bring it near me,' he said, and the detective leaned in close; but it was only one or other of the fevers talking. Emil's breath smelled as if he was already dead, as if all those nightmares he couldn't have were hanging round him like a gas. 'I'm sorry, Emil,' Aschemann said eventually. 'You would have been interested in what I worked out.'

Downstairs, Edith was sitting on the floor, sorting intently through a box of notebooks in all sizes, full of deranged handwriting and diagrams in different inks, their covers faded and water-stained. They had an air of being handled harshly, folded into pockets, dropped and trodden on, bled into, lost and found, over the years. She would take one out, open it in two or three places at random, riffle through all the pages in one movement as if she was hoping something would fall out, then put it back in the box. There was a smell of real dust in the air. When Aschemann appeared, she shut the box and pushed it away. He thought she was in a better mood. 'Don't get up,' he said. 'I have to go.'

'Do you want that other drink?'

'No. But this is for you.'

Edith gave him a vicious look. 'It's not money we need,' she said. She put herself between Aschemann and the door. 'Remember how I used to sit in your lap when Emil first brought me to Saudade?' she reminded him. 'Those were the days! Sit on your lap in your private office with you.' She laughed derisively, but it wasn't clear which of them she was laughing at. 'You shouldn't have let yourself be persuaded. You should have locked him up forever, so his life would be saved now.'

Aschemann couldn't think of a reply to that.

'I'll call a rickshaw,' he said.

She shrugged and stood out of his way.

'Another thing,' she called after him, 'I don't like you going after Vic the way you do. He's a moron but he never hurt anyone.' After a pause she was forced to concede, 'Not deliberately anyway,' but by then the detective had gone.

Aschemann had always admired Bonaventure's generation, though his admiration diluted itself over the years. They thought of themselves as uncut diamonds, in reality they were drunks, junkies, sky-pilots and entradistas. But in their day the site had only recently fallen to earth. It was unmappable to a degree. No one knew a dependable route through the aureole – which was more active then – or, if they made it through, where they would end up inside. They weren't even sure if inside/outside concepts had meaning. Despite that they launched themselves in there daily, on foot, by air, and in every kind of cheap local petrol-driven vehicle. They came home, if they came home, three weeks later, only to find that twelve hours had passed outside. Just as often it was the other way around. No perspective, no data, no count of any kind could be depended upon.

As for artefacts, they were scooping them up off the ground in open contravention of common sense. They were digging them out of earth as ripe as cheese, fetching them down on the run with a variety of anaesthetic darts and lite particle beams. As a result they died in numbers, of odd diseases or inexplicable accidents inside and outside the site, leaving wills too exuberant to understand and last testaments tattooed on their buttocks. These treasure maps, whose psychic north pegged itself to equally unreliable features of the Kefahuchi Tract in the night sky above, always proved worthless.

'But, hey,' Emil Bonaventure would say, in the tone of voice of a survivor about to bring forth the sum of his and others' experience – then, after a longish pause, shrug perplexedly because he had forgotten what he was talking about.

Aschemann had the rickshaw take him to his ex-wife's bungalow. 'Go by the noncorporate port,' he told the Annie. Traffic was light. The port seemed reassuringly inactive, its fences intact under the halogen lights. By the time he got to Suicide Point the night's offshore breezes had started up and were blowing the mist back out to sea. There was a light oiliness to the water, and from round the curve of the bay he could hear something being loaded on to a ship. A few Point kids, upped on cheap AdAcs, were running about the beach in an aimless way. Aschemann spoke to them briefly and as a result got in touch with his assistant.

'I'm puzzled that you would come here,' he said, 'without asking me.'

The assistant felt ambushed. She felt slow and confused. She had spent her night off in a C-Street tank farm. There, a hundred per cent immersed in the role of housewife in the moderne world of 1956AD, she had mopped a floor; gone for a spin on a fairground ride called the Meteorite, then, in an inexplicable third episode, discovered herself posing in front of a wardrobe mirror dressed only in loose transparent satin briefs. Her breasts were heavy, with big brown aureoles; the rest of her body, by the standards of her own day, soft and running to fat. After a little while, she pushed one hand deftly down the front of the briefs and began to practise saying, 'Oh Robert, it's so nice to have you in there. Are you going to fuck me, Robert? Are you fucking me?' until quite suddenly she came, with a sharp blue line of light cracking across her vision, and felt exhausted. As a night off it was different, but less fun than she expected. It was an 'art' experience. In the end she had preferred the Meteorite, which consisted of a wheel like a huge flat openwork drum, mounted on a bright red steel arm which levered it seventy or eighty degrees from the horizontal. You entered, the Meteorite began to spin, faster and faster. You were pinned against the wall by simple but implacable physical forces.

'It was a mistake I made,' she apologised to Aschemann. 'I thought you said you would be there.' She glanced at the data flowing endlessly up and down her arm; for a moment, despite all her training, she couldn't do anything with it. I was trying to understand you, she thought of explaining: but in the end only advised him, 'You should get some sleep,' and cut the connection.

After Aschemann left, Edith Bonaventure went to her father's room, stood looking down for a minute or two at the blue hollows behind his collar bones, then took him by the shoulders and shook him until he woke. 'Listen to me, Emil,' she said. 'Listen. Look at me and help.' He coughed suddenly. 'I'm sorry to do this, Emil,' she said. She pulled him forward so that he lolled against her, weightless and rank, his chin on her shoulder taking the weight of his head like a baby's, while she felt around, first under the pillows then under his hot skinny buttocks. 'I need it and it has to be here somewhere.' Suddenly she shoved him away and began to beat his chest with her fists. 'I'm serious,' she said, 'I'm serious, Emil.' Emil made vague defensive motions.

'Hey,' he said thickly. 'There's no need for this.'

'*Where is it?*'

There was a longish pause and she thought he had passed out again. Then he laughed.

'It's under the bed.'

'You bastard, Emil. You fuckhead.'

'It's under the bed with the bottles. It was always there,' Emil said. 'You could have looked any time.' His laughter grew quieter and stopped. 'It won't do Vic Serotonin any good,' he warned her. 'There's no good giving it to Vic.' Contempt came into his voice. 'Why? Because he's a tourist.' He leaned carefully over the side of the bed and vomited a thin line of bile on to the floor. 'Sorry,' he said. He hung there exhausted, his face a foot from the boards, sentient tattoos crawling for cover like lice between the sores and shadows of his ribs. His skin was rich with a smell she couldn't explain. Edith hauled him back into bed and mopped up. She wiped his face, which had once had the power to solve every problem for her, but which now seemed all bone and stubble, hurt eyes like a boy. It was a face which for sixty years admitted desire but not alleviation. He had always moved on to the next thing; he had never taken shelter, and as a result he didn't know how. She clutched him and rocked him. 'You were always useless,' she told him. 'You were a useless father.' She began to cry. 'I don't know what to do,' she said.

'I'm sorry about your life,' Emil whispered.

She let him fall, and sat back in disgust. 'Won't you grow up even now?' she shouted.

The journal was there, pushed as far as he could reach into the darkness under the bed, where the only way to find it was to sweep your hands to and fro in blind disgust until one of them touched it. What else was underneath? Edith didn't want to know. 'Spew up on me while I'm down here,' she warned him, 'I'll kill you.' No answer. But as soon as she had the book and stood up to go, he grabbed her arm and drew her down towards him. She was astonished by his strength – understood, for the first time, that everybody in his life had been too.

'Where's Vic?' he said.

'Vic's not here, Emil.'

'I never went deeper,' he said. 'This is the record of it. A year inside the site, and this book is everything I saved.'

'Emil—'

'Fifty of us set out, two came back. We travelled to the heart of it. Where's Vic Serotonin been? Nowhere.'

'Emil, you're hurting me.'

'It was worth it,' he said.

His eyes went out of focus very suddenly and he let go her arm. 'A year passed in there, Billy boy,' he shouted, 'less than a day out here. What do you make of that?'

After she had calmed him down she brought the journal to her own room. It looked worse in the light. Her father's adventures had aged it the same way they aged him. Its covers were bruised and greasy; like Emil's, its spine was rotten. Every page was stained, spattered, slashed; some had been torn in half longitudinally, to leave only curious groups of words – 'emergent behaviour', 'sunset of the amygdila' and 'outputs accepted as input'. But these were just problems of legibility. The site being as it was, an electromagnetic nightmare, writing was the only way to get anything out: but how do you write the fakebook to a place that is constantly at work to change the ink you write with, let alone the things you see? Her father's script tottered into the gale of it, stumbling off the edge of one page to fall by pure luck on to the next.

He tried to remain calm. Of a misfired attempt to go in from the sea using inflatable boats, he recorded, 'Two miles from [illegible] Point, wrecks show themselves at half tide.' Then, 'Satnav and dead reckoning both unreliable here but keep Mutton Dagger in line with the derelict fuel refinery and you might clear the sand. Ben Moran says he went in hard and got two feet clearance at low water.' Scribbled across this, in a hand so distraught it looked like someone else's, was the instruction, 'Forget it.' Then underneath: 'Something ate Billy in the fog. We lost the [illegible] & had to walk out. Four days in here, a week passed outside.'

And then: 'How do we know that what we come back to is the same?'

Edith shut the book there and then. To read any more would be to read too far into Emil. *How do we know that what we come back to is the same?* Less a cry of horror than of triumph. In plain fact her father was only alive when he was in there, where everything was toxic, indefinable, up for grabs. Whatever he said about it – whatever he said about himself – it was the anxiety he loved. He loved the shadows, the wrenched way the light fell, the unpredictability of it all. So what he wrote in the journal was nothing like the assured face he showed the world, or even the one he showed himself, and that was why his handwriting had this disordered, scribbled, racing look about it. As for Vic Serotonin, he was the same. Despite Emil's bad opinion, Vic was the same, so maybe the book would be a help to him. Maybe, after all, it would give him the edge in his situation with Lens Aschemann and Paulie DeRaad. Whatever that was.

'Vic, you moron,' Edith said gently, as if he was in the room with her.

When she looked up, the accordions glared at her from the walls; out the window she could see the street full of cats, their black and white fur untouched by the fierce gold needles of rain falling through the streetlight. Despite these omens Edith tucked the book away, put on her maroon wool street coat and found her umbrella. 'I'm going out!' she called up to her father. For the longest time there was no answer; then just before she slammed the outside door, Emil, who had lain there alert and intelligent with a curious hard smile on his face since she took the journal, called down:

120

'It won't do him any good. My advice, give it to Aschemann, at least he's dependable.'

'Emil, you love Vic!'

This made her father laugh; the laugh turned quickly into a cough. 'So what?' Emil Bonaventure asked the ceiling when he could speak again. You can love a disappointment.

Earlier that evening, Vic Serotonin had walked into Liv Hula's place in time to hear Liv say to Mrs Kielar:

'Sometimes I could do without that.'

He had no idea what they were talking about. Reduced to essentials by the strong overhead light, leaning towards one another from each side of the zinc bar, the two women made between them a shaped gap, a Rubin's vase illusion. Though none of their differences could be said to be resolved by this, it gave them something in common for once: more, at any rate, than Elizabeth Kielar's cup of chocolate cooling on the counter by her hand; more than either of them might have in common with Vic Serotonin. Vic was surprised to catch that glimpse of them. They spoke for a moment longer, then, becoming aware of him, seemed to move languidly apart and break the spell.

'Hi, Vic,' Liv Hula said. 'Get you something?' Then, as if he couldn't already see, 'Your client's here.'

It had been a quiet night. Earlier, a few tailors from the franchise chopshops along Straint came in to celebrate a win at the fights; they had been followed back from Preter Coeur by some tourists off a Beths/Hirston ship – probably the *Pro Ana*, to which, outbound on her twice-yearly loop of creatively selected Beach destinations, Saudade was little more than a fuel stop. For twenty minutes this was the cause of unhealthy excitement among Liv's shadow operators, but then one of the tourists remembered the name of a new venue off Antarctic Boulevard and they all left. That was the bar trade in a nutshell, Liv thought, as she tidied tables, added up the money in the till, and washed the empty glasses, letting the warm water lave her hands. She had the blues for her old life, which was different than this. That afternoon, in her room upstairs, two things had happened.

First, she had encountered herself by accident in the mirror. The face she saw was too much her own, and too little like Elizabeth Kielar's face. It was tired of never owning a fur coat. It was tired of always being what it was. Its eyes looking out were no longer calm. Up in the Halo you could beat that, you could always reinvent, move yourself on. Because empty space is kind. Everything's negotiable out there. There's so little to run into. But down here your room is what you are.

The second thing that happened to Liv was this: waking from a shallow sleep, she sat on the edge of the unmade bed and looked out the window and saw Antoyne Messner walking past with Irene the Mona on his arm. Irene had on a new outfit, cropped mohair bolero, latex pedal-pushers, acrylic stilt-heels, all in popular neoteny pink; while the fat man was wearing the pale blue suit she made him buy when he started working for Paulie DeRaad, with his hair arranged in a ridged oily wave on top of his head. They looked ridiculous, but at the same time mysteriously dignified just by being together. They looked like the king and queen of the affect. Seeing them in that unaccustomed light, she had wondered if she should run downstairs, ask them why they never drank at her bar any more. Now, as she watched Vic Serotonin usher his client to a table by the window where they sat down and began to talk earnestly, she found herself thinking the same thing she had thought about Antoyne and the Mona:

Those two believe they've discovered something new. Good luck to them then.

In fact Vic Serotonin was saying, 'Maybe in four days we can risk it,' and Mrs Kielar was already beginning to shake her head, no. It had to be sooner for her, she said, this was such bad news for her.

Her nerves were worse. She wasn't sure, she said, she could wait another day. 'I'm not sure I can wait an hour.' And it was true, he thought. Whatever was consuming her from inside had upped its ante since she fucked Vic in the Hot Walls apartment.

'Three days, then,' he offered.

She shook her head. He took her hand, which she was already beginning to pull away as he reached for it, and explained, 'It's only because things are going on here I don't understand.'

'No,' she said.

'Two days,' Vic said. 'Two days, Mrs Kielar, you can allow me that. Something's wrong with Paulie, something's wrong in the site. The police are all over everything like a cheap suit.'

Mrs Kielar, trying to avoid this information the way you would avoid a physical blow, got to her feet so suddenly her chair toppled over. She stared down at it as if a chair being knocked over was already the worst thing that could happen to either of them.

'I can't,' she whispered.

At that point Vic didn't see a way forward. He was as puzzled by his own behaviour as by hers. 'I'm waiting for something to happen,' he remembered her saying, 'and I don't even know what part of my life it will approach from.' He got up and put his arm round her and set the chair back on its feet. 'Look,' he said, 'there. You see? It's OK. It's no problem.' Where his hand touched it, he could feel the whole thin apparatus of her right shoulder rigid and trembling. He was aware of the hot bones, *Elizabeth Kielar* inscribed through every one of them. 'We'll be in there in forty-eight hours time,' he said. 'I promise.' She was like a hologram; if you looked, every part of her would prove to contain the whole you didn't understand. He tried to persuade her to sit down again. She clung to him instead. They ordered more drinks and sat on opposite sides of the table, not speaking but holding hands. Much later, when Edith Bonaventure walked into the bar dressed in her maroon wool coat and holding her father's site-journal, that was how she found the two of them.

'Vic, you cheap shit,' Edith said.

She went over and asked Liv Hula to give her a drink. 'I'll take that here at the bar,' she told Liv. 'You don't mind if I sit on the stool and talk?'

'You're the customer,' Liv Hula said.

'That's good, that's nice,' said Edith. 'It's nice because if I face you I don't have to look at that shit by the window.' She assessed the bar a moment. 'It's a nice business you have here,' she advised Liv Hula, 'but a little kicked about. It needs a refit. It needs a theme, something cheerful.' She put down half her drink in one swallow and wiped alcohol out of the faint down on her upper lip. 'Hey, Vic,' she called, holding the journal up high in one hand so he couldn't mistake what it was, 'Emil was right about you. See this? I walked all the way across town to give it you, now you can whistle.'

'Jesus,' Vic said.

'You can fucking whistle for it, Vic, because you're a cheap toilet and in the end where have you been? Nowhere.' Edith finished her drink and stood up. 'Thanks for that,' she said to Liv Hula. 'I enjoyed that. Goodnight.'

Vic Serotonin was on his feet by then. He got to the door first and caught her by the wrists.

'Edith, we can talk,' he said.

Edith laughed lightly. 'No we can't, Vic,' she said. 'You made an error there.'

Vic tried to think what to say to her. 'Listen,' he began, 'whatever Emil says, something is changing in there.' He already saw that this wasn't what she wanted to hear, but he couldn't stop. 'All our experiences of it might be false.'

'How nice it would be if you grew up,' she said wistfully, 'either of you.'

'Edith—'

'You know what this reminds me of?' Edith asked him, and her gesture seemed to take in all of it, Mrs Elizabeth Kielar, Liv Hula's bar, the long perspective of Straint Street that she wasn't even looking at, Saudade itself which was nothing but sand on the Beach, a refuelling stop on someone else's big tour. 'It reminds me of the fights.'

'Edith—'

'It reminds me of that night at the fights,' she said.

She looked down at his hands imprisoning her wrists, then back up at his face. 'I don't give a shit what's in there, Vic.' Unable to reply, he released her and she walked off down Straint in the rain, stopping once to add without turning round, 'And you know it isn't about Emil either,' after which the sound of her heels diminished along some simple, exact, inevitable accoustic curve. Vic watched her go. Back inside he found that Mrs Kielar had smashed a glass against the wall and was now sitting huddled like a child on the blackened floorboards by the window, staring along Straint Street towards the event site aureole – which could be seen, at the limits of vision, as a line of rusty walls, broken windows, concertina wire – and refusing to speak.

Liv Hula patiently swept up the broken glass.

'I'm losing my sense of humour for this,' she told Vic. 'Maybe you should find another office.' While she thought to herself: This afternoon I was just down. Afternoon is a bad time to be alone anywhere.

SEVEN

Space Noir

Vic took Mrs Kielar to Hot Walls in a rickshaw. On his way home the next morning he was arrested. The arrest was quick and deft: a Cadillac convertible, travelling quietly against the grain of the traffic, pulled up alongside the kerb, its front passenger door swinging open just far enough ahead of him for Vic to walk into it. 'Hey!' he said. By that time Aschemann's assistant was out on the sidewalk with him, grinning right in his face and saying, 'Get in the car, Vic.' It was already a nice day, with a light but lively onshore breeze. The sunshine glittered off a wing mirror, slicked along the Cadillac's perfect finish and into Vic's eyes. He must have had an unpredictable look about him that morning, because the assistant's smile broadened and he saw her tailoring cut in, a ripple of nanomotion, subcutaneous and subliminal. Her eyes blanked over. Data poured down her arm, full of excitements of its own.

'Vic Testosterone!' she said. 'Vic, you can try me out, or I can call down a fire-team—' here she glanced meaningfully skywards '—or, how would this be, you could just come with me and no one would be killed at all. What do you say?'

Vic shrugged and got in the Cadillac.

She stared down at him expressionlessly for a moment, then shook her head and shut the door.

'Use the seatbelt,' she advised.

Vic expected to be taken to a holding cell. He expected to be processed. Instead, she drove him around in the light traffic for perhaps five minutes, enough to make him wonder what was happening, then said suddenly:

'You must have known Lens a long time.'

'Who?' Vic said.

'Did you ever meet his wife?'

'Ask your arm,' Vic suggested. 'Maybe it can tell you.' He didn't know what she was talking about. Even if he had known, he wouldn't have wanted to go any further into it. 'Or does it just get the fight results?'

'He's here,' the woman said into her dial-up.

'This is a nice car,' said Vic, as if there was a third person in the Cadillac with them, perhaps in the back, 'and I enjoy the smell of the real leather bench seats.' He turned a chrome knob on the dashboard, music came out. Station WDIA, Radio Retro, airwaves to the planet. Aschemann's assistant, still talking into her dial-up, reached across and switched it off again.

'No,' she said, looking emptily at Vic then back at the street, 'he isn't a problem.'

Vic was left alone for about ten minutes in an office on the second floor of the police bureau at the intersection of Uniment and Poe. It had been sprayed recently to smell of authentic furniture wax; the blinds were down, though enough narrow strips of sunlight fell through them to make visible the used, uneven but shiny surfaces of everything, the brown leather chair, the knocked-about steel desk and filing cabinets, the polished floor of green linoleum. One or two shadow operators emerged from the corners as Vic sat down, looking worn and under-used at the same time. 'He isn't here yet, dear,' they apologised. 'Would you like a cup of tea?' Vic started to go through the desk drawers. He found some packets of letters written on flimsy pale blue paper which folded cleverly to make its own envelope. They were brittle with age. One of them began, 'My dearest Lens,' but he had no time to read it, only stuff it back in and close the drawer, because Aschemann walked in the room.

'Vic, don't get up,' the detective insisted. 'It's good to see you so relaxed. If these operators bother you, just say.'

'What am I arrested for?'

'I'll hang my coat up here on this hook,' Aschemann said, 'to get it out of our way. Vic, you aren't arrested yet.'

Serotonin got up and went to the door.

'It was nice to see you again,' he said.

'You aren't arrested yet, but this is Site Crime, not a bar on Straint Street. Sit down, talk, is that so hard?'

Vic sat down again, taking the good leather chair behind the desk, which left Aschemann the hard one in front. If he felt any irritation at this reversal of protocol, the detective didn't show it, only hitched the trousers of his light brown suit – the worn cuffs of which fell back to reveal short black socks, white calves with the beginnings of varicose ulcers – to save their knees, and asked, 'Vic, what's it like inside the site?'

'You're kidding me.'

The detective nodded to himself, as if this was an answer he had expected; as if it was one of several possible answers, all worth consideration, all, perhaps, in the end, of a similar weight. It hadn't, after all, been a fair question. 'I'll sit here and smoke my pipe, if you don't mind,' he said, 'while you think about things.'

Poor-quality black-and-white footage of Vic now began playing across one wall. It was like a show without sound, Vic Serotonin walks down a street in Hot Walls, Vic Serotonin plays the fights with a plump woman on his arm, Vic Serotonin buys a hat. Vic walks down his own street, the hat tipped back on his head. His life is comprehensively represented: in one shot he threads his way through the VIP crowd at Paulie DeRaad's Semiramide Club, stopping to exchange a word with Paulie's best girl; the image vanishes abruptly at the door of Paulie's back room and now Vic's all the way over town at the Long Bar, where you can see, through the fog and scratch of irresolvable bad data, the Café Surf two-piece playing a tune of their own, a little thing of their own they've called *Decoda*. This visual record had intelligence, it had narrative, it had edit. It followed Vic into the toilets, passing over chipped paint and chequered linoleum, and then out again, where it caught up with him staring, puzzled, across the damp sand behind the bar, past the line of demarcation into the site. Aschemann watched Vic watch himself. He smoked his pipe. After a few minutes he froze the footage.

'So,' he said. 'Next is what happens most nights at this venue. Vic, you aren't in this footage, but perhaps you could pay attention to it as if you were?'

Up on the wall figures lurched about in half dark, their movements uninterpretable; a doorway at one angle, the neon sign *Live Music Nightly* at another; another doorway, and then the sea. Nanocameras swarmed in the seafront light like milt. Vic saw what looked like brand new people moving hesitantly away from the Café Surf, unformed, emergent, puzzled but as yet unwounded, full of expectation.

'Maybe it happens in the day too, maybe we don't watch closely enough.'

Two boys in dress shirts. A girl who dances inexpertly on the sand. They link elbows, ascend Maricachel Hill towards the centre of the city. They try to talk, but it's better they lean together and sing snatches of tunes learned twenty minutes ago in the Café Surf. After that, they find what they're looking for, one by one: and vanish. They stare thoughtfully at the neon signs, they regard the street junctions with soft and meditative smiles, then slip into the ink joints and porn parlours. One minute they are in camera – in a million cameras – then the city has absorbed them. The cameras all have blinked.

Aschemann switched the wall off abruptly.

'Are they artefacts?' he asked, 'or people? Maybe you can help, Vic, our equipment can't make the distinction. Whatever they are, they don't have any practice at life, literally, they're without praxis. They don't have a grip on reality.' He paused for a moment. Then he leaned forward, put his pipe on the desk next to the ashtray and said, 'My wife was a little like that.'

Vic stared at him. 'What?'

'There's a fierce attrition rate, Vic, most of them worn to nothing inside an hour. But the ones that survive!' Aschemann shook his head. 'How can I describe that? They learn how to eat, Vic, how to dress. They learn what the city wants from them. They get a room—'

He shook his head in admiration.

'Vic, I have to know what part you're playing in this.'

'Is this what you think we're doing, Paulie and me? Smuggling these people in? This has nothing to do with us!'

Aschemann shrugged. Vic stared at him angrily. No one was saying anything. Up near the ceiling, the shadow operators clung and shifted, pulling themselves one over another like a colony of bats. Grainy images began to unreel across the office wall again: Vic Serotonin was seen to enter the Long Bar, he was seen to tip his new hat back on his head, exchange a word or two with the barkeep. He was seen to exit through the lavatories and peer across the wet sand towards the event site aureole, which the cameras rendered as a greyish luminescence. Aschemann nodded his head as if these pictures offered not simply new evidence but *scienza nuova*, new ways of looking at things. Then he said:

'Vic, I have to apologise. I understand now from this film that you were never in the Café Surf, or especially out in back by the rusty wire, a stone's throw or less from the site itself, which you don't deny entering on numerous occasions—'

Vic laughed resentfully.

'I was never in the Café Surf until I heard you thought I was.

I went to check it out. Believe me, it's the worst jump-off joint I ever saw.'

The detective, impressed by the professionalism of this explanation, seemed to consider it. But whatever conclusion he came to, he put to one side, and when he next spoke it was to continue an earlier train of thought. 'Suppose they *are* fitting in, Vic? Why? What happens to them next?' He didn't know how to answer that, so he sat there contemplating it instead. Eventually he said, 'Vic, I'm not the man for this. I need your advice here.'

'I'm just a travel agent.'

Even as he made this claim, which neither of them pretended to take seriously, Vic suffered a raw flashback to the site, and his encounter with the artefact he would subsequently sell to Paulie DeRaad. The artefact was watching him from ten yards away. It remained nervous but it had made eye contact. Vic had taken two or three hours over the journey through the aureole and was by this time perhaps five hundred yards into the site proper, standing under a cherry tree which he knew to have been in bloom for six years. There were the usual smells, as rank as rendered fat; the usual distant animal noises. The bits of music you thought you knew. The sense you had of a voice reciting something. The sense of everything fallen away from sense. It was one of those memories that folds itself quickly out of sight; but it made Vic think, and suddenly he didn't want to be in the detective bureau any more.

'Nice to talk,' he said. 'Maybe we'll see each other around.'

Quickly for such an old-looking man Aschemann got between Vic and the door. He clutched Vic's wrist. 'Don't go, Vic,' he said urgently. 'There's more. I went to see Emil today, but he's gone a long way down. He's gone a long way down.'

'What is Emil to do with it?'

'Vic, this footage of you can be explained to everyone's satisfaction. I can forget everything you've done. Even now.'

'So what will it take for that to happen?'

'I want to go in there. I want you to guide me in there.'

'Jesus,' Vic said. 'You're as fucked as me.'

He looked into the detective's face, with its Zipped-in signature features of pouchy cheeks, shocked white hair and amiably drooping eyelids. An inexplicable excitement made the eyes watery and vulnerable; it slackened the corner of the mouth. In forty years, no one had seen through the tailoring to Aschemann, not his assistants, not his superiors, not his wife; now he disclosed himself for no reason to a cheap travel agent, in a shabby empty office in the middle of the morning, with the shadow operators curled up in the corners like dead leaves. Everything that made him the police detective, everything that had made him such a reliable antagonist when Vic met him on the street, was undermined. His obsessive commitment to Site Crime revealed itself, through one simple inversion, to be the very same obsession that had derailed Emil Bonaventure's life, or Vic Serotonin's. Vic's instinct was not to confront this understanding. Instead, he pushed past the old man and out of the office. He didn't want to know Aschemann's motives. He didn't want to know what had changed so suddenly. He didn't want to look into a psyche as weakened and visible as his own, in case the encounter reduced his freedom to act.

'Arrest me or let me go,' he said. 'I'm not comfortable with any of this.'

'No one is comfortable,' Aschemann reminded him, 'out here in the Halo.' He watched Vic walk away down the corridor. 'You should take care from now on,' he called, 'in case I can't protect you from yourself.' He dialled up his assistant. 'Put every camera we have on him,' he ordered. But the orbital component of the surveillance system, a smart fog of microsatellites sold on from some small war ten or twelve lights along the line, was down for service. 'Those pSi engines burn too hot for their own ceramics,' the assistant informed him. They would be out that day, she apologised, and all the next; consequently there would be a reduced service. There would be some loss of coverage. Even as he flagged down a rickshaw in broad daylight at the junction of Uniment and Poe, Vic Serotonin was becoming as invisible as his friend DeRaad.

'I thought we were arresting him,' the assistant said.

'We changed our minds.'

Police work, the man who looked like Einstein always tried to teach his subordinates, is an activity drained of romance yet suffused with every possible kind of mystery. It was the opposite life, he believed, to the one his wife had lived: although he knew that his ability to see himself clearly – to encounter himself as a continuity – had, quite early on in their relationship, been corrupted by his attempts to bring her into focus. Did that matter, now that he had begun to understand what was happening in the teeming epistemological gap between Saudade and the event site?

Vic Serotonin went straight from the detective bureau to the Semiramide Club, the nearest place he could think of to get a drink. It was like a warehouse at that time of the morning, with much the same ambience if you discounted the smell of high-end pheromone patches and low-end liquor. The cleaning service was in. A few people of Paulie's, disconcerted by his absence, sat around tables at the back, among them Fat Antoyne Messner and Antoyne's squeeze Irene, who were discussing the hottest subject in the Halo at that or any other time – what they would do with their lives if they ever got off-planet. Irene could envisage herself owning a little business. She had as many ideas what that might be, she confessed, as she had smiles; but she knew just what she'd call it, however her good fortune turned out: Nova Swing. That was a name the fat man could appreciate, indeed he received it as he received all Irene's plans, with the look of someone already convinced. On his part, the suggestion was they buy a ship. *Nova Swing* would be as good a name for a rocket, he believed, as for a boutique; and a rocket was, whatever angle you looked at it from, a business. Antoyne would always know how to make money out of a rocket. At which Irene gripped his hand across the table and smiled with every part of her body.

'We only could get our start, Antoyne, there'd be no limit to the things we did!'

That was how Vic found them.

'Hey, Fat Antoyne!' he said, pulling up one of the many empty chairs so he could sit down. 'I was just thinking of you on the way over.'

This approached the truth, although what had engrossed Vic most, as the rickshaw girl plodded through her midmorning low, was his promise to Elizabeth Kielar. Now wasn't a good time to take a client into the site. On the other hand, he had no doubt that circumstances would soon make it impossible for him to go in at all. He wasn't sure which he was most afraid of: being caught in whatever operation Paulie DeRaad was running through the Café Surf (because now he was certain it must be Paulie's op, financed for their own purposes, perhaps, by his shadowy backers in EMC); or allowing himself to be sucked into the meltdown of psychic confusion and professional misjudgment Paulie had triggered at Site Crime. Thinking too much about this had caused Vic a crisis of confidence. That was why he was glad to see Fat Antoyne, though a moment's consideration might have changed his mind about the offer he now made.

'I was thinking of how you always wanted to go into the site,' he said. 'Well now you can.' He beamed at Antoyne, who did not reply, and then at Irene, who gave him an unfriendly look and said:

'Excuse me, I got the urge for the powder room.'

'It's work, Antoyne, if you want it.'

'I work for Paulie,' Antoyne pointed out. 'Also, I don't see you for days, maybe weeks, suddenly you want me to go in the site with you. You never wanted my help when I offered.'

'That was perhaps insensitive of me,' Vic allowed.

Antoyne only repeated, 'You never wanted my help when I offered.'

'I see that,' Vic said. He knew it wasn't enough, but he didn't know what else Antoyne wanted him to say. After a pause he went on, 'Paulie's not feeling well. I expect you heard.' He shuddered. 'I got it from Paulie himself, you don't want that experience. He doesn't look good, Antoyne. It will be a while before there's work for anyone in that direction. Look around you.' He indicated the gun-kiddies, desultorily threatening to shoot one another over a dice game called Three Dick Hughie. Every time someone came in the front door they all looked up at once, their little six- and seven-year-old faces full of light, in case it was Alice Nylon with news. 'These guys know that. Hey, what about a drink?'

Vic sat back. Antoyne stared at him as if he was in the middle of planning what to say. They remained in that position until Irene returned from the powder room in an improved mood and accepted a cocktail, as she put it, on both her and Antoyne's behalves. 'You two men can still be friends,' she judged, after the drinks arrived, 'if you just but trust each other. You know I'm right.' She tried to catch Vic's eye.

'That's nice, Irene,' Vic said, looking away. 'That's as true as anything I heard. I was thinking of going in tomorrow,' he told Antoyne.

Some discussion followed – on how they would meet, exactly where and when the jump-off would take place, what Fat Antoyne might expect in the way of remuneration – and then Vic went home. 'That is a very lonely man,' Irene concluded as she and Antoyne watched him leave the Semiramide, 'whose journey is always the long way round. Antoyne, there's something I have to ask you, and I want you to think hard before you answer because it could mean so much for our hopes and dreams.'

In one corner of Vic Serotonin's South End walk-up, on a small wooden chest of drawers hand-painted dark green, were arranged some items he had brought out of the site. There was nothing fatal about them. Look away from an artefact and you always feel for a moment that it lives another life – that in fact it *takes the opportunity* to live another life. But these were not artefacts, or at any rate they did not announce themselves as such; they were ordinary objects he had picked up in there – a brass lizard three inches long; a bowl full of beads in hot colours; one or two dusty ceramic tiles featuring pictures of fruit.

Vic examined them for a moment or two, thinking how they stood out in some reassuring way from the cheap repro which otherwise filled the room. Then he sighed, pulled open one of the drawers and unwrapped his Chambers pistol from the soft cloth he kept it in.

He swept the top of the chest clear, unfolded a second cloth and laid the gun out on that in pieces; these he inspected, cleaning the mechanical parts carefully before reassembling them. Throughout the process, the weapon itself reminded him in a gentle, persistent voice that its non-mechanical parts weren't user-serviceable. A chip was supposed to keep the physics under control, but the Chambers pistol was known as a particle jockey's nightmare, feared by humans and aliens alike. Vic had his at a discount from Paulie DeRaad, who had it gratis with a crate of other stuff from an EMC armoury sergeant up the line; they'd been in some war together. Every time he cleaned it, Vic heard Paulie's voice advising: 'Treat that fucker with respect, maybe it'll kill someone else instead of you.'

Once the job was finished, Vic didn't seem to know what to do next. The light moved round the room to afternoon. The air cooled and there was a mist over the far edge of the noncorporate port. Occasionally he would get up and look out the window down into the street, but mostly he sat on the bed, wrapping and unwrapping the pistol until Mrs Elizabeth Kielar knocked at his door and he let her in.

'I felt so afraid,' she said.

She stood awkwardly just inside the room, as if she was expecting a further invitation. 'I walked, I don't know why. I went to the bar but then I remembered you wouldn't be there.' Before Vic could speak she said quickly, 'Are you all right with this?' She turned up the collar of her coat, then turned it down again so that the light from the window accentuated the sharp line of her jaw. 'You did tell me to come.'

'Don't you ever say what you mean?' Vic asked.

He touched her where the light fell. Both of them went very still, and she looked up at him with a bemused expression.

'We never know what we mean,' she said. 'We act it out, moment to moment. We never know what we mean until it's too late.' Then, when Vic let his fingertips slip until they found the pulse in her neck:

'Why don't you fuck me? It's what we both want.'

Vic woke up later in the dark from a thick and disturbing sleep, half-convinced that someone had that moment dialled him up with the kind of message no one wanted to hear – a change of plan, a debt called in, a dead parent, the kind of message that could only divert your attention from the feelings that made you real to yourself. Elizabeth Kielar's satin underclothes were on the bed, pooled slippery as water. Elizabeth herself was kneeling close by, turned away a little from the waist, feet tucked under, iodine shadows delineating each muscle and rib. There was a harsh, dry smell about her, which Vic, excited, took to be her sex. She had opened up her diary and was holding it towards the window so that the street light caught the pages. When she saw he was awake, she smiled.

'Why do I do this?' she asked.

'Only you can answer that.'

'I looked out of your windows while you were asleep,' she said. 'And I looked through all your things. Was that wrong of me?' She shivered, staring ahead as if she could see a long way off. 'I write because I don't remember anything about myself. Do you remember your childhood, Mr Serotonin?'

'I'm Vic,' Vic said.

He put out his hand and touched her arm above the elbow. 'You don't have to panic,' he said. 'Read me something.'

'I'm afraid of what will happen tomorrow,' Elizabeth said.

'Are you reading that or is it what you feel?'

'I'm reading it and it's what I feel,' she said.

'You don't have to go in there,' Vic suggested, though he knew she did. She shut the diary and dropped it on the bed, began to put on her clothes. Vic picked up the diary, smelled its pages, leafed through them. He could feel her watching him, trying to anticipate what he would do. When he found an entry he could almost understand, he read it aloud. '"Some sea-travellers,"' she had written, '"never regain their land legs. They come ashore but from now on, for them, walking will always be as difficult as walking on a mattress. But it's worse to sit still, or try to sleep. At least when they move about the symptoms are minimised."'

'Don't,' she said. 'Don't!'

'"They call this *mal de debarquement*."'

She put her hand over his mouth to stop him. 'What do my fingers smell of?'

Vic laughed. 'The sea,' he said.

'Well then, make me wet.'

He turned her hand over, licked the inside of the fingers and placed them against her sex. 'You do that,' he was beginning to say, when his dial-up cut in and Alice Nylon's voice filled his head without warning. 'If this is Vic Serotonin,' Alice said, 'Paulie wants to talk to you,' and after that, Paulie himself came on. Vic pushed Mrs Kielar away.

'Hey, Paulie,' he said.

*

Among Paulie DeRaad's bolt-holes he kept an apartment on the top floor of Beddington Gardens, a system-built beachside tower in retro-Socialist chic circa 1965AD, its cracked curtain walls accurate down to the wads of newspaper the original contractors had used as separators in place of cement. A bald rectilinear space with inset lighting, its window a single sweep of glass taking in the full curve of the bay to Suicide Point, the apartment was furnished and styled moderne, with the wet bar at one end and at the other racks of what resembled *faux*-wooden TV consoles from the historical times, connected to the FTL routers by which Paulie kept abreast of his interests up and down Radio Bay.

White carpet was fitted throughout.

Alice had brought her boss there two days before, and she had been looking after him ever since. She made what food she knew how, mainly ordered-in falafel and brownies, but Paulie wasn't interested in eating. She mixed him drinks from the wet bar, but, inexplicably, Paulie wasn't drinking. When he was asleep she wiped his forehead with a cloth, or stood up on tiptoe to admire his possessions. She liked best the white singlets and underpants he kept nice and clean in a drawer, which she buried her face in when she first found them, but only looked at thereafter in case she spoiled them. The rest of the time she spent talking to the Semiramide people, intercepting problems, cleaning house across the city, trying to gauge how panicked everyone was. 'He's all right,' she told her friend Map Boy, who, because he wasn't one of that crowd, she could open up to a little. 'On the other hand you don't want to get close to him. I'm cautious about it. You know?'

The brief spells Paulie was awake, he didn't pay her a lot of attention, uplinking instead with his offworld contacts. Nothing much came of this, so to start with she was relieved Paulie got hold of Vic. She stayed in the pipe in case either of them needed her, but with a hope that the conversation would take the weight off her.

That was a short-lived hope, because when Vic said, 'Hey, Paulie,' all Paulie replied was:

'Don't hey me. Who are you to hey me, you cheap fuck?'

Vic told Paulie he should steady down.

DeRaad gave a thick laugh. 'Can you believe this?' he asked Alice Nylon. Whatever else was wrong with Paulie, he remained sharp enough to know she had stayed in the pipe with him. Security was always first things first with Paulie. She said:

'I can't believe this, Paulie, no.'

When he heard Alice's voice, Vic sounded relieved. 'How are things going?' he asked her.

'You don't fucking talk to Alice,' Paulie shouted, 'while I'm still here. You fucking talk to me.' No one could afford for things to develop further in that direction, so there was a silence on all sides. 'Cheap fuck,' Paulie said into it, not to Alice or Vic but maybe, given his present situation, to himself. Then he went on in a calmer voice, 'What are you doing to help me, Vic? I'm hiding from my own people. I'm sick. I'm losing trade. It's in me, Vic. I feel it there, I hear it trying to talk to me. They say "shit it out" but when I can't have a bowel movement that's great advice. Meanwhile what are you doing to help?'

'Paulie, I don't know how to answer that.'

It was easy to appreciate the position Vic found himself in. Paulie had lost perspective on things, Alice could see that – she was still his best girl, but it was easy to see he had lost his perspective on things.

'If I brought you a daughter,' Vic was saying, 'that's the risk you always knew you took.' Alice could feel him searching around for something else to say, but in the end he only added, 'I'm running a client in tomorrow from the Baltic Exchange, just after dawn. Maybe I'll find something in there to help you,' and all three of them knew what that was, speaking of shit. There followed another silence, then Paulie DeRaad said, 'Vic, you're fucked with me,' and broke the connection.

'Alice?' he called. 'Are you still my best bet?'

'You know I am, Paulie.'

'So set me up a pipe to Lens Aschemann. I got some information for him.'

The first night they were at Beddington Gardens, Paulie had
screamed for four hours solid in his sleep while lights seemed to
crawl up his own arms and into his mouth. Next day, he sent her
to Voigt Street to fetch the sick kid he kept there, who had started
all this and who had radioactive blood or whatever. When she got
back, which took all morning with the kid stinking and throwing
up and falling out the rickshaw and wandering off into shopping
malls singing to itself while its face shone with an exultation Alice
did not envy, Paulie had rigged up a curtain to divide the main
room in half. From then on he passed his time behind that with
the kid and wouldn't let her come through, or look at him again.
They had a chemical toilet in there. She had to pass things round
the curtain to the two of them. She did once see that the bed was
slick, and they were slick too, with something which resembled a
clear resinous liquid. Maybe they spewed up this stuff and that's
why Paulie wouldn't eat the food she made him. After perhaps
eight hours a smell started to fill the room; also, since Paulie went
behind the curtain something was wrong with his voice. It started
out each sentence with thick tones, as if it was far back in his throat
or he had been eating Roquefort cheese; then halfway through it
jumped an octave into a music kind of sound. Alice knew that
sound. She didn't like it.

'He's here now,' she told Paulie when the police detective came
on. This time she stayed out of the pipe. You never knew what
operators Site Crime might be running in there.

Perhaps an hour before Paulie called Vic, certainly not more, Lens
Aschemann could have been found walking briskly along the
Corniche to the Café Surf where, instead of entering the Long Bar

and occupying his customary seat in the corner, he took shelter in the darkness under the condemned pier behind the building, tapping his foot to the faint jazz music that leaked out into the night, until he saw Antoyne Messner approaching him along the beach.

'So,' he called. 'A nice night, Fat Antoyne.'

'It's just Antoyne,' Antoyne said.

He looked doomed and sodden, as if someone had recently pushed him in the sea. The foldaway rainwear ballooning up around him in each gust only partly covered his royal blue suit. The night's weather had pursued him from bar to bar, The World of Today to The Breakaway Station, lacquering his hair across his reddened face: every time he went in somewhere, the rain eased off; every time he decided to move on, it got worse. Now he stopped short of the pier and, eyeing its pitted cast-iron supports, said, 'I won't come under there, thanks.' And, failing to take heart from the detective's smile: 'I been walking up and down for hours in case I missed you.'

'This was the time we agreed.'

'I was never good with time. I got anxieties around it.' The rain lashed at him suddenly. To avoid it he stepped without thinking into the shadow of the pier.

'You see?' murmured Aschemann, as if Antoyne had proved something to him. 'It's not so bad.' They contemplated the junk that had gathered beneath the pier, too heavy for the sea to move; then the line of rusty barbed wire and barely discernible fluorescence at the eastward extent of the event site itself.

'Are you afraid of it, Antoyne?'

'I don't care about it one way or the other.'

Aschemann pretended to give this some consideration. 'I thought I saw something move over there,' he said. 'Just before you arrived.' He couldn't quite decide if it was the kind of movement you would expect from, say, a rag, or a bit of wastepaper tumbling briefly across mottled sand; or whether it was more animate than that. 'Everyone cares about it,' he said. 'Otherwise, what would we talk about?' Antoyne shrugged. Aschemann struggled to light his pipe, then gave up and suggested that, since nothing was happening now, they went into the Long Bar. 'It would be warmer there, we could get that cocktail drink you introduced everyone to.' But Antoyne didn't want to be seen in the Café Surf.

'I came to give up Vic,' he said.

'That will put a different gloss on it,' the detective admitted. 'Also, I remembered you don't like the music there. Come with me then, let's stare this thing right in the eye, you can tell me everything you know.' He took Antoyne's arm and urged him to look across the old fence into the site, marvelling, 'A piece of the Kefahuchi Tract! A piece of the heart of things that fell to earth! I'm afraid of it, Antoyne, I don't mind admitting; I'm afraid of what it means to us, and that's why I asked you how you felt.' All he got in response was the white of Antoyne's eye. The fence wire was so rusty it fell apart at a touch, into a kind of wet grit. Rubbing a little of it between his fingers, the way you might crush a leaf of mint, Aschemann smelled the strong iron smell. 'No one's replaced this since the original event,' he guessed. 'Antoyne, why would you want to give up Vic Serotonin?'

'I don't like it here,' Antoyne decided suddenly.

Aschemann kept hold of his arm. 'But you're used to it, a man like you. Vic's been in and out by this route all year.'

Antoyne laughed.

'No one in their right mind would go in from here,' he said. 'Is that what you thought? Vic would jump off from here? Look at it!' There was no aureole to speak of, there was only the thinnest skin between the different states of things. You would be straight into the worst of it without warning. 'Look at the air over there!'

It was like a heat shimmer, only cold and dark, and its very existence seemed to bring home to Antoyne the falseness of his position. 'I'm hanging by a thread here,' he complained. After a short struggle, he detached himself from Aschemann's grip and began to walk rapidly away from the wire, out from under the pier and into the wind and rain, his rainslicker flapping and cracking wildly. 'I never went in there with Vic or anyone else,' he called over his shoulder.

Aschemann, stumbling after him, heard none of it. Even as they talked, something had been changing on the other side of the fence; halfway to the safety of the Café Surf the wavefront bowled them over. Fat Antoyne knelt in the wet sand opening and closing his mouth, while the detective, temporarily unable to order his legs, stopped and stared out to sea, where he believed he could see, moored in broad daylight, two or three ancient, rusting cargo vessels. An electric current appeared to be arcing between his clenched jaws. 'Irene won't like what you've done to your nice suit,' he made himself say. At that, Antoyne's face turned up, dead white in the streaming rain.

'I got the information. Where Vic'll start from tomorrow. Who the client is. But it's reasonable I get money for it.'

Aschemann continued to stare out to sea.

'I could find you something,' he conceded vaguely.

The rain drenched Antoyne. It poured down his face. His hands and knees made large smooth dimples in the sand, spacetime curves in a surface that seemed elastic with water. 'More than something,' he said. 'I supported Vic in his ambitions, like all those Black Cat White Cat people. But I got to admit now he didn't truly reciprocate, and it's time to take back from him the responsibility for my life.' He looked up at the detective. 'It was a waste of my heart the day I tried to be friends with a man as lonely as Vic Serotonin, and this is the only favour he'll ever do me.'

But Aschemann wasn't listening; his eyes were focused off to the side, in that vague way people have when they are taking a dial-up.

'Hello, Paulie,' he said.

Only shortly after these events, across the city in Globe Town, Edith Bonaventure woke guiltily from a dream in which she was thirteen years old and nationwide, a dream like the glitter of accordion chrome in smoky light, expanding and contracting as queasily as accordion bellows in that way which seems to the listener to bear only the most cursory relationship to the music produced: a repeating dream which, despite its general noise and dancing and evident nostalgic glamour, she sometimes thought, did not have her best interests at heart. Globe Town, by contrast, presented to itself – or at least to the waking Edith – as quiet and dark, a little triangle of gentrified streets still faintly resonant with some recent displacement of air, some implacable release of energy, some out-rage committed on one kind of physics by another. A great tour ship (probably, Edith thought, the Beths/Hirston *Skeleton Queen*, destination Santa Muerte, brochured as 'Planet of the Alphane Moons', fifty lights or more down the Beach) had just left its berth for the parking orbit.

Edith got her feet over the side of the bed. 'If you think I'm believing any of that,' she told her dream, 'you're wrong.' The floor was cold, her nightdress tangled around her waist, as if making music in your sleep was as much of a struggle as making it awake. She knew better than to blame the *Skeleton Queen* for waking her; more probably it was Emil's kidneys. 'Hey,' she called up to him, 'don't do anything, I'm on my way. It's OK. Leave it to me. It's OK whatever you did.'

No answer.

'I'm coming,' she called.

Emil had crawled under his bed and become wedged at the hips. She attempted to haul him out. 'Hey, are you trying to help?' she said. 'Because don't.'

'We're fucked, Billy. Those things out there aren't human. Whatever we do now is the end of us.'

'Come on, Emil, it was only a cruise ship.'

'Look at that fucker! That's better than any floating pile of shoes!'

The room was dark, though random blue and green lights crawled across the walls: hard ultraviolet, absorbed from the tour ship's exhaust flare by a system of fluorescent butterfly-scale pigments and tailored Bragg reflectors in Emil's smart tattoos, now re-emitted in the visible spectrum. The departure of the *Skeleton Queen* had also brought on a mild fit, during which his bowels, it seemed, had let go. Edith, exhausted and suddenly depressed, began to wonder what she was doing here – what either of them had ever been doing, wherever they were. She lay on the floor near her father and started crying. 'You don't help me,' she said, turning angrily away from him like a wife. 'I have to do all this myself.' And then, turning back, 'We came in from the stars, Emil, but the stars were our home. We gave up all that fun so you could go mad.'

Emil returned her stare dubiously. 'This isn't the only bed I've ever been under.'

Edith wiped her hand across her tears and laughed.

'I know,' she said.

'You know why I think I get this?' he said. 'Neuronal soft errors. We're all brain-fried in Globe Town. Seriously, we should move somewhere safer. Those departures are a quantum jockey's nightmare.'

'You get this because you left your mind in the site.'

'That too,' he admitted. Then: 'If anything, the arrivals are worse.'

'Jesus, Emil, you really smell.'

'If you pull my arm I think I can push with my other leg.'

Eventually, in the weird fading light his tattoos had stored up out of the physics bounty of the *Skeleton Queen*, she extricated him and cleaned him up. She spread fresh twill sheets on the bed and got him back into it. She propped him against the pillows and sat beside him. He looked nice. 'You look nice,' she told him, 'like a proper old man. You even have that thin white hair the best old men have.' When she was sure he was asleep again, she went downstairs and sat in a chair leafing through a volume of his site journal dated fifteen years before. The room cooled. It stayed night. Looking up occasionally at the rows of teen costumes on the walls, like afterimages of herself in some scientifically inexplicable medium, Edith found she had forgotten where she was, or what part of her life she was in. 'Go to sleep in here, you dream entirely in tiny mad paintings,' Emil had written. 'This is what I got last night: a man spews up a snake, someone else is helping him. They entwine, bent in the shapes of alien body language.' She was dozing over this when Vic Serotonin dialled up.

'Hey, Edith,' he said.

'Funny you should say that, Vic,' she replied, and closed the pipe.

When Vic came on again and asked how Emil was, which she had known he would, she answered, 'He's fine. He's happy. You can always see what Emil's thinking, through the holes in his head.' There was an ominous rhythmic croaking sound in the pipe, along with a common type of visual interference which made things spin out sideways from under her gaze. She felt fine with her eyes closed; but when she tried to look at things, they slipped away from her. It was the story of her life. 'Why'd you call me, I wonder?' she said. And before Vic could reply, 'Well, you just want to say you're sorry. You're going into the site tomorrow. Maybe I would change my mind about the book.'

'Edith—'

'But who's there with you, Vic? You see, you don't answer that one.'

This time it was him who broke the connection.

'So no diary for you, then, my boy,' Edith whispered. She waited a little, as much to give him the benefit of the doubt as to clear her

147

head. Inshore winds drove the rain down the street towards the corporate port. A smaller ship left the ground on a line of light like a crack across things. The world stopped spinning. When he didn't get back to her she opened a new pipe and said to the voice at the other end:

'I want to report a site crime.'

Upstairs, Emil Bonaventure was propped upright against the pillows like a corpse, his skin yellow in the streetlight from the window, his old ribs slatted with shadows. The energy had drained out of his smart tattoos and he was breathing ever so lightly. Edith watched the pulse in his neck. She *could* almost see the life through the skin, the thoughts in his head, and what were they but the dreams he couldn't any longer have? Shallow water over cracked chequerboard tiles and cast-off domestic objects, books, plates, magazines, empty tunnels smelling of chemicals, a black dog trotting aimlessly round him in his sleep on some dirty waterlogged ground neither in nor out of anything you could think of as the world, while a woman's voice mourned open-throat from a house not far enough in the distance.

'Emil,' she whispered. She meant: *I'm here.* She meant: *It's OK.* She meant: *Don't go.* After a moment he opened his eyes and smiled.

'Where's Vic?' he asked.

'Vic won't be coming to see us any more,' Edith said.

Later that night, down by the seafront, the wind dropped. The rain turned to drizzle and then stopped; in its place, fog stole in across the Corniche, muffling the sounds of merriment from the Café Surf. A man who looked like the older Albert Einstein sat on the cold sea wall for a while, content, it seemed, to watch the rickshaws come and go in the oystershell lot, or exchange scraps of talk with the Monas in their lime-green tube skirts and orange fake-fur boleros. He liked them to flirt with him, and in return showed them pictures of someone they took to be his granddaughter. The limits of visibility fell, give or take, at a pleasant twenty or thirty yards, describing a comfortable, colourful space lit from within by flocks of smart ads. Everyone, really, was having fun, when into the lot wheeled a pink 1952 Cadillac custom roadster, blessed or cursed, according to where you stood on the subject, with the low skirts and frenched tail lights of a later, impure aesthetic, a giant vehicle which blunt-nosed its way between the rickshaws, scattered the ads and see-sawed to a halt on its real mechanical suspension, while from an unimpeachable white leather interior the sounds of WDIA, Radio Retro, Station to the Stars, thugged their way in solid blocks across the voice of some hysterical commentator at Preter Coeur.

'Very impressive,' Lens Aschemann congratulated his assistant. 'I'll just fold my wet raincoat before I get in, if you don't mind, and put it in the back here.'

'Those Monas seem to know you well,' the assistant said.

'It's charity work. Let's drive a little before you take me in.' He fastened his seat belt. 'Go anywhere you like since we'll only be killing time. By the way,' he said, 'are you back at Sport Crime? If not, you needn't listen to this indifferent music the fighters like.' He leaned across and switched off the radio. 'Later we can have a proper breakfast, maybe you'd like to go to Pellici's which I know you enjoyed before. Then I'll let you do what you always wanted: arrest Vic Serotonin.'

He chuckled. 'That Vic,' he said, 'Betrayed three times in the same night. It's hard not to laugh.'

They took the coast road. At first, when the assistant looked up into the driving mirror all she could see was the nacre reflection of her own headlights diffused around the car; further along, though, the fog, stirred up by temperature differentials out at sea, broke into patches. As soon as Aschemann saw where she was taking him, his mood changed. He folded his arms and stared ahead. 'You drive too fast,' he complained. 'How can anyone enjoy themselves?' About fifteen miles out, they got perfect visibility. Shortly afterwards, the assistant pulled into a headland viewpoint and stopped the car facing out to sea.

'It's a long time since I sat here,' Aschemann said.

Cold air filled the Cadillac, but he wouldn't allow her to close the roof. Instead, he stood up with his hands on the top edge of the windscreen and watched the big ocean waves shovelling the remains of themselves into the bay. Far out, the assistant could see the single, desolate fluttering blue light of some lost rickshaw advertisement: otherwise, the headland was black, the sky and the sea different shades of grey. 'Was this place on the record?' he said eventually. 'I'm surprised. It was never part of the investigation.'

'You're thorough,' she said. 'Everyone says that. You came here the day they found her, so you had it recorded.'

'It looks nicer in daylight.'

There he stuck, staring out over the sea.

Alerted by neighbours, the uniform branch had found the body of his wife, six o'clock on a hot summer evening, sprawled among the broken furniture, boxes of clothes, the piles of local dope-sheets, fashion magazines and old record albums which had divided the floor of the bungalow into narrow waist-high alleys, filled at that time of day with the rich yellow light filtering between the millefeuille slats of the wooden blinds.

'They called me immediately,' Aschemann said. 'It was hot in there.' Up from all the yellowed pages, stronger than the smell of the corpse, came a stifling odour of dust and salt. 'It got in your mouth as well as your nose.' She had fallen awkwardly, wedged sideways with one arm trapped beneath her and the other draped across a copy of *Harpers & Queen*, her left hand clutching an empty tumbler, her cheap sun-faded print dress disarranged to show a yellow thigh: but not one of those piles of repro-shop junk, the uniformed men remarked, had been disturbed by her fall. There were no signs of a struggle. It was as if her murderer had been as constrained in here as anyone else. Tattooed in her armpit were the lines: *Send me a neon heart/Send it with love/Seek me inside.*

When they turned her over, she proved to be holding in her other hand a letter Aschemann had sent her when they were still young. Invited reluctantly to the scene by an investigator several years his junior, Aschemann examined this for a moment – giving less attention, it seemed, to what he had written than to the thin blue paper he had written it on all that time ago – then went and stood puzzledly in the centre of the maze. The assembled uniforms spoke in low voices and avoided his eyes. He understood all this but it was as if he was seeing it for the first time. If he peered between the slats of the blind, he knew, he would be able to see Carmody, Moneytown, the Harbour Mole, the whole city tattooed stark and clear in strong violet light into the armpit of the bay.

'What could I do?' he now asked his assistant.

'They were right not to allow you to investigate.'

'Were they?' He shrugged, as if at this distance it didn't matter. 'I told them, "Do a good job." I said, "Bring me the details to my office later." Then I had someone drive me up here, someone as bright and ambitious as you, who could speak just as many lan-guages. I was a suspect, though I never worked Carmody or knew tattooing.'

He looked around.

'It's nicer in the day. Nice light.'

Nice light, a warm wind at the edge of the cliff, the whisper of the tide far below. A few eroded bristle-cone pines, a patch of red earth bared and compacted by tourists' feet. An extraordinary sense of freedom, which he had regretted every day since.

'Take me back,' he told her. 'We won't have breakfast after all.'

*

On the drive back he was as preoccupied as he'd been when Vic Serotonin left his office the previous afternoon. At the bungalow he stood with his sodden raincoat over his arm and watched her K-turn the Cadillac so she could head back up Maricachel towards the centre of Saudade.

'You got this from my shadow operators,' he accused, 'that was clever. I hope it was what you wanted.'

'I will never understand you.'

'No one ever understands anyone,' he said. 'We should both get a little rest.'

All her ambush had achieved was to drive him further back inside himself, a place the assistant now understood as a maze which made the one his wife had lived in look simple. Instead of going home, she made her way across town to C-Street and the tank farm. Against reason, she had begun to enjoy the flabby, rather slow-witted version of herself the tank had proposed. She cleaned 1950s house; chose 1950s clothes, especially silk knickers; and waited for 1950s man to come home, wondering what he'd say to her if he ever did. Mostly, she imagined his blunt, nicotine-stained fingers on her. The tank's flexible programming enabled her to do the shopping in Aschemann's Cadillac, though she refitted it with a rolled, peaked and vented hood, reshaped rear-quarter scoops and lowered skirts; and – after considering paint chips both authentic and inauthentic – resprayed it the pearlescent blue of a boiled sweet. She had the steering wheel chromed, but otherwise kept the chrome down to the fenders and grille. The front bench seat was long enough to lie full-length on in the fairground parking lot, so she could watch the Meteorite spin violently above her while she masturbated, and after ten minutes or so come with a deep sigh. It was as good as a sleep.

While she was telling herself that, Aschemann sat listening to the sea and trying to fit what he knew about himself and his wife into what he knew about the event site. As part of giving up Vic, Edith

Bonaventure had rickshawed her father's site journals over to him. It was something, she said, she needed to do. Leafing through them (a little puzzledly, because, despite all his experience on the other side, Emil had so clearly lacked the one understanding Aschemann now came to), he fell asleep almost as if by accident, and for the first time in fifteen years found himself dreaming of something other than the dead woman: water flowing as cool as early daylight over his feet and around his ankles; voices laughing in excitement. It was, he assumed, some memory of childhood.

EIGHT

Boundary Waves

By the time the cats began to pour back into the event site, up Straint Street and past the yellow window of Liv Hula's Black Cat White Cat bar, it was raining again. Five in the morning. A few people would be out once the street had cleared, workers who used Straint as a short cut through to the ion works. A few shop assistants and clerks with rooms nearby, making their way down into the city proper; a few fighters making their way back from Preter Coeur. But generally Straint was unfrequented, and every morning at that time, the light seemed less to be coming back into things than leaving them for good. Liv Hula's window was the only lively thing in that part of Saudade. It illuminated the sidewalk. Seen from outside, two or three all-night drinkers, isolated by its rectangularity so that they seemed to have nothing to do with one another, could look like a warm crowd. They looked like people you might enjoy to know.

Liv, watching the cats go past and wondering why her life seemed like a lot of separate pieces of reasonable worth which hadn't yet added up to anything, would include herself in that picture: she was someone you thought you might like to know when you were walking up Straint, when the colour was bleached out of everything else, the kerbstones, the cats, the two-storey buildings with their chipped, greying storefronts. That was the sum of her.

'The cats never get wet,' she said. 'You notice that? Whatever the weather is, they never get wet.'

Vic Serotonin, who had come in about ten minutes previously, now stood with his elbows on the zinc bar, staring hard at his hands as if it was an effort for him to remain alive. His client had walked in five minutes before him, and was sitting at a table on her own. Vic had a small bag with him, and he was wearing a dark-coloured watch cap. Mrs Kielar had on a short belted leatherette jacket over fitted black slacks; she looked tired. They were drinking coffee with rum and pretending, for the nano-cameras, not to know each other. It wouldn't have fooled a dog.

When Vic didn't answer, Liv poured him more coffee, adding milk from the covered jug, and said, 'You're in early, Vic. It a jump-off day? You're always in early on a jump-off day.'

No answer to that, either. She shrugged and went behind the counter, which she wiped carelessly with a rag. She looked over at Mrs Kielar and raised her voice. 'Don't say anything, then, Vic,' she said. 'I don't want to hear what you say about yourself. I heard enough about that.' She switched the lights off, then on again, then off. Without them, the air in the bar reverted to a sepia colour – although the objects it picked out often seemed without colour themselves and as if they were lighted in some way from inside. 'Is that bright enough for you, Vic? Can you see well enough in this light?'

When Vic refused to take the bait, Liv moved away and stood in the shadows at the back of the bar.

The travel agent and his client continued to ignore one another in their obvious way. They were there about fifteen minutes more, then Mrs Kielar pushed her chair back, turned up the grey fur collar of her jacket and left, and Vic threw some money on the zinc counter and he left too. As soon as he'd gone, Liv Hula stepped out of the shadows and counted the money. Her hand went to her mouth. She rushed to the door and called, 'Vic, it's your whole tab. There's no need to pay your whole tab!' But they were already too far up Straint to hear her, following the black and white cats into the aureole of the event site.

'Good luck, Vic!' Liv Hula called. 'Good luck!' But neither of them looked back.

If it was cats on Straint, it was dogs across the city at Suicide Point: Lens Aschemann woke just before dawn, with the confused impression that he had heard them barking as they lolloped through the surf. A trip down the hall and into the kitchen, which had the best seaward view, showed him the tide was on the turn under fast grey clouds; while rain blew suddenly this way and that across an empty beach. He stood for a minute or two listening for the loose sound of the swash; he could still hear the dogs, but they were moving away. It occurred to him that he wasn't entirely sure he was awake. This idea made him smile faintly and dial up his assistant.

'Do you hear dogs?' he asked her.

'What?'

Sand, blown in under the kitchen door during the night, had stuck to the soles of Aschemann's bare feet. He brushed at them ineffectually, first one then the other, with the palm of his hand. 'Every part of the year,' he told her, 'is filled with unacknowledged acts of memory, cued by the smell of the air, the seasonal fall of the light. Do you follow?' Silence in the pipe. Perhaps she did, perhaps she didn't. 'There are dogs in everything. They aren't real, but neither are they only a metaphor. We're dogged by the things we've forgotten.'

'I'm not sure I—'

'Do you see what I'm saying? The investigator must always allow for this. The older we grow, the louder their voices, the more inarticulate they are.' She made no further attempt to reply, so he said, 'At least I don't hear them in this datapipe, that's a blessing,' and then asked her to run the nanosurveillance from Straint Street, which she seemed relieved to do. After a few minutes following the life of the bar, he shook his head.

'Is this all that happened overnight?'

'Three or four a.m., the system went down again. There's some footage but it's not informative.'

'I can believe that,' Aschemann said.

'We should have put people in.'

'Who would we use? This woman knows everyone who drinks at her bar. She's no fool, even if Vic is.' Liv Hula stood motionless at the zinc counter; she leaned her elbows on the zinc counter. The footage jumped, and she leaned on the zinc counter again. She stared emptily ahead. She looked tired. 'Switch this off, for God's sake.'

Aschemann brushed at the sandy soles of his feet as if this action might clarify his life, or at least connect him to it. Two hours' sleep in an armchair had given him kidney pain, but it couldn't explain the feeling that something was approaching him, racing towards him from what part of his past he couldn't even guess. It couldn't explain why his hands were so stiff, as if he'd been clenching them tightly in his sleep. Only the dogs could explain that. 'At least we know where they're going,' he said. 'We have an embarrassment of confirmation on that.' Just before he closed the dial-up, so that the assistant would have no time to reply, he said, 'By the way, did you enjoy that sleep of yours you had in the twink-tank?'

'Watch out for the dogs you hear.'

Aschemann took his kidneys to the toilet, chuckling. 'One day I'll give that tank a try,' he promised himself.

'How will we know we're in there?'

Vic Serotonin stopped to allow his client to catch up. 'Sometimes you don't,' he said carelessly.

The event – the fall to earth, whatever you described it as – had taken place a generation or more ago, in the city's old industrial quarter, the warren of factories, warehouses, docks and ship canals which at that time connected Saudade to the ocean. Commerce had ended instantly, but its characteristic architecture remained as a fringe about half a kilometre deep, a maze of empty buildings with collapsing corrugated roofs and broken drainpipes, their iron window frames bashed in and emptied of glass. A mile or two past Liv Hula's bar, Straint narrowed to a lane; the cobbled cross-streets became little more than industrial alleys, pitted and rutted, littered with lengths of discarded cable and balks of timber. Everything smelled of rust and precursor chemicals. The blue enamelled signs on the street corners had long since corroded into unintelligibility. Elizabeth Kielar studied them and shivered.

'I'll know,' she said.

'Then why ask me?'

'I'll feel it.'

'All that happened last time,' he reminded her patiently, 'is you lost your nerve.' The only reply she offered was an angry look; as if he were the unpredictable one, the one both of them had to be careful not to trust.

Over the years, Vic had given the question more thought than his tone implied. You knew you had entered the aureole when the weather changed, that was his view. Turn a corner between two factory yards in winter: sunlight would be falling into the well of the street while insects described fast, wavering trajectories from the brassy light into the darkness of the buildings. If it was sunny in Saudade, patches of fog drifted through the aureole. Or the wind would, as now, pile up a few cold soft short-lived flakes of snow in the gutters. Whatever else happened, the shadows struck at absurd angles for the time of year, as if geography was remembering something else. 'The lines of distinction aren't sharp,' Vic concluded. You had to use your intuition as to when something like that became important.

'When the Kefahuchi Tract first fell to earth, they tried to build permanent controls. Walls, ditches, concrete blocks. But that stuff would be absorbed overnight.' Something went wrong with the air, and next morning your border post had gone and you were looking across a fifty-yard waste lot covered in cheat weed and cracked concrete, at what appeared to be a huge, motionless, empty fairground in the rain. 'Now they have a more relaxed attitude. Take the wire up every so often, put it down somewhere else: they call it "soft containment". Still trying to explain himself, and thinking of the complexities of his relationship with Emil Bonaventure too, Vic added, 'Even in the aureole you need luck. I'm not one of those people who believe they'll have street light in there by next Wednesday.'

'Do any of you understand anything at all?' she said angrily. 'Why do you all act as if you know something when you don't?'

'This area's thick with police. So try to keep up.'

Twenty minutes later it was full dawn, and the first patrol of the day had caught up with them. Vic hurried Elizabeth through the nearest door and into a derelict warehouse – puddles, ripped-up concrete and foul earth, holes that gaped down into cellars and sewers, everything of worth stripped out long ago – where he pushed her to the floor and put his hand across her mouth. Elizabeth stared up at him in a kind of puzzled supplication, as if she didn't understand why humiliation should be part of this search for her own nature, while matt-grey Site Crime vehicles forced themselves down the narrow accessway outside, repeatedly occluding the light then allowing it to splash in again rich with steam cooked out of the standing water by the waste heat of the nuclear engines. The air shuddered with the din of it; above that, you could hear the faint realtime shouts of the foot police coordinating their sweep through the buildings.

'They're not looking for us!' Vic shouted into Elizabeth Kielar's ear. Nevertheless he made her lie there, listening, until long after the engines and the shouts had passed. Then they left, Elizabeth brushing irritably at her clothes. After that it was more of the same, rusting tracks, flooded rocket-docks with vast discarded machinery visible just beneath the surface of water stinking of the sea but so glamorised by exotic radiochemicals it would glow faintly in the dark. They made good time, and Vic Serotonin was pleased by the professional way things were falling out for once. But as they passed, everything – each alley and abandoned wharf, each collapsed or melted gantry, even the Site Crime patrols – seemed to settle, shift and morph indiscernibly into something else. The aureole was all around, like a wave propagated through everything. Everything was up for grabs. Half an hour later, when rain caught them at the edge of the site itself – a shower which slanted in, mercurial against the direction of the light, to pass within minutes – you couldn't, as Vic said, be sure where it came from, or how. Though on the face of it things looked simple enough.

Independent of the patrols, Lens Aschemann's pink Cadillac nosed its way down the pot-holed alleys, waited at each junction, then, accelerating briefly but wildly, left the road and bumped its way through the tall weeds of a concrete lot as if its driver had lost control of the clutch. With the detective himself at the wheel, the car's character changed. It became like a big, blunt animal, some species adapted neither for stealth nor pursuit but which, despite Darwinian constraints, had decided to learn them both. Aschemann drove as if he couldn't see well, gripping the wheel tightly and thrusting his face close to the windshield, while his assistant suffered in the passenger seat, steadying herself with both hands and offering him an expression of open hostility.

'I don't understand why you're insisting on this,' she said.

'Now you think you're the only driver in the world?'

'No!'

'Everyone drives. We all like to drive.'

'This is because of yesterday.'

'I won't dignify that with an answer. Sometimes we have to drive, sometimes we have to ride. Don't spoil a beautiful day.'

Aschemann's face looked more than ever like the older Einstein's, the eyelids even more drawn-down, the cheeks pouchier, with a greyish tinge from lack of sleep. His eyes were veined and watery. They gave him a look of confused enthusiasm. The Cadillac's front wheels left the ground briefly, then banged back down so hard the suspension bottomed out. She clutched the windshield edge reflexively: this stimulated a response from her forearm dataflow. 'Are you familiar with the term "lost"?' she said. Satellite navigation signals were still available, but her software could no longer distinguish between several possible sources, ghost emissions, particle dogs, accidents of atmospheric lensing. They might be real, they might be not. At least one of them seemed to be in the site itself. 'As of now we don't know where we are.'

Aschemann smiled.

'Welcome to the aureole,' he said.

'This *is* about yesterday,' she accused him.

He leaned over and patted her shoulder. 'After all, can we ever say we know where we are?'

There was more orbital traffic than usual that morning: military traffic, alien traffic, surveillance traffic. If you just knew how to look, you found EMC up there in numbers. High-end assets in hair-trigger orbits, calculated to keep an eye on some dubious investment of middle management's. She had her own investment in play. She followed the data as it bled endlessly down her arm, pausing only to say:

'Please keep both hands on the wheel.'

Along with the agency, its goodwill, and his South End walk-up, Vic Serotonin had inherited from Emil Bonaventure the use of a bolt-hole on the top floor of the old Baltic Exchange building which faced the event site across a bare expanse of concrete called 'the Lots'. This comprised a room twelve feet by fifteen, once an office with frosted glass dividers. Over time Vic had been obliged to defend it against other travel agents: in reprisal, two or three of them, led by a woman born Jenni Lemonade but known in Saudade as Memphis Mist, had used a hand-held thermobaric device to rip a hole in the middle of the floor, through which you could, if you felt like it, contemplate a thirty-foot drop into standing water. Despite this it remained a serious professional location, offering views of the Lots where they rose gently towards the faint thickening of rain-wet air which marked the interface. It offered a place to wait while you assessed the situation. Vic had slept there once; the dreams he experienced convinced him not to do it again. Now he stood at the window, which possessed neither frame nor glass, and was puzzled to hear Elizabeth Kielar say:

'Did you ever want children?'

The view frightened her. She had averted her head as soon as he brought her in and, careful to keep facing the hole in the floor, inched her way round the walls to the corner in which she now squatted, her arms wrapped round her knees. When Vic spoke, she smiled at him confidingly, as if he'd caught her in some even less dignified position. What little oblique, dirty light fell on the side of her face served to occlude rather than disclose. Close to the site something was always wrong with the light anyway; it struck as if refracted through heavy but volatile liquids, aromatics on the edge of evaporation.

'I had children,' she said, 'but I left them.'

She laughed at his expression. 'To be honest, they were more grown up than me from the start. They were often impatient.' She fidgeted. Looked down at her hands. 'I left them,' she said, 'because I saw they'd be all right.' Vic didn't know what to make of this, so he didn't reply. After a moment, she asked:

'When do we go?'

'Soon.' A certain amount of waiting was inevitable. The wise thing was always to remember the client and not be too hard on her in that way: but, as everyone remarked, Vic stayed well through the exercise of caution. Some adjective from the complex vocabulary of the place, a change in the light or the density of the sounds you could hear, would sooner or later reassure him. He wasn't anxious, because he wouldn't commit until he had that reassurance. It was the professional course. 'It's not like waiting for a door to open,' Emil Bonaventure had once advised him. More something you could interpret as permission.

'Come and look,' he invited Elizabeth Kielar.

'I don't know,' she said.

Vic shrugged as if it didn't matter. Then he said, framing the experience for her in the voice he reserved for clients:

'This is what you came to see. This is it.'

After a moment she stepped primly round the hole in the floor and joined him, and they stared across at the event site. You were never sure what you were looking at. Beyond the wire, beyond the remains of the original wall, with its fallen observation towers, prismatic light struck off the edges of things. There was a constant sense of upheaval. Loud tolling noises, as of enormous girders falling, or the screech of overdriven machinery, competed with the sudden hum of an ordinary wasp, amplified a million times. It was like a parody of the original function of the place. But also there were snatches of popular songs, running into one another like a radio being tuned through some simple rheostat. You smelled oil, ice cream, garbage, birchwoods in winter. You heard a baby crying, or something clatter at the end of a street – it was like a memory, but not quite. Sudden eruptions of light; dense, artificial-looking pink and purple bars and wheels of light; birds flying home against sunsets and other sweet momentary transitions between states of light. Then you saw things being tossed into the air, what looked like a hundred miles away. Scale and perspective were impossible to achieve because these objects, toppling over and over in a kind of slow motion – or so the eye assumed – were domestic items a hundred times too large and from another age, ironing boards, milk bottles, plastic cups and saucers. They were too large, and too graphic, drawn in flat pastel colours with minimal indication of shape, capable of liquid transformation while you watched. Or they were too small, and had a hyper-real photographic quality, as if they had been clipped from one of the lifestyle-porn magazines of Ancient Earth: individual buildings, bridges, white multi-hull sailing ships, then a complete city skyline toppling across as if it had been tossed up among flocks of green parrots, iron artillery wheels, tallboys, a colander, and a toy train running around a toy track. Everything in a different style of mediation. Everything generating a brief norm, reframing everything else. At that time, in that instant of watching and listening, in a moment savagely and perfectly incapable of interpretation, they were all the things that fly up out of a life, maybe your own, maybe someone else's you were watching. Day to day, you might have more or less of a sense that the things you saw were describable as 'real'. In fact, that wasn't a distinction you needed to make until you crossed inside.

Vic Serotonin felt nothing but relief each time he arrived at the Lots. At this point you weren't committed, you could always turn around and go home. But it was another chance to engage, and as a result a kind of peace went through you. You felt stabilised again. You felt both excited and relaxed.

'It's quiet today,' he said.

Elizabeth smiled uncertainly. 'This is awful,' she whispered. 'I can't bear this.'

'Will you be able to do it this time?'

'I can't bear not to.'

'Well then,' he said, 'we should start.'

He went to the door calm and happy, but when he looked back she was still at the window. 'This is the right time to go,' Vic encouraged her. When he took her by the shoulders, though, there was that tautness so permanent, so designed-in, so far down in her it was like touching some stretched internal membrane and pausing to wonder what you would do next. Elizabeth seemed to understand this. Caught between Vic and the window, she twisted into him; pulled his face towards hers and bit him sharply. 'Fuck,' Vic said. He let her go and put his hand to his cheek. She knelt down, worrying inefficiently at his clothes, then her own. 'Yes,' she said, 'fuck. Fuck. Get in me, Vic,' she said. 'I want something to take in with me.'

He stared at her.

'Christ, Vic, don't you see? *Fuck me while I look at it.*'

That was how the man who resembled Albert Einstein found them. He arrived in the doorway – excited from driving his Cadillac, a little out of breath from the stairs – and remarked to his assistant who was standing next to him giving Vic her flat smile:

'They're hot, these two. I never saw two this hot.'

'We're always getting lots of Vic on Elizabeth action,' she agreed. 'Lots of girl on girl.'

Vic reached for his Chambers pistol. The assistant's tailoring, which had reactions down in the millisecond range, turned itself on in response. There was a blur of motion from her, during which she seemed to be in several places at once, and then an actinic flash, in the aftermath of which nothing much could be seen at all except Aschemann by the door looking old, white-faced, perplexed; and Elizabeth Kielar, who jumped neatly into the hole in the floor and vanished, only to reappear a little later sprinting and weaving across the Lots towards the site boundary. Aschemann's assistant strode calmly to the window and began to shoot at her. Chambers bolts curved slowly down through the rain, making a noise like defective neon and setting fire to the thin vegetation.

'Stop that,' Aschemann said. His voice tones shut down the assistant's tailoring and she stared at him angrily.

'You see?' he appealed to Vic.

'Yes,' Vic said. Something had happened to his arm; it was numb to the shoulder and he hadn't even seen her move.

'Vic, I told you she could drink you with a glass of water!'

Vic rested on the floor. He stared out the window. He'd been arrested before, but he had no dependable sense of what would happen next. Meanwhile Elizabeth Kielar was nowhere to be seen. *Fuck me while I look at it.* In the end that was what most of his clients wanted. They never got any further than the Lots. They had sex with you in open view of the thing out there – as if that was how they understood it; not as a state of affairs but as a live thing, perhaps even a conscious thing, they wanted it to be watching when they came – and then didn't speak on the way back. To them it was just a choice that made life more interesting. Vic wouldn't say he made his living from that impulse, or that he had any opinion about it; but the risk was lessened for everyone when that was what the client wanted. Though her resources were in disarray, he didn't think it was like that with Elizabeth Kielar; and he was beginning to regret how little he had discovered about her sense of herself.

They took Vic out on to the Lots and put him in the back of the pink '52 Cadillac repro while Aschemann sat in the front and lit his pipe. At the same time the detective got a dial-up to the police bureau. 'It's no problem,' he said, shaking out a match, pulling open the dashboard ashtray, smiling and nodding at Vic. 'The weather's more of a problem this morning. He's here, he's fine, we kept him in one piece. No, that's other business.' While Aschemann was talking, the assistant walked impatiently up and down outside the car. Every so often she stopped and peered across at the event site, as if she had seen something no one else could. The outline of her body rippled a little as her tailoring, pumped and excitable from its encounter with Vic, cut in and out; the datableed ran red and green pictographs interspersed with jet-black oriental-looking characters in rows down her forearm. She leaned into the car and smiled amiably in Vic's face, as if she would like to start a conversation.

'Vic,' she said, 'what I've got *switches off* what you've got. Do you follow? That's why your arm hurts so.'

'Go and look for his client,' Aschemann ordered.

Vic said, 'Her name's Elizabeth. She's nervous; it might make her difficult. Please try not to shoot her for that.' The assistant glared at him, then down at her datableed. Then she jogged off through the rain.

'Don't go in the site,' Aschemann called after her.

He examined the bowl of his pipe, then – as if they were of equal value in a wider context – turned his attention to the event site. Something vast and orange-coloured flew up into the air, but you could barely see it through the rain. It hung there for a moment then folded itself sectionally until it disappeared. The whole incident was over in forty seconds, and there was no way of describing the accompanying noise. Aschemann watched with a kind of calm approval. 'A slow day today,' he said. 'A few hours ago, it was quite different. Down by the Café Surf, it bowled me over.' He seemed delighted by the memory. 'Literally, physically. Our friend Antoyne too. Today, I think a wave is coming, nothing happens.'

Vic Serotonin shrugged. 'You wouldn't find it so quiet inside,' he predicted. He wanted to make it clear that while the detective was perfectly entitled to an opinion, of the two of them Vic had the bulk of the experience. 'How was Fat Antoyne?'

'A little upset.'

'Antoyne feels things more than he'll admit.'

'I still want to go in, Vic.'

'Why?'

'Because my wife's in there. What we're seeing is the life-cycle of a new species of artefact, and I think my wife was one of them.'

Vic made so little of this he didn't know how to respond. 'What species?' he said eventually.

'Walk round the centre of Saudade any night, visit the clubs, the shooting galleries, the music venues. That species. Or come and see them in the holding cells, fresh from the Café Surf and still gazing around like idiots, wondering how they came to be on our side of things. They love it – who wouldn't? Who doesn't love sex, fried food, hard drugs? The tough ones do what anyone would, get a room, go to ground, wait out their appetites, pupate; they look wounded but that's because they're just not us. They try to make contact, they try to strike up a conversation with our world, or someone in it. They're here for a change of state, but we're too much who we are to have any idea what that might consist of. While you think they're human you see them as having interesting qualities, but they're only confused. They're like insects, Vic: after a few years whatever instinct drove them out of the site takes over and drives them back in again.'

It was a two-way traffic, he said, one which, as a result of their own anxieties, people like himself had overlooked from the outset. 'Ever since the Tract fell to earth, we thought we knew what an escape looked like. It didn't look human. It looked like a catastrophe. We were clear on that, we could make rules for that. You've seen them in the quarantine centres, Vic: half-flesh, half-artefact, falling to pieces, speaking in tongues while the daughter code pours out of their mouths like light to infect a whole city block. We weren't prepared for anything more subtle.'

'Your wife's dead,' Vic said. 'Everyone knows that.'

Aschemann stopped talking immediately. Tears ran out of the corners of his eyes.

'I'm sorry,' Vic said.

They stared at one another in discomfort.

'This rain,' Aschemann said, holding one palm out flat. 'Do you ever wish you were on some other planet?' He wiped the rain off his face, which looked tired and unkempt. He fiddled with the dashboard ashtray. Then he had a brief exchange with his assistant by dial-up, which he concluded by telling her, 'Come back now. You're wasting everyone's time. Vic wants to get his arrest over with, and be put in a nice cell.' A minute or two later she appeared quietly out of the Lots, her face, hands and gun beaded with water. 'You can sit in the car,' Aschemann said, patting the bench seat beside him. 'Come and sit here in the driver's seat, the way you like. Put the convertible roof up if you're wet.'

'We're all wet,' Vic said.

'Shut up, Vic.'

They watched appreciatively as the convertible roof, which was the same shade of white as the upholstery, closed slowly over their heads. Then Aschemann said, 'Vic, this woman here had a fire-team set up to bring you in.' He chuckled. 'That's how determined she is. They're still up there in the fog somewhere, trying to find their way home. Visibility's down to ten yards and the site is cooking their communications. She expected more trouble from you. To be honest, so did I. How's your arm? That numbness will wear off.'

When this didn't get a response, he shrugged. 'The reason you're in custody is this: you didn't give me what I want. Never under-estimate that as a cause for arrest.'

'What about the tourist?' the policewoman wanted to know.

'We'll have to leave the tourist,' Aschemann said, without much reluctance. 'After all, they come here for the risk.' He leaned over the back of his seat and said to Vic Serotonin, 'You know, I could wish it was Emil sitting here instead of you. Emil would be more interested. He never saw the site as a career opportunity; it was always an adventure he couldn't extricate himself from. I respect that. Vic, how was Emil last time you saw him?'

'He wasn't good.'

'He wasn't good the last time I saw him either. But Edith seemed fine.' To his assistant Aschemann said, 'Start the engine. Let's take Vic away.'

*

This proved more difficult than he could have imagined. They were in the middle of one of the Cadillac's wallowing long-wheelbase turns when a rickshaw lurched round the corner at the other end of the Baltic Exchange and sped towards them, trailing a stream of ads in colours that crackled against the soft wet air, lighting up the puddles around the Annie's thudding feet. She pushed hard into her shafts, breathing like a horse. Vic could hear a voice calling from inside the rickshaw, but not what it was saying; nevertheless, it gave him the sense that things had become too complicated to control.

From the other end of the Exchange, two dozen figures emerged wearing the signature rainslickers and waterproof hats of gun-punk chic. As soon as she saw them, Aschemann's assistant knocked Aschemann off the seat beside her and pushed him down into the footwell so that the engine was between him and the danger. Then she shoved open the driver's door and rolled out into the rain, shouting commands into her dial-up. Her tailoring had cut in by now; she was visible only as a sort of fibrous blur. Aschemann, his neck bent at an odd angle, blinked at the carpeted transmission hump. 'What's happening?' he asked Vic. 'Can you see what's happening?' Meanwhile the Cadillac continued to swing through half a circle, slowing down as it went, until it halted side-on to the approaching rickshaw. The driver's door now hung open to its full extent, allowing Vic to recognise the little figure of Alice Nylon riding the rickshaw step.

'This is a fucking disaster,' he said to Aschemann. 'Warn that lunatic of yours not to shoot at anyone.' He leaned forward and stuck his head out. 'Alice,' he shouted. 'For fuck's sake, Alice, it's me. It's Vic.'

'Hi, Vic,' Alice called. 'Look at me!'

'Call your kiddies off,' Vic told her. 'No one wants an incident. And don't ride the step like that,' he added. 'It's not clever and you'll only get hurt.'

Before Alice could respond, the rickshaw pulled up.

'Three-up's two too many,' the rickshaw girl said, 'even for a pony my size.' She leaned forward in the shafts, vomited with practised accuracy between her own feet and examined the result. 'Nothing a dexamil won't cure,' she decided. 'I got plenty if anyone else wants it.'

A thick yet curiously musical laugh came from the rickshaw's interior.

'Nice car, Vic,' the occupant said.

'It *is* a nice car, Paulie,' the rickshaw girl agreed. '1952 roadster. Pushrod V8, 330 ft lbs at 2700 rpm, I respect an engine can pull. You know?'

'Jesus,' Paulie DeRaad said. 'Everyone an expert here on Retro Radio. Open this thing up, Alice, so I can get a look at my old friend Vic.'

'Paulie, don't have anyone shot,' Vic said.

'Paulie me at your own risk,' DeRaad promised him. 'What are you fucking looking at?'

When Alice Nylon unlatched the hard apron of the rickshaw, a faecal smell rolled out and you saw immediately that Paulie was in a bad way. They had crammed him in with the remains of the Point kid and the two of them were embracing awkwardly, as if it was new to them despite all the practice they had. They were breathing gently into one another's eyes. Neither of them had much on, and their china-white bodies were covered in a thin, slick, resinous film which, though it looked liquid when you first saw it, was constantly hardening and cracking off, like something they exuded to protect them from the air. Paulie was still roughly the right shape, but the boy had begun to fatten, soften and blur. He had aged thirty or forty years since Vic first saw him in the building at Suicide Point. However you looked at him, he seemed to be out of focus. He had no idea where he was, or what was happening to him. Despite that, he came across as happy. Every so often, motes of light emerged from his mouth like very small moths, accompanied by a note or two of music.

Paulie, less satisfied with his condition, flailed one arm about. 'Alice, it's fucking stuck to me again,' he said.

Alice peeled them apart carefully so her employer could get out of the rickshaw. It made things difficult that Paulie couldn't bring himself to look at his own body. 'You got to help me, Paulie,' Alice begged; but he kept looking up and away from himself, and from Alice too. He didn't want to admit she was helping him. Eventually she manoeuvred him on to the concrete in front of Vic Serotonin, where he stood swaying and stinking and opening his arms. Part of his face went out of focus, then back in again.

'Do you see, Vic? Do you see what you did?'

Vic was saved from answering by Lens Aschemann, who clambered out of the Cadillac on the passenger side buttoning his overcoat. 'This rain,' the detective complained, 'will never stop. You should stay out of it, Paulie, because you don't look well.' He gave Paulie a thin smile. 'Better still, go to a Quarantine bureau, where I'll be able to find you.'

Quarantine wasn't a realistic option for DeRaad because of what would happen to him there. Leaving him to contemplate that, Aschemann went over to the rickshaw and stared down with a kind of puzzled anger growing on his face. 'Don't you want me?' the Point kid sang out in his three voices. It wasn't clear how, but he could feel the detective there. He laughed. 'No one wants me.'

Aschemann stayed bent over the rickshaw for some time, like an old man studying a baby. 'What you've done here isn't good for anyone,' he told Vic Serotonin without looking up.

Out on the Lots, a wary truce had developed.

Alice Nylon's gun-punks patrolled restlessly, whispering to one another in a gluey-sounding battle language they had refined from the fight argots of Preter Coeur. Aschemann's assistant wasn't prepared to try them out, despite the superiority of her chops. Things couldn't change, she decided, while her fire-team remained trapped up there by a conjunction of bad weather and site-side interference. But the situation wouldn't last forever and then she would see what happened. In keeping with this decision she had switched herself off and now lounged against the offside rear-quarter scoop of the Cadillac, from where she could exchange sneers with Alice Nylon, or stare with a kind of amused distaste at what had happened to Paulie DeRaad. Things could only get worse for Paulie. If he survived another twelve hours, which seemed un-likely, Hygiene would sequester him in an orbital facility. There he would be intubated in every natural orifice, plus some extra. They would run a bunch of wires up through the roof of his mouth and into his brain, in the hope some heavy-duty operator might gain access and fry the code before it became a full-scale escape. Either way he was dead. Meanwhile he presented as a danger to everyone around him, and without Alice's support he would be running out of friends.

'Bad luck, Paulie,' the assistant said.

'You should keep your eye on the prisoner,' Aschemann advised her, 'if you want something to do.' He treated DeRaad to an apolo-getic look. 'What's your interest in this, Paulie? You gave Vic up, that's the end of it.'

Vic stared at Aschemann, then at Paulie, to whom he said, 'You gave me up? Paulie, I'm hurt you did that.'

DeRaad ignored him. 'I appear like this in person, it's not in my best interests,' he said to Aschemann, 'plus the pain and humiliation I got to suffer. But Vic goes down for bringing out an artefact and selling it on. *You're* hurt?' he screamed suddenly at Vic. Spit came out of his mouth and Vic stepped back in case he got infected by whatever Paulie was incubating. 'Fucking Jesus bastard, *you brought me a daughter.* Look at me!' Screaming only tired Paulie out. He shook his head disgustedly. 'You fucked me, Vic, so I fucked you. So much for friends.'

'You fucked yourself, Paulie,' Vic said. 'I was only the bearer of the bad news.'

But Paulie was already making his way back to the rickshaw in the piss-wet rain, leaning heavily on Alice Nylon's shoulder. He left behind him a feeling that the edge had gone off the situation. Aschemann had Vic. Paulie had his revenge. Aschemann's people would talk to the people who took care of Paulie, and the additional problem he represented would be solved at some other, higher level. Even Paulie accepted that. EMC would send someone for him and he would not bolt, because it was important to him to protect his brand – he was, after all, the last man out of the wreck of the old *El Rayo X*, which you could watch a genuine holographic record of the incident any evening at the Club Semiramide. He had a myth to manage. As a result, the escape would be contained. Everyone on the Lots that morning could back down without loss of face.

So it would have remained, but the weather changed. Onshore winds peeled the cloudbase back in raw hundred-metre slabs. Inside the cloud unpredictable gusts and eddies came and went, full of rain and daylight one minute, wet snow and night the next. Electromagnetically disoriented and still awaiting instruction, the Site Crime fire-team – comprising code jockeys, weapons specialists and a human pilot hardwired into the DBH delivery vehicle – found itself drifting sideways at a brisk seventy knots into the event site. No one wanted that. The pilot weighed things up, shrugged, and side-slipped blind into the first gap that offered itself. She was out of there, she said, for a fact.

'Abort, abort,' ordered Aschemann's assistant.

The DBH breached the cloudbase, clipped the southeast corner of the Baltic Exchange and, condensation swirling off its asymmetric weapons pods, shot low over Aschemann's Cadillac, ploughing shortly afterwards into the concrete.

Since there was no correct interpretation of this move, everyone used their initiative. Vic Serotonin got down behind the Cadillac. Alice Nylon's gun-kiddies engaged the remains of the fire-team with hand-held thermobarics and Chambers guns. The fire-team, unable to respond at that time, called for help. Alice Nylon got off a shot at Aschemann's assistant, but the assistant had tailored up and was already speeding across the concrete towards the wreckage of the DBH, shedding curious frozen images of herself where she had paused just long enough for your eye to retain some detail. Each of these pauses represented one of Alice's little troops taken up, damaged, and thrown down in a disjointed attitude.

'None of this was intentional,' Aschemann told Paulie.

'You fucks are all dead for this,' Paulie told Aschemann.

Inside the DBH, the situation was out of everyone's grasp. The hull had been breached. The code jockeys were dead. The pilot's roof-of-the-mouth implant, ripped out by G-forces, hung from the console, a mass of fine gold wires, each one tipped with fresh brain matter. In an attempt to save itself, the ship had disengaged. In an attempt to save the pilot it had pumped her full of epinephrine and SSRIs, but her eyes were looking in different directions and her smile was as unplugged as her hardware. Worst of all, code had begun to leak through the compromised navigational firewalls and crawl over the living personnel who, hampered by their impact injuries, were kicking and screaming and struggling to crawl away from it.

Aschemann's assistant paused in the breach and assessed all of this. They saw her through the drifting sparks of light, consulting her forearm datableed. They were begging and pleading with her. If you had asked right then what they made of her expression, they might have described it as 'blank'. But what did that mean? She was a policewoman, aiming her pistol from the approved stance. She was a policewoman, shooting the survivors before she used a high-temperature incendiary to torch the wreckage. She had an aptitude for that practical kind of thing. She was a policewoman, who thought she would watch the thick white smoke rise a moment or two longer, just to be sure, before she let her tailoring take over again and guide her on to the next thing.

No one wanted another escape on their hands.

Annie the rickshaw girl stood around, filled with a kind of awkward dismay at the way things were going and wondering what her fare would want to do next. She couldn't catch his attention, so she got out of her shafts and went behind the Cadillac, which she recognised from all over the city, especially downtown, and tried to strike up a conversation with the guy Vic who was sitting on the wet ground with his legs stretched out in front of him unwrapping a gun from a bit of oily rag.

'Is this your car?' she asked him.

'No.'

'Only you'd have thought it was, from what Paulie said. I seen it around. 1952. You got your V8 pushrod, 330 cubic inches, bore & stroke 3-13/16 x 3-5/8. Best engine they ever made. Nice body, too.' She trailed her fingers down the smooth candy-and-pearl blends of the rear quarter. 'And you got your wide whites. Fact is,' she said wistfully, 'I'd rather be one than own one. So, are these here your friends?'

'Not really,' Vic said.

'Only I work for Paulie most of the time.'

'No one more generous than Paulie,' Vic said, 'when he's on the right side of himself.' He said, 'You should keep your head down now.' He worked along the body of the Cadillac until he could stick his own head out past the front fender. That moment the fuel-cell of the Site Crime vehicle went up with a kind of damp crump and a lot of white smoke trails curving randomly into the sky. Bits and pieces began clattering to earth. Vic winced away, then made himself have another look. 'Fuck,' he said. 'She's still alive.' A little later he added, 'In fact I think she's the only thing alive out there.'

When he said this, he appeared puzzled but also as if a small sluice of panic had opened inside him. He crawled back to the rickshaw girl. 'If she comes this way,' he advised, 'you should make it a point to leave.'

'I got no fare,' the Annie said. 'I don't leave without a fare.'

'Suit yourself.'

Weird mint-coloured light broke through the overcast, angling down on to the Lots where the policewoman, uncharacteristically still, continued to stare at the burning wreckage as if she was failing to understand something. This made Vic impatient as well as angry, so to divert him the Annie said, 'Paulie has a good heart, but he's often a little too focused, you could say that of him. You know, I hate gunfire. I *would* leave, but for another thing they got this boy in my rig, no one seems sure what to do with him. I pulled him around a lot in the last couple days.'

'So there's your fare,' Vic pointed out.

'He ain't so much a fare as a liability,' she said. 'You smell him? Jesus.' The fact was, she said, she felt sorry for him, he was nothing but a Point kid who did no harm to anyone – though she believed there were always two sides to that kind of passivity – and she wondered if he would get home all right. As a result, when Vic said that, it was like having permission. No one else was interested in her – they were just standing around in shock waiting to see what the policewoman would do next – so she went over to her rig, got between the shafts and wheeled it round to Vic's side of the Cadillac. Vic was back to sitting with his legs in front of him.

'I could take you too,' she offered.

At that moment, Alice Nylon stepped round the trunk of the Cadillac. 'Paulie wants you to know he's had it with you, Vic,' she said formally. She thought for a moment. 'We been good friends you and me, and I'm sorry I got to do this.' Even with Vic sitting on the floor, she had to point her gun up at his face, gripping it hard in both hands and squinting one eye across the sights at him. 'But

I'm being as tuff about it as I can.'

'For fuck's sake, Alice,' they heard Paulie call out, 'just kill him. I got a right to feel betrayed here.'

'You can see his point,' Vic told Alice. 'Paulie should be on his way home to Beddington Gardens now, in the hope he can get baked enough to forget what's happening to him.'

'Fuck you,' DeRaad said. 'I heard that.'

During all of the foregoing, Paulie had walked about nervously, sweating and gesturing; or sat on the concrete for a minute or two with his hands between his knees and followed everything that was going on, his expression quiet and knowing. He stared up at the Baltic Exchange building, then down at his own skin, leaden and white at the same time, and as shiny as if it had a resin laminate, and, once, across at the site. He said, 'I think it's in my legs. I can feel it in my legs somehow.' Then he was up again and lurching around, thrusting his face into the face of Aschemann the police detective, to whom he spoke only when he needed a break from sneering at Vic Serotonin. 'You and me, Lens, we're above this crap,' he said. He examined the façade of the Baltic Exchange once more, as though puzzled by its iron pillars, its rows of windows in the blue-grey weather light. Then he added:

'We're at another level from crap like this.'

Aschemann's arrival on the Lots had nothing to do with Paulie DeRaad; it had, especially, nothing to do with DeRaad's mythology. So when Paulie spoke to him like this, he couldn't think what to say in return, but stood with the rain in his white hair, feeling disarranged and contentless, while smoke from the wrecked vehicle caught in his throat and Paulie shouted in his ear. Nothing was happening for Aschemann's intelligence to get leverage on; it wasn't his kind of situation. In a moment everyone might be dead. 'Paulie,' he managed to say finally, 'things here have tipped in the worst possible direction.' But Paulie's attention had wavered and moved on. A level of ADHD was written into his cuts, as a professional requirement. He indicated the policewoman, locked in her inexplicable fugue out on the Lots; shook his head to illustrate that, despite his depth of experience, even he could be at a loss.

'Lens, those chops of hers aren't military,' he guessed.

'She came to me from Sport Crime,' Aschemann admitted, glad to find something they could talk about, 'on a one-month trial. God knows what she had them do to her there.'

At last Paulie looked worried. 'Shit,' he said.

'To be fair, she drives well and she's good at languages.'

'I got connexions could switch her off,' Paulie offered. 'If that's the problem.'

Aschemann had a clear little vision of DeRaad's connexions, floating in restless fragmentary orbits somewhere miles above, dipping down at random so their stochastic resonance software could slice through the electromagnetic clutter from the event site. Unlike him, they knew exactly where they were; where everything was. Miles away seemed too close. 'Paulie, Paulie, you frighten me!' he said, although it wasn't Paulie he could see so well in his mind's eye. 'I won't need that,' he promised hastily. 'It's generous of you to offer, but I won't need that.' He dialled up the assistant again. 'For God's sake, answer,' he begged her. He was already opening a second pipe in case he needed more help. Meanwhile, he laid his hand on DeRaad's upper arm in what was intended to be a reassuring gesture.

Of late, Paulie's tailoring package had been preoccupied. Its dialogue with the daughter-code wasn't going well. Nanopatches bolted on to Paulie's adaptive immune system, back in the *El Rayo X* glory days, had not held up. Now the daughter was chewing its way through the system itself (slowed only by the discovery that in Paulie's case the military Zip had used, in place of the usual immunoglobins, proteins with leucine-rich repeats generated from lamprey DNA). Nevertheless the package overall had been excellent in its day, and despite these difficulties remained aware enough of the world outside Paulie to misinterpret Aschemann's motives. Nerve impulse propagation speeds ramped up by factors of four; simple instructions were issued to the rags of Paulie's central nervous system. The conscious mind processes at forty bits a second, the CNS at millions. Disorder is infinitely deep. Before he even knew he what he was doing, Paulie DeRaad had kicked the detective twice in the upper torso and once each in the throat and left ear. He looked down. He looked surprised. He shrugged and said, 'Fuck you, Lens.'

Then he said, 'Hey, I honestly didn't mean to do that. Sorry.'

Across the concrete, the policewoman woke up in a startled way and looked around her just in time to see Aschemann stumble backwards and fall over. She took a generous millisecond to assess the situation, then disappeared into the weather and reappeared quite suddenly in front of Alice Nylon.

'Uh oh,' Alice said.

The assistant smiled and let her tailoring take over. After it had finished with Alice, it blurred its way over to Paulie DeRaad and put him down too. Then somehow she was back on Vic's side of things again, kneeling shoulder-to-shoulder with him, so close he could feel her skin on his, staring in the same direction as him – her body quivering, the air around her soupy with waste heat from her mitochondrial add-ons and exotic ATP transport upgrades – as if she wanted to see exactly what Vic was seeing. She smelled as sharp and sour as an animal cage. She had a look on her face he couldn't interpret. She was smiling. 'Come on, Vic Testosterone,' she whispered. 'Try me out. Show me your special move.' Vic shivered. He kept as still as he could. The minutes passed. He closed his eyes until he felt her chops shut down and she laughed and ran one finger lightly across the pulse in his neck and said, 'Hey, Vic, you're safe now,' and moved away. Next time he saw her she had dragged Aschemann into the back of the Cadillac, where she could work on him out of the weather. Except for the datableed running its perpetual Chinese chequers down her forearm, she seemed so ordinary. She was some Sport Crime tailor's experiment or joke, laid like an ambush for people like Vic. She was something new.

Vic had a struggle to get to his feet.

He felt cold and stiff from sitting in the rain.

Alice Nylon lay in a shallow puddle, one arm flung out, her blue slicker ballooning up intermittently in the wind to reveal pink pedal-pushers. Her hat had fallen off. A single line of blood ran from the left corner of her mouth. Alice had bitten her tongue when she fell, but the damage was elsewhere. Vic found guarding in the muscles of the abdomen and lower back – she was as hard as a pear down there. The whites of her eyes were yellow. His diagnosis, the spleen had let go; there were ruptures to other organs too. Not a mark on her, but everything was puréed inside. Her eyes looked tired, her teeth were rotten from speed use, her spoiled, peaky, unlined little face looked very old.

'Shit, Alice,' he said.

Her eyes opened. 'I lost my gun, Vic,' she whispered.

'Paulie will buy you a new one.'

'You know what?' she said.

'What, Alice?'

'Me and Map Boy did it. We had a fuck, Vic!'

She chuckled. A small convulsion went through her.

'I'm that bit younger than him,' she said, 'so I wasn't so interested. But he's nice enough, and at least I got to do it before I died. Vic, you ever meet Map Boy?'

'I never did, no.'

'He's cute. Vic?'

'What?'

No answer.

'Alice?'

Paulie DeRaad was kneeling on the concrete, muttering into a dial-up. Vic went up to him and said:

'Alice is dead, and to an extent, Paulie, I blame you.'

During his encounter with Aschemann's assistant, both of Paulie's shoulder joints had been popped. His arms didn't work, which, if nothing else, gave him some trouble maintaining position – each time his body threatened to fall forward, he left it to the last moment then writhed his torso in a curiously graceful motion to stay upright – but despite this he didn't seem upset or even interested. He let them dangle, like the sleeves of a coat. His face was grey, though patches of high colour sprang up where the old radiation burns had thinned the skin.

'I got a bad mouth ulcer, I know that,' he said. 'You want to just pull down my lower lip and look?'

'Jesus, Paulie.'

'That police fucker won't leave me alone. Everywhere I go, he's there first. He's asking questions, he's taking names. You remember Cor Caroli, Vic? K-ships on fire across half the system? Wendy del Muerte tried to make planetfall in an Alcubiere ship with the drive still engaged? There won't be anyone like Wendy again.'

'I wasn't there,' Vic said.

'Yeah? I love it!' Paulie said, and laughed as if Vic had brought to the table some reminiscence of his own they could both enjoy. His eyes lit up, then almost immediately took on a perplexed cast. He had forgotten who he was. 'I love all that stuff,' he said. He leaned over, vomited weakly, and fell on his side. Vic made sure he was alive, then left him there.

'I want you to know I've had it with you, Paulie,' he called back over his shoulder.

The job was fucked as far as Paulie was concerned; compared

to him, Lens Aschemann, sprawled awkwardly across the rear seat of his car, head tipped back, mouth open, looked like a brand new morning. He was conscious, and dabbing at his ear with a wet cotton handkerchief. His eyes followed anything that crossed his field of vision, but his discomposure was as evident as his brown suit, and he seemed too tired to speak. Paulie's kicks had burst one of his eardrums and bruised some ribs. 'It's good to see you, Vic,' he said, 'and know you got through this. Don't worry about me, I'm more shocked than anything. A little deaf perhaps. Vic, it's good you didn't run away.'

At this, the assistant gave a little smile. 'Vic won't be running away,' she said.

Eighteen miles above their heads, one of DeRaad's connexions fired its *f*RAM engine for 7.02 milliseconds, flipped lazily onto its back and, with the first wisps of displaced atmosphere already flaring off its hull like an aurora, raced earthwards. That was how Paulie knew he was still a good investment. The sky opened. A flat concussion ripped the overcast apart. A single matt-grey wedge-shaped object, its outline broken up by intakes, dive brakes and power bulges, shot across the Lots at Mach 14 and halted inside its own length perhaps thirty feet above the Baltic Exchange. Parts of the roof blew off, but the structure held. The K-ship *Poule de Luxe*, on grey ops out of a base in Radio Bay, hung motionless for a moment, hull boiling with everything from gamma to microwaves, then pivoted neatly through 180 degrees to dip its snout attentively in the direction of Aschemann's Cadillac.

Paulie was on his feet, dancing about on the concrete, shouting and yelling and trying to wave his arms.

'Oh *fuck*,' he shouted. 'Just fucking *look* at this!'

With the care of a living thing, the K-ship lowered itself to earth in front of him. A cargo port opened. Paulie stumbled towards it, his arms swinging out haphazardly. 'Hey, Vic,' he called, 'what do you think of her? It's the old *Warm Chicken*. Is she ugly, or what?' Tears ran down his face. He struggled up the cargo ramp, turned round at the top. 'Can I tell you something, Vic?' he said. 'Just before I go? Even the *paint* on this vehicle is toxic.' Someone pulled him inside suddenly and the hatch closed.

The K-ship raised itself a little and slid smoothly forward, nose down, until it hung just above the hood of the Cadillac. There was a frying sound – the air itself being cooked – as its armaments extended and retracted in response to a change of government fifty lights down the Beach. In the Cadillac, Aschemann and his assistant felt its heat and steady gaze upon them. Every time either of them exhaled, the K-captain, buffered and secure in its proteome tank at the heart of the machine, knew. It wanted them to know that it knew. A minute stretched to two, then three. While they sat there wondering what to do, it mapped every strand of their DNA; at the same time, its mathematics was counting Planck-level fluctuations in the vacuum just outside the photosphere of the local star, where the rest of the *de Luxe* pod remained concealed. It gave them a moment to appreciate how capable it was of these and other divergent styles of behaviour. Then it revolved lightly around its vertical axis, torched up, and quit the gravity well at just under Mach 42, on a faint but visible plume of ionised gas.

Lens Aschemann sighed. 'Who'll save us from the machines, Vic?' he asked.

No answer. The driver's door swung open in the wind.

Paulie DeRaad's rickshaw girl had watched all this from a couple of hundred yards away on the city side of the Lots.

She didn't know what to make of it. She wasn't prepared to say it was the grossest or most interesting thing she'd ever seen, because everyone saw new things all the time. 'And when you pull for a living,' she remarked to her fare, 'you see it all.' In this case, 'all' meant bodies were scattered over the Lots. White, thick, gritty smoke was still going up from the crashed vehicle. Two small figures, kiddies you'd say, were helping each other crawl away. She wasn't sure what happened to Paulie DeRaad, though he didn't look well when she last saw him.

One thing: a breeze had got up for a change, so maybe they could look forward to better weather. Another: as the K-ship took off on its line of light like a crack right across the solidity of things, a figure in a black watch cap was sprinting away from the Cadillac. It was the guy Vic who she had talked to. 'He can run, that guy,' she was forced to admit. 'He has a nice action if he would train a little. Or, easier, he could get a package.' The rain turned to sleet as it moved away to the west, which briefly made visibility even poorer than before; but she could see he had his bag over his shoulder and his gun in his hand. After a minute or two, the Cadillac's engine started and it rolled slowly over the concrete as if it would follow him. But they never got out of first gear and soon drifted to a halt. Shouting came from inside, some kind of disagreement was in progress. The driver's door opened and a woman got out. Then she got back in again and slammed the door. Vic Serotonin put the Baltic Exchange between him and the Cadillac and disappeared into the event site. Don't blame me, the rickshaw girl thought. I offered the guy a lift.

'Did you see that?' she said. 'He went the wrong way.'

The fare, who had something wrong with his voice to add to his troubles, made a noise like three notes of music played at the same time. 'Moths mated to foxes,' he said, 'fluttering into their faces in the desert air.' He laughed. A few dim motes of light issued from under the rickshaw hood to join its shoal of sponsor ads. 'The faces of the foxes are like flowers to them, they circle closer.' The Annie shrugged. Some fares wanted your input, some didn't. That was another thing you learned.

'Hey, are we going to haul?' she wanted to know. 'Because we got no business here.'

'Let's haul,' said the three voices, one after another.

'It's your ride, hon.'

She took one more look at the pink Cadillac and sighed. That sure was her favourite car. With its subtle paint blends and frenched tail lights, it had been the best part of her day so far. 'I'd just once like to be that pretty,' she told herself. Then she turned the rickshaw around and trotted off towards Saudade at a steady pace. 'Don't you worry,' she reassured the Point kid. 'I know where they kept you.'

'Let's haul.'

NINE

Black and White

Liv Hula's room had a blush-pink princess washbasin on the wall opposite the door.

You walked in, and on the right was the white-painted iron bed with its clean oatmeal-coloured throw and its plain wood blanket chest at the foot. Facing that was the window, which had a view over sloping ground, across wet rooftops, lines of narrow streets, pokey yards, to factories and a narrow segment of the event site.

In front of you would be the washbasin mirror, about eighteen inches square, chipped halfway down one bevelled edge; and below that the washbasin itself, shaped and fluted like a clamshell, with its piece of lavender soap and single coldwater tap. In the basin beneath the tap a permanent limescale stain had been artfully added at the point of manufacture, tadpole-shaped, but the crusty greyish-yellow colour of the sole of a foot. Liv owned plenty of other things, but if she asked you up there with her, that was the item you noticed, and it was so ugly you wouldn't understand why she chose it. When she arrived in Saudade, the room had been her bulwark against all the Liv Hulas she had already been. She would shut the door and look in the washbasin mirror and smile, while the cheap repro tap ran cold water on any previous idea of herself.

Liv stayed out in the street long after Vic Serotonin and his client had disappeared. Every so often she stood on her toes and craned her neck because she thought she had seen them again in the distance. It was as if the two of them were still moving away from her in a straight line, so all she needed to do was to resolve them, detach their image somehow from the background with which it had merged. After perhaps an hour, the sun came out. The traffic increased on Straint. Then a thick white plume of smoke began to rise from somewhere in the aureole a point or two to the north and Liv's uncertainty gave way to dullness.

I can't stay here forever, she thought. I can't stand in the street like this. But she didn't want to be in the bar either. It was too early to have a drink. If she stayed in the bar, she would only clean the counter and count the bottles. So she went up to her room instead, and tried to wrench the washbasin off the wall.

Dust sifted down. The basin made a cracking noise and pulled away a little. But the pipework held it in place; so, even though what her muscles needed was to feel it tear loose by their unaided effort, she went to look for something to help her break it up. About then she heard the long sonic boom of an ascending K-ship, thunder which seemed to roll all the way round the world and meet itself coming the other way. She glimpsed the ship through the window. It was gone so quickly! A line of light across everything, then only the afterimage downshifting from violet to purple then black, flickering up again, bright sharp neon-green as she blinked, then dimming away for good. Liv Hula's eyes followed it thoughtfully. She strode over to her bed and stripped the bedclothes. She opened the window and tossed them out into the air, where a breeze caught them so that they ballooned and folded and sideslipped as they fell. Then she went back to the sink and wrenched and wrenched at it. Nothing, except she could see herself in the mirror, red face, shoulders pumped.

Under the bed she kept a heavy tin box, enamelled black, with gypsy-looking red and yellow handpainted roses. This she hauled out, and used it to bang at the washbasin until the washbasin shattered into three large pieces, two of which fell off the wall. Only then did she go and sit on the bed and look around her angrily. The box stayed where it had fallen. For the moment she couldn't remember where she had put the key to it. She sat there until the morning was over.

Vic Serotonin arrived at the abandoned checkpoint on the edge of the Lots. He'd heard Aschemann's Cadillac start up behind him, then stop again. He knew he was safe. Whatever happened to him next, he could forget all that. He followed the fence a hundred yards north to where houses had collapsed across it from inside the site, leaving a steep shingle of bricks and broken tile thinly grown with local weeds. The interface mist closed round him, damp and absorbent. He stood still. Just the other side of things, he could hear water drip; further off, the rhythmic banging of a door in the wind. He smiled, closed his eyes and pushed his face forward as if to receive air kisses. Gentle pressure on cheekbones and lips, as if they were stretching some membrane; it felt cool like the mist.

Perception of a state is not the state.

The phenomenology of the site, Emil Bonaventure had often reminded him, as if Vic needed reminding, was this: what could be observed from the outside, you rarely encountered inside; inside or out, what could be seen or smelled or tasted bore no relationship to physics data collected by EMC's many expensive orbital assets. As a consequence – for Vic as for Emil and all those earlier Saudade entradistas with their particle guns, their scars and their easy air of knowing something no one else knew – the moment of transition was the moment of maximum uncertainty, maximum payback. That was the rush for him, Vic was ever willing to admit: but it was not a simple one, and you could not write it off entirely to body chemicals or temperament (although on any given day both might be involved). Neither was it the kind of rush people experience from contemplating possible injury, madness, death or sudden personal disfigurement (although a proportion of those things might easily happen to you inside); because consequences always seemed negotiable – in fact reusable to a degree.

So what kind of rush was it?

'How can I explain?' Vic would have to ask in the end. 'You should go in there one day and get it.'

When the membrane broke, there was a smell like a pile of woollen coats and a taste in his mouth like a bad avocado, and he knew he was inside. Vic opened his eyes. The slope was where he expected. It was as barren and dusty as if the houses had just fallen down. No mist. The air was cold. Halfway up he could see the cherry tree in blossom. White petals flushing to pink, bathed in light. An organ sound.

Wind chimes would be acceptable. Wind chimes were within the margin of error, but if ever the petals seemed to emit a soft light of their own, you went some other way; or you left things where they were and went back to Liv Hula's bar. Otherwise something bad would happen. Your options would close out. Vic struggled up the slope, which fell away from his feet at every step in loose musical cascades of broken tile. Luck was an issue at this point. But if you entered from the Lots, closed your eyes as you passed beneath the cherry tree, turned round three times then opened them again, you would be likely to find next that the slope had turned into a short flight of internal stairs.

Water ran down its yellowed left-hand wall, under intermittent flashes of light. Between one step and the next, day changed to night and back again; while in the room at the top of the flight, it was always afternoon, with unreal warm-coloured light streaming in through the open window. There was always the question of what you might see in there, and the day of the week seemed to have bearing on that: for instance, Vic had noticed early in his career that if you left the Lots on a Wednesday, the room would be empty, but there would always be a cigarette burned halfway down in an ashtray on the windowsill. It was hard not to feel someone had just left, in which case you could only suspect they'd passed you on the stairs.

Today the room was slow with the tick of a mechanical clock. Every flat surface – the gate-leg table with its green chenille cloth, the huge brown furniture, the mantelpiece, the shelves, everything but the floor – was covered with black and white cats.

You smelled their sour cat smell in here the way you never would in Saudade; it was as heavy and thick as talcum powder. They sat motionless, pressed together too tightly to move. Wherever Vic went in the room, they were facing away from him. Even Emil Bonaventure agreed: if you entered between dawn and dusk, from the Lots, these cats would be filling the outer regions of the site. Accounts varied, as they always did: but you would, in Vic's experience, always have some cats in your life; and in places they would come to resemble a thick fur on everything, a kind of deposit. They were always motionless, turned away from you, sitting on their haunches with their faces pressed into the walls, the corners, the cobwebs, each other. It was as if they were ignoring you. But it was also as if they had no choice – wherever your gaze fell, they had to face away from it. Emil believed that this was evidence which, though anecdotal, might one day be correlated with science from outside the site.

Vic Serotonin had no theory about the cats.

He stood in the middle of the room.

A street ran left to right just below his eyeline. There was a real sense of bustle down there. Laughter. Women's heels tapping back and forth. Rickshaws rang their bells. Deep summer lunchtime, and the old New Nuevo Tango issued from every open door. There were the smells of *Café electrique*, Calpol, and other exotic stimulants from the history of Ancient Earth. There was hammering and banging, the scrape of spades through wet cement, trowels through mortar, the rattle of construction machinery. Everyone down there was busy, or they were having a working lunch, pears in brine with a really interesting small salad of alien leaves. It was always like that until you went to the window and looked out. Then the noises cut off instantly and you saw that something was wrong with the street. It was a representation. Curving sharply away in both directions to identical early sunsets, the offices and shops, the sidewalk cafés and street lamps, were *drawn on*, in unrealistic sunshine tones, thick poster yellows cut with blues and reds, strong blacks to make the outlines.

It was empty. It was silent. Vic stared out.

After a minute or two, an accordion started up, then, half a bar into *Hernando's Hideaway*, stopped again; and he saw, as he had hoped he would, Elizabeth Kielar struggling away from him down the middle of the street. Time doesn't pass the same way in there, and sometimes luck will help you with that, and sometimes it won't.

'Elizabeth!' he called, 'Elizabeth!'

When she turned, her face was rubbed-out white, the features gone, and he wondered for a moment if it was her after all. By then he was in the street and Elizabeth was twenty yards away, walking fast, as if she wanted to get away from him, as if Vic was part of the place, just another weird thing you couldn't depend on and didn't want to engage. Nothing was the same down there, but Vic had expected that. The street looked real again, but it looked older and dirtier too. Ripped awnings over the shop windows. Brick with a hard finish, a metallic, clinkered look. When you passed an open doorway, smells of old carpet, leather chairs, furniture polish, some insistently medical smell you couldn't name. Elizabeth stopped suddenly and waited for him to catch up.

'I'm frightened. How did I get here?'

'I thought I'd lost you,' Vic said. When he tried to embrace her, she backed away.

'No,' she said. 'Look, I was on a beach. And now it's this.' She stared around her with a bruised expression. 'I didn't pay for this. Where have you been?' She put her hands in the pockets of her coat. 'Where have *I* been?' she asked herself.

'Perhaps you could tell me what it was like,' Vic said.

'I don't remember.'

'Do you remember anything at all after you left the Baltic Exchange?' He meant, *I warned you.* He meant, *It's dangerous to come here looking for any part of yourself.*

'I was on a beach,' she said. 'A man was exercising two dogs.' She had watched him walk his dogs backwards and forwards, backwards and forwards, over the same two hundred yards, even though he had miles of beach available. His reflection kept pace with the reflections of the dogs along the wet sand. Every so often, she said, he seemed to stop and, cupping his hand, splash their undersides with seawater. 'They were so patient and accepting!' They stared ahead in whatever position they had come to rest, and eventually one of them curved itself into a taut, elegant hoop and tried to defecate. After that, all three of them trudged away up a steep shingle bank, the rain dissolving them into a single wobbling cipher.

'You followed them. It was evening, you saw lights.'

'No.'

'You found yourself here,' Vic said.

'They were as fastidious as schoolgirls, those dogs,' she said. 'I had to laugh.' She said, 'I felt like a little girl again.'

'It wasn't a beach. They weren't dogs.'

She turned her back on him and began to walk away. 'I'm going in, whatever you say.'

'Elizabeth, you're already in.'

'Do you know *any*thing, any of you? Anything at all?'

He couldn't answer that.

*

Smoke was still rising from the Lots half an hour after Vic Serotonin had made himself scarce. Bodies lay in extreme positions where they fell. One of the surviving gun-kiddies had died. The other had stopped crawling and begun to make a peculiar thin keening noise; it had suffered significant head injuries. Site Crime was arriving in numbers, mainly local uniforms in their huge patrol vehicles, responding to the original conflagration: but also specialist teams from Hygiene, Quarantine and Surveillance; teams whose job it was to co-ordinate with EMC; and teams whose job it was to co-ordinate teams. They held informal meetings on the Lots to discuss protocol, collars raised against the rain; or stared up at the roof of the Baltic Exchange, which had collapsed shortly after the departure of the *Poule de Luxe*. A group of them gathered round the punk, some taking bets, some repeating in loud voices, 'Can you hear us?' and, 'Can you tell us who did this to you?' then advising each other tiredly:

'Forget it, guys, this one's fucked.'

They avoided Aschemann's car, although they sometimes tried to catch the eye of his assistant, whose reputation had reached them via one Bureau pipe or another. On her part, she had nothing to say. She leaned against the rear quarter of the Cadillac, radiating heat from her ramped-up metabolism – which, like most contemporary Preter Coeur product, had a stage by which it burned forty per cent of its own cellular waste – and treating everything but her datableed with contempt. She hadn't spoken since Vic got away.

'I'm feeling very shaken up,' Aschemann told her.

He put his hand on her arm. 'Thank you for everything you did; perhaps next time you could kill a few less people.'

She shrugged.

'Are you angry?' he said.

'This was never an investigation. It was a mess.'

Her eyes went out of focus; she said something flatly into her dial-up. She had called down another fire-team; but it was too late to catch Vic, and Paulie had never been her responsibility. When Aschemann reminded her of that, she levered herself angrily away from the Cadillac and stood off a few paces, looking in any direction but his. She knelt next to Alice Nylon and tidied the hair out of the peaky, dead little face. 'I don't understand why any of this had to happen!' she said to Aschemann. 'I don't understand why you have to pretend to be old, and get driven around in a car from the historical times. No one in this culture has to be old any more.' She lifted Alice by the shoulders, shook her lightly – as if Alice had gone to sleep on some secret which if she had shared it would have changed both their lives – then allowed her to drop back again. 'An *escape* is involved here,' she reminded Aschemann. 'I don't understand why you can't investigate the way everyone else does.'

'I'm sorry,' Aschemann said.

This response caused her to return to the car, look in at him in a thoughtful way, and say, 'What's your name?'

'Pardon?'

'What's your *name*?'

'You shouldn't have to ask,' he said. 'Aschemann.'

'And that's how your wife spoke to you, is it? Aschemann, pass the hummus, Aschemann, slide the chair over to me so I can stand on it and fetch down this bottle of dark rum. Aschemann, we're old and will die one day.'

Aschemann felt hurt at this.

'It's Lens,' he said.

'Well then, Lens, it's been nice. You never once asked me my name, but at least now I asked yours. I resign.'

'I don't—'

'I'm in for a transfer as soon as this disaster winds itself up.'

He didn't seem to hear.

'When I left Utzie,' he said, 'she would dial me up and say, "People think it's a failure to live alone, but it isn't. The failure is to live with someone because you can't face anything else."' He chuckled.

'Two days later it would be, "Cooped up with yourself twenty-four hours a day, that's life, without remission. Lens, the worst thing in the world is to be inside yourself, you don't even want to be rescued. Yet to be as happy as we were – to be so open to someone else – invites the failure of everything."' One minute she would be phoning to tell him her plans, she was going to have a garden behind the bungalow – wallflowers, poppies, an iris modified to smell of chocolate – the next her brother had died of bowel cancer. Who died of bowel cancer since the twenty-first century? It was a choice. That whole family had disaster as a lifestyle.

'No one has to lose anyone now,' Aschemann said to his assistant. 'Perhaps I wanted to know what that was like. Utzie—'

'I know all about Utzie,' the assistant interrupted.

Aschemann stared at her. 'Who made you responsible for me?'

'You make everyone responsible for you.'

He watched her walk away and get into conversation with the uniforms. They were all clustered round the dying child now, he couldn't see why. 'You were a good assistant,' he called after her. 'What are you afraid of, that you might learn something? How could you, when you know everything already?' Then he slid behind the wheel and started the car. He was happy enough with the way things had gone. He had lost Vic, but he still had Emil Bonaventure's notebook. He thought he would drive with the roof down, it was a nice enough day. He picked up first then second gear, nice considerate changes with the unhurried old engine well below its red line. Despite that, he was soon up to fifty or sixty miles an hour. He dabbed the horn at knots of uniforms. People were beginning to shout into their dial-ups. All across the Lots, they watched with mounting puzzlement as the roadster plunged across the concrete and into the interface mist. The assistant – who, if she were honest with herself, had all along expected something like it – loaded her tailoring to its operational limits in an attempt to cut him off; but it was already too late.

Perhaps ten minutes after Vic caught up with her, Elizabeth Kielar discovered abandoned in the road a plaster mannequin meant to represent a child of five or six years old.

It was naked, bald, a greyish-fawn colour, with a sweet, strange expression, the sort of demonstration piece you saw in the window of any Uncle Zip, outfitted with a black uniform beret from some recently glamorised interstellar war, torso crawling with colourful live pins, the proteins for which had been derived from phyllobate DNA. Its arms were jointed at the shoulders to allow movement, but otherwise its body was moulded in one seamless piece. To the best of Vic's knowledge it had been lying there for a year and a half. He had to persuade her not to pick it up. She looked mutinous then smiled and said:

'How sad he must be that he has no genitals!'

The shadow of an unseen bird flickered across a window at the end of the street.

'Vic, let's go that way!'

'Do you know why you're here?'

She wouldn't say. It was a contest of wills. 'It's safer,' he tried to explain, 'if you keep your expectations low.' But Elizabeth was already working them in deeper by the minute, her expedient simple: if he disagreed with her she simply walked away. The further off the beaten path Vic got, the more nervous he became and the easier it was to persuade him to take another wrong turn. It was what he had always feared.

The landscape continued to change, one moment residential and deserted (though you saw women waiting expectantly at a corner in their best clothes, they were gone as soon as you reached them); the next industrial and derelict. Flares rose from something like a coking plant in the distance, but everything close at hand was fallen down and overgrown. Old separation tanks became shallow lakes, with mudbanks streaked a dark chemical maroon.

Something huge passed across the sky: you winced away from its shadow, then saw it was a toy duck looking down – looking *in* – at you from above with its intelligent bright-blue painted eyes. It was a hypermarket of the meaningless, in which the only mistake – as far as Vic could discern – was to have shopping goals. The idea that you might map things in there in terms of your needs was what had so entrapped and confused Emil Bonaventure's generation. It was safer to learn how things worked, then assemble the portfolio of habits, behavioural tics just this side of the psychotic régime, that stood in for having a clear frame of reference and kept the travel agent from harm.

'Everything smells of sulphur,' Elizabeth said. 'Does it smell of sulphur to you?' She said, 'Do you ever go into a building while you're here? Vic, let's go in one of these buildings! We could fuck in a building, wouldn't that be nice? Wouldn't you be excited by that?' He explained to her why it was a bad idea. Soon after, her mood deteriorated. She was silent for long periods, then said bitter things in a tired, desolate voice, as if she was in conversation with some ex-lover. 'Don't you see,' she said, 'that I can't talk now? Here?' Vic hadn't asked her to talk. 'The life I'm living now,' she said, 'the life I've been living: I wasn't like this, but now I am.' She said:

'It never gets any further away.'

'What?'

'That factory. You know, Vic, we walk towards it but it never gets any further away.'

'You'll find that in here,' he said, just to contribute.

Eventually they were driven off the streets by the rain and the approaching dark. Vic wasn't keen to enter any space he didn't know – they could so quickly become the arena of your worst expectations. But it was night as Saudade knew it, and Elizabeth was cold. She looked up into the rain, which seemed to fall towards her through layers of unsourced light, then down at her clothes. 'I'm shivering, Vic,' she said in a surprised voice. 'Take me home now.' Somehow it was the least human thing she had said all day.

Everywhere they tried was full of cats, facing into the corners, lined up along the walls, balancing on the arms of chairs, pressed together too tightly to move. Vic was relieved to find them at such densities. 'It means we aren't too far in yet.' The ground floor of the building he chose had no internal walls, although you could see the stub brickwork where they had been. A recent flood had left it banked with dirt, which had a packed and crusty look until you touched it, when it fell in on itself in soft wafery structures marbled with colour. There was some kind of expansion chamber fifteen or twenty feet below, through which they could hear volumes of water rushing at intervals. Otherwise it was empty but for echoes. Elizabeth listened for a moment, then nodded as if acknowledging the inevitable. 'I remember snow falling very slowly,' she said, 'the size of coins. Into the long garden in the dark. I remember trodden snow on the pavement outside. Then I remember a street market, a dead cat in the gutter.' Vic thought she was describing a process, a sequence, not the memories themselves. He put his coat, then his arm, around her shoulders. They huddled against one of the walls, as far away from the sound of water as they could get. She held his face and began kissing him, then opened her legs and guided his hand down there.

Later, when he asked, 'Where were you born?' she answered, as he had expected she would, 'Vic, I don't know.'

A little over a month after they gave up Vic Serotonin to Site Crime, Fat Antoyne and Irene the Mona sat at the Long Bar in the Café Surf. Antoyne had on a new suit – yellow double-breasted drape with hologram buttons of Irene laughing and saying how Antoyne would always be a star to her – and they were drinking Boiru Black with chasers of something local Irene had never tried before, which she called 'dickweed', although Antoyne thought he could have misheard that. It was early evening after a day of sunshine and showers along the Corniche, both heartbreaking and heartwarming; a day, as Irene said, which allowed you to see the true, beautiful balance of things, with both positives and negatives of your mood reflected back to you in the weather.

'It's good,' she told him now, 'that we take part in the great see-saw of life, but never forget, Antoyne, that the balance for this girl must always be on the positive side.'

It was a slow night under the *Live Music Nightly* sign. Twenty minutes ago, its equipment assembled, its gin rickey appreciatively swallowed, the two-piece had begun chasing down a groove via the twenty-minute interrogation of a tune of their own they called *Adipose Annie*. But Annie wasn't disclosing herself to them or anyone else tonight. Offered a solo, the saxophone shrugged no. They took fours briefly, restated the theme, and left town on the first rocket out, while the paying clientele shook their heads judiciously and dug into their reserves of goodwill. Band and audience saving themselves for later on: a recipe for mutual misunderstanding. Antoyne and Irene clapped desultorily, along with the rest, and Antoyne ordered more drinks.

'I am blue,' he said. 'I admit that.'

'And I know why, Antoyne,' the Mona said, resting her hand on his forearm. 'Don't think I don't. At least,' she said, 'it's good to get an evening away.'

When Paulie DeRaad's connexions came down to Saudade two days after Vic and Paulie disappeared, the first thing they did was take over Paulie's club. The Semiramide was less fun after that. As Irene said, the work was there but you missed Paulie, who always had something to say to a girl. All these EMC guys wanted was to track down Paulie's bolt-holes, which no one could tell them much about; also his habits after he got ill. They stayed in the back office all day; they had filled it with FTL routers, also they were going through Paulie's shadow operators with heavy-duty professional software, looking for something, they wouldn't say what, perhaps they didn't even know. All this would be fine, Irene said, but they didn't do much business themselves, whereas until his illness Paulie was always interested that way.

'That man was as unsparing with his money as he was with himself,' she concluded. 'He had the knack of making you feel wanted.'

Antoyne looked into his drink.

'He'll be missed,' was all he could think of to say.

'Antoyne,' the Mona told him, 'you lost the art of enjoying yourself since all this. How are we going to get that back?'

Antoyne shook his head and looked away.

The bar now made its long day's journey into night. In addition to her signature dish, chocolate lasagna, the chef offered Emmenthal & capers in choux pastry followed by a cappuccino of chickpeas; as if in response, keyboard and saxophone discovered their missing groove hidden in a chamame remix of the popular standard *Barking Frog Buzz*. Smells, music, kitchen heat: a sea-change could now take place in the room, shy and emergent at first, in little pockets all around, then catastrophic, irreversible, global. Noise levels rose. The regular clientele, settling into the irradiated zone under the *Live Music* sign, began volume consumption of Ninety Per Cent Neon and Giraffe Beer. Soon it was like any other night at the Surf. Deep into the first set, figures began squeezing themselves out of the space between the band and the bar. They were tentative – unsure what was required of them or what they required for themselves – yet young, pliant, labile, willing to dance. Their faces were as yet unwritten-to, their eyes only reflections of the lights in the bar, lights flickering off glass and bottle, reflections of reflections which though warm had no expression you could read. At first it was as if they were meant to be viewed only under this kind of illumination – and only for a moment, before your eyes took in something else. They had appetites, but didn't yet know what they were. They blinked in the neon, they drank thirstily at the bar, they struck up the quick friendships of children or animals and, arms linked suddenly, adventured out into the night.

Looking, Irene wondered, for what?

She thought love. She thought fulfilment. 'Don't you think that too, Antoyne?'

Antoyne said he had no opinion.

'But don't you hope that's what it is?'

He could only reiterate what he already said, Antoyne told her. Then he stood up so suddenly he knocked over his stool. 'Jesus,' he whispered to himself. He tipped back his drink, wiped his mouth on the back of his hand and, without a word to Irene, pushed his way through the Long Bar crowd until he could stand trembling on the Corniche looking down at the beach where, a month before, he had sold Vic Serotonin to Site Crime. The tide was high. Two women and a man were trying to have sex on the thin strip of sand under the Corniche lamps. Laughter rose in the cold air. 'Here! No, here!' Someone sang two or three bars of tango music. The man's face was a white smear of pleasure under swept-back black hair. Antoyne wanted to call out but could not. He felt as if he was frozen in some other kind of time. As he watched, they came up from the beach adjusting their clothing and, arms linked, wandered off into the lamplight.

Irene found him standing there, staring along the Corniche towards Saudade. Tears ran down his face.

'Antoyne, honey,' she said, 'what is it?'

'It was Vic. I saw him.'

'Honey, you didn't. Vic is gone now and he won't return. He was too inner a man to know another way. Don't do this to yourself any more! Vic Serotonin had no heart, but Antoyne, you have all the heart in the world! Come back inside. Please come back in.' Antoyne shook his head no, but allowed her to lead him back to the Long Bar. The two-piece played, the people were squeezed out into the room. He watched them leave.

'Life always goes on, Antoyne. It always goes on.'

That was the crisis for Antoyne Messner. It got easier for him after that, and he was increasingly able to learn the gifts of happiness and self-belief.

Momentum ran the Cadillac halfway up a long bank of broken earthenware tiles before it slowed suddenly, slid a little way back, then rolled on to its driver side in a cloud of dust. For a minute or two, as the slope restabilised itself through the medium of small random avalanches decreasing in force and frequency, the man who looked like Einstein did nothing. He was content to rest, hanging awkwardly against the seatbelt with his chin pushed into his clavicle.

A bluish, sourceless illumination lay over everything. Everything seemed mixed together. Just as fluids trickled out of the car, all sorts of thoughts and images trickled out of his mind. 'This was never an investigation,' he heard his assistant complain. His wife said, 'Aschemann, you would give the world the whole of yourself – if only you could find it.' Meeting her for the first time, he had thought the same of her. That was on the Corniche, late one summer afternoon, with the light on the sea like mild steel. She was sitting outside a café, in a yellow silk frock and glasses so dark that she had to raise them to see him, eating an ice. Her air was one of disorientation, her eyes looked as bruised as if their life together had already occurred. An hour later she was sitting on his lap in the back of a rickshaw, with the silk frock up round her waist.

Aschemann smiled at this memory.

He extracted himself from the seatbelt, and then the Cadillac.

He turned over the broken tiles with the toe of his shoe. 'So now you're inside,' he thought, 'whatever happens can't be good.' Then, opening a page of Emil Bonaventure's journal at random, he attempted to compare it with the landscape, as if Emil's memories could be used as a guide to his own relationship with the world.

'Vehicle broke down immediately,' Bonaventure had written. 'We slept in the old outfall pipe. G woke often, heard rats in the night. His ulcers no better. Four litres of water remain.' This was accompanied by something between a map and a drawing, in which dotted lines connected various roughly sketched features in an arrangement without perspective, height on the page replacing distance from the viewpoint. 'The expansion chamber flooded repeatedly, & we were forced to retrace our steps. Lupercu records "parliament of insects" here, but I saw only woods on high ground, and an [illegible].'

'Emil, Emil,' Aschemann chided, as if the old entradista was at his side. 'None of us does anything for the right reasons.'

He threw the book away and walked off in the direction he was facing, which happened to be upslope. After that, he seemed to wander about for some weeks. He didn't get hungry or thirsty, although he was cold at night, and his clothes fell apart rapidly. What he took to be devastation stretched away under what he took to be moonlight. Waves of difference passed through the landscape, but it remained obstinately coated with buildings. Though many of these remained intact, their doors and windows had been stripped out, and they had been emptied of anything domestic, or even human. You could see down into basements filled with tight flattened clusters of large bone-white lice, or an ionised slurry of broken smart ads like ectoplasm. To begin with, black and white cats lined the gutters, all facing away from him. There was always a note in the window; a rickshaw disappearing round a corner; a laugh but no one there. There was a smell over everything like rendered fat, which made him recall a conversation with Vic Serotonin, that corrupt tour-operator of the soul.

'Only the simple ever claim it's simple down there,' Vic had said. 'And what do they bring back? Fuck all. You couldn't pay for a motel room with sheets that used. The air's like lard. It's the smell of code. You see something, you break the rules, ptoof: death. Worse than death. Never pick anything up. *Never let anything pick you up.'* As if to confirm this, or at least to gloss it, the dying advertisements detached themselves from their basement slurry to make him half-remembered promises, offers no one could ever accept or fulfil:

We carry all sex medds at bargin price

99% approval rate

to take advantage of this Limited Time opportunity do not reply

They were the tidal dogs, the unremembered memories, of a place never the same place twice. The most determined of them followed him for days, taking the form of small coloured lanterns or, less often, drawings of small coloured lanterns, which bobbed in the air slightly behind his left shoulder. The attrition rate was fierce. Soon only one was left. *Such eloquent timepieces,* it tirelessly informed him, *are supposed to be owned by gorgeous females*. And: *You can get your deploma today.* Did this count as being picked up? The detective couldn't tell. He had lost his assistant. He had lost his car. He had lost his purchase on the ordinary. In return, the site awarded him this wispy companion, lacking in stamina yet full of persistence. He wasn't sure yet what it would require of him in return. When he lay all night half-asleep in some shallow stream, he drew comfort from the ad's simple tune and soft mothy flicker; he came to feel an equally simple affection towards it.

What is a daughter?

Late one evening eight weeks after Vic Serotonin and Lens Aschemann disappeared, Edith Bonaventure squeezed into the costume she had worn at seventeen years of age and took herself to the gates of the Saudade corporate port. There, she opened an accordion case on the cement sidewalk, strapped on the instrument it contained, and began to play. Cruise ships from all the major lines were in, towering above her like a mobile downtown, their abraded, seared-looking hulls curving gently into the low cloudbase. That time of night it was both raining and mist. The port halogens shone out blurry white globes, the pavement was black, slick, cut with transitory patterns of rickshaw wheels. Edith's costume, stiff faux-satin a fierce maroon colour, still fitted; though it made her look a little stocky. Unaccustomed excitement reddened her cheeks and bare thighs. For once, Edith had left her father to his own devices. He could choose to fall out of bed or he could choose to stay there: this evening, she had informed him, that was up to him. It was everyone's right to choose.

'Emil, you can watch the tour ships lift off, or maybe enjoy throwing up on yourself. Me, I am off to The World of Today to pick up a man.'

'If it's convenient, the two of you can bring me back a bottle—'

'You wish.'

'—then do what you do quietly for a change.'

Emil seemed well, perhaps he was getting over Vic's defection. Why she told him such a lie, she didn't know. All she was sure of, she wanted this other thing, she wanted to play. She had picked an accordion to match the outfit, maroon metalflake blends under a thick lacquer finish, with stamped chrome emblems of rockets and comets which caught the spaceport light like mirrors. Sometimes, as a child, Edith had less wanted to own an instrument like this than to be one, to find herself curled up inside one, like a tiny extra dimension of the music itself. Edith played *Abandonada*. She played *Tango Zen*. She played that old New Nuevo standard, *A Anibal Lectur*. She was quick to merge with the night, to become part of its possibility for the paying customer. Rickshaw ads fluttered round her the colours of fuchsia. The rickshaw girls called out requests as they passed; or stood a moment listening despite themselves, puzzled to be still for once, their tame breath issuing into the wet air. While up and down the rickshaw queues, the offworld women shivered – as the sad passionate tango songs made, in cheap but endlessly inventive language, their self-fulfilling prophecies of the entangledness and absurdity and febrile shortness of life – and pulled their furs around them. It was the briefest *mal de debarquement.* Saudade! Its very name was like a bell, tolling them back to their true, enjoyably complex selves! They laughed to wake up so far from where they started, so momentarily at a loss in the face of night and a new planet, yet so in control of the brand new experiences awaiting them there. In search of a gesture that could contain, acknowledge and celebrate this inconsistency, they threw money into the salmon-pink silk interior of the fat, odd little busker's open accordion case. Sometimes the banknotes they threw floated around Edith herself like confetti at the marriage of earth and air, while she played *I Am You, Motel Milongueros,* and an up-tempo version of *Wendy del Muerte* she learned in a pilot's bar on Pumal Verde. She had no idea, really, why she had come to the gates. She was forty-two years old. She was a black-haired woman with wide, blunt hips who couldn't afford to be anyone but the self she had chosen at eleven and who, consequently, blushed up quickly under her olive skin. She was a woman of focus, a woman of whom men said to each other:

'You can't blame Edith. Edith understands her own needs.'

When the stream of rickshaws had abated and she felt she had had enough, she gathered up the money, packed the instrument in its case and shuddered suddenly, struggling into her old maroon wool coat. 'The winds of memory,' she misquoted to herself, 'approach this corner of my abandonment.' At least it wasn't far along the side streets to the bar they called The World of Today, by then, a little like herself, just a lighted yellow window from which all custom had fled. Edith pulled up a stool and counted her cash. It was more than she hoped, less than she imagined when she saw those fur coats, the cosmetics by Harvard and Picosecond, the Nicky Rivera luggage custom-stitched from alien leathers.

'Give me a bottle of Black Heart to go,' she suggested to the barkeep; then, 'in fact, why don't I drink it here.'

'It's your party,' the barkeep said.

Later she asked him if he thought she was too old to get a smart tattoo. Still later, unable to remember his answer, she found herself on the sidewalk in front of an Uncle Zip outlet two doors down.

Uncle Zip the gene cutter had turned out to be his own most successful product. Years after his mysterious disappearance in the Radio RX-1 wormhole, you found an Uncle Zip franchise, maybe two or three of them, on every Halo planet. You found the man himself on a stool inside, sweating with his own energy, a fat clone with a sailor's mouth who'd tailor you by day then – well known to be the patron saint of the piano-accordion – play his music all night. His cuts were still fresh and new. He was cutting for EMC, he was cutting for the glitterati and the common man alike; he was cutting, they said, for alien beings. He was nationwide, all the way to the Core. If there was a religion of the Beach stars, Uncle Zip was its theologian, because he showed you how you could always change and move on, how you never needed to be an old-fashioned fixed entity, with all the gravitational penalties that might incur. Uncle Zip was tender to you, as he was tender to everyone, in that if you hurt you could stare in his window, the way Edith was staring now, and see liquid new possibilities for yourself in a thousand drifting holograms which looked as beautiful as boiled sweets, or ancient postage stamps glowing in the true colours of dragonfly and poison dart frog. You just had to have them! You could be Audrey Hepburn in *Roman Holiday* and sit cute and hungover on Gregory Peck's lap wearing his pyjamas. You could be Princess Diana and sing like a Bronx nightingale at the fatal Kennedy fundraiser in your see-through Givenchy gown. You could go missing from your own life as someone no one ever heard of, by courtesy of DNA pulled at random from a prison hulk at Cor Caroli. You could go half alien, or, it was rumoured, whole hog. You could have the cheapest smart tattoo (known traditionally as a Fifteen Dollar Eagle); or you could get neural chops complex enough, and comprehensive enough, for a management position in the supply-side sex economy of Radio Bay. Whatever you chose, the almost spiritual light spilling out of Uncle Zip's window suggested, you would come out not just new. You would come out someone else and go far away.

Edith shrugged.

She stood there a moment, asking herself if she had truly worn her heart on her sleeve in this life. No answer came. 'You had your turn at being new,' she told herself. She felt good. She felt like going home and saying to Emil, 'When you named the daughter-code after me, you were wrong. While a daughter is all of those things you implied, she's none. She is what comes out of you, why do you need to go in the site to look for her?' But when she found him waiting up for her like any father, in the blue darkness of his room, what she actually said was:

'It's raining again.'

Across the bed lay scattered the remaining volumes of his journal. All of them were open, some flat and broken-spined, some with their yellowing pages fanned out stiffly in the streetlight. Smart diagrams in sharp bright reds and greens. Minute brooch-like maps which would speak when you knew the code for them. Directions to places that shifted and vanished twenty years – or twenty seconds – ago, if they could ever really have been said to be there at all. So much of it put together after the fact, which as everyone in this life knows is far too late. Emil's eyes were inflamed from trying to read his own history written this way, caked at the corners, deeper-set than when she left the house. Over the last two days, he had developed a small growth on one eyelid. It was fantastically delicate, convoluted and infolded like petals of flesh, and in some lights resembled a rose.

Edith sat down on the edge of the bed with her elbows on her knees. She felt tired now.

'So read me something you wrote,' she said.

'You read. Half a lifetime is in there, I can't even understand my own handwriting. Here, you can read this.'

'H. claimed to have made a drawing in Sector Three. Expected [illegible] but got more. A rolling, endless landscape of tall grass. In the foreground, lying in the grass in front of a bench, something that looked partly like a woman partly like a cat. Though it seemed immobile at first H. said it was slowly changing from one shape to the other. H. said he was "struck silent" by the potential of this. He was "full of a tranquil sense of his own possibilities". Cat a kind of ivory-white colour.'

As she read, Emil's face became loose and unfocused, like a face seen at the bottom of a stream. Eventually she saw he was crying. She put down the book and, taking his hands in hers, brought them together so he would be in touch with himself for once. 'Are you entradistas always as brave as this?' she said. Emil tried to smile, then something caught his attention, some flash of light on the walls too quick for Edith to see, and she knew he was back in there, with his plans falling apart before he had a chance to put them into practice. He said:

'I dreamed of Vic. I dreamed that Vic came back.'

'You never dream, Emil.'

Vic Serotonin and his client spent their third night site-side in an abandoned cafeteria. It was in a curious state. Loops of power cable had been dragged out of the walls by some event you could only describe as visceral, while at the same time the stainless steel ranges and glass-fronted food cabinets remained intact and spotlessly clean. Snow fell steadily from near the ceiling, below which, for a couple of hours around midnight, the body of a child about eight years old materialised, wrapped in a crocheted shawl so that only its face was visible. The snow never reached the floor. Elizabeth Kielar stared up at the child and would not look away. He was careful with her after that. In the morning, sun poured in through the knocked-out windows. Vic woke up and found her kneeling in the middle of the black and white tiled floor staring into a flat clear trickle of water. At first she seemed fine. 'Look! Look!' she called excitedly. 'Fish!' There were smudges of dirt on her face, but her smile was radiant. 'Two tiny fish!' By the time Vic joined her, the sun had gone in, so all he saw in the water was his own reflection. It seemed tired, and under some strain, and its hair had turned grey. He looked away before anything else could happen to it.

'That's nice,' he said.

'Do you think we can drink this?'

'If you're thirsty, drink the water I brought in. Nothing here is what it seems.'

'After all, the fish drink it.'

'The fish,' Vic explained, 'aren't fish.'

'I used that water to wash myself. If you fuck often you have to stay clean.' She shrugged. 'When one fish turns the other turns with it. Did you know that everywhere in the universe shoaling is controlled by the same very simple algorithms?'

Vic stared at her, unsure what to say next.

It was a difficult morning. Though he tried to persuade her, she wouldn't eat anything. Before they could leave, the child was back, wrapped tightly in its shawl, spinning this way then that below the ceiling like a chrysalis in a hedge. Elizabeth crouched as far away as she could get from it, and when he tried to put his arm round her, bit his hand. It was behaviour he recognised from their previous trip. The sensible thing would be to leave her and try to make his way back to Saudade, but they were too far in, and he had broken too many of his own rules. Without personal goals, he was at the mercy of whatever had driven her into the site.

'You must be careful of me, Vic. I'm not really here.'

Vic stood up, rubbing his hand. 'Where are you then?' he said.

'I don't know.'

'Where did you come from?'

When she didn't reply, only staring up at him as if he ought to know the answer to that already, he shrugged and went outside and sat in the warm sunlight and cool air. The cafeteria, a single-storey white building that looked as if it had been built for some heavier duty, lay on the bank of a tidal inlet, held in a crook of hills and woods. Gulls, green weed, dappled sunshine on the hummocky ground between the trees. The tide was low, the light so bright on the revealed mud he couldn't look at it. The trees tumbling down the opposite shore of the inlet vanished into a dazzle of reflections in which stranded multi-hulled ships rested like insects tired after some long intense flight to mate. Beyond that, it was two or three kilometres of dried-up chemical ponds, then long rolling slopes of tall grass. Vic felt hollowed out – as if the site was about to present him, if he wasn't careful, with a self he didn't want. After an hour or two, he went back inside in the hope of persuading her to eat, or leave, at least make some decision he could take a position on. It was cold in there. Elizabeth had spent some time squeezing into the gap between two food cabinets. She was still staring up at the ceiling. Something happened to the light when it reached her. It was wrapping itself around her in a way that made her face smooth and eroded, less featured than you would expect. The rest of the room looked ordinary enough.

'Elizabeth?'

'Don't come near me, Vic.'

He caught her hand, pulled her out; she broke away and huddled in a corner, watching him intently. All afternoon, white-faced but quick and deft, she kept the room between them, always moving off to the next corner if he got near her. Vic was cautious. He didn't think she would harm him, but he didn't want her to harm herself. He thought that eventually she would tire, although he had no idea what he would do then. Nothing he already knew about her seemed to apply. After an hour or two, she began to pull off her clothes, as awkwardly as if she had forgotten how clothes worked, or as if she had never known in the first place.

'I don't want these,' she said. 'Why should I want these?'

'Elizabeth,' he said. 'Please.'

She laughed, then crouched down to urinate fiercely. 'No,' she said. 'You don't know enough to stay safe, Vic.'

'Elizabeth!'

'I got your sperm anyway.'

By dark, her skin had deep, ivory qualities, as if each layer had accreted over time then died, achieving a dull shine. She smelled of distress and unknown hormones. She lay panting from a heat Vic couldn't feel, watched him sidelong as she lapped up water from the black and white tiles. The light in the room frightened him. He was only a facilitator here. He thought again of leaving; but when he looked outside, the inlet had curled itself away like a missing dimension, and all he could see was a dune-like landscape with isolated patches of fog, protruding rocks, a litter of fluorescent white bone. There were flickers of what might be lightning, or rocket-exhaust on the horizon. She called him back. Her voice, always a pure contralto, had taken on harmonics, as if someone was speaking in unison with her but not quite loudly enough to hear. She positioned herself in the centre of the abandoned cafeteria in the loose darkness, adopting one desperate, open posture after another.

'Vic,' she said, 'people lose their way as an act of defence. Then they panic and decide they have to find it again.'

She darted past him and out of the door, moving away quickly into the drifting chemical fogs, her gait already not quite human, her skin fluorescing in the dry fitful lightning glare.

'Elizabeth!'

All night she ran aimlessly back and forth across the faces of the dunes. It was hard to say at what point she became something else. This thing – pivoted sharply at the hips so that it could walk on all four limbs with the palms of its hands flat on the ground, its head too small and streamlined, somehow, to accommodate the great blue candid cartoon human eyes – called Vic's name until he put his hands over his ears and went inside. Next morning he set out to follow its tracks; but he lost them quite soon, where the dunes turned to rolling purple grass.

Over the dusty months and years of searching that were to follow, Vic Serotonin penetrated the site deeper than he, or anyone, had ever done before. He threw away his gun. He ate what he found. He lived a life in there. Every day he walked until he found somewhere safe to sleep, somewhere he liked, and at night he grew used to the sound of radios shifting randomly from station to station; girders tolling as they fell; the intrusive quack of the plastic duck. He heard the landscapes swing apart and grind themselves together again. The empty rooms no longer smelled foul to him. He never met anyone else, though he woke one morning in a deserted plaza to the sound of a woman's voice singing some passionate open-throat lament. Pigeons flew up; they flew up again. The cold air was perfectly still, but full of old shoes – old shoes cracked and wrinkled, soles hanging off, floating around one another as if they'd been lifted up on a strong wind – as if shoes were an organism, one which, given the correct conditions, could exhibit flocking behaviour. Vic knew then that Emil Bonaventure had been right about one thing; but he understood too that neither this location nor any other could be said to be the centre of anything. Vic aged. Wind and sun whitened and bleached him. His memories of Emil and Edith, his memories of caning it nightly at the Black Cat White Cat bar with his friends Liv and Antoyne, eventually even his memories of Vic Serotonin, faded. But he never forgot his client, and he searched for her until the day he died.

*

Aschemann the detective followed rising cindery ground for a week, only to find himself facing a three-hundred-metre vertical drop into what seemed to be a vast replica of the Long Bar at the Café Surf. This he took to be a metaphor.

He stood at the edge. His coat blew out behind him in a gale of music and light. He held on to his hat. He looked down thirstily at the Black Heart spirit optic, glittering in the warm barlight. Everything around him tottered on the edge of change, but when the wave came it was Aschemann who fell. He saw an architect's drawing. Pies. Polaroid snaps of dogs. A man's bracelet chronometer, very large. He saw playing cards. A wooden toy penguin with rubber feet. Then his old friend and sparring partner Emil Bonaventure, asleep on a mudbank in rising water. He saw bluebirds and chipmunks against a sunset. In response, a kind of seizure overcame him and when he recovered from it he was lying a few metres downslope, unable to move his legs. It was only what you expected in here, where plate tectonics held sway and one reality was always sliding beneath the next. It was night. He examined his legs: nothing seemed untoward, but he couldn't deny they felt peculiar, perhaps with all the walking.

'Something has happened to you,' he acknowledged. 'You can't do anything while you don't know what it is.'

He was able to accept that. He lay there a long time. Night replaced day replaced night. Equally regular pulses of change propagated through the ground beneath him. From upslope, close and comforting, could always be heard the sounds of a lively evening at the Long Bar. He was content; but the smart ad, which had accompanied him thus far without demur, grew increasingly anxious. *You can have the pe[nis] of y0ur dre ams*, it suggested, and: *Call out Gouranga be happy*. It roamed upslope and down, straying further and further away, fading to the ghostly blue and orange of burning alcohol; a marsh light as lost as its victim, an ignis fatuus in reverse.

Finally it gave up on him and drifted off.

'Send me a sign,' Aschemann called. 'Seek me inside.' This made him chuckle. On balance he felt more sympathy for the ad than he did for himself. 'Send me a neon heart.'

This made him think about his crime. About his wife, expecting everyone to come to her in her minotaur's cave; about the Marilyn Monroe look-alike, going out along the high wire from her room to everyone. He thought about the damp sand at the back of the Café Surf, squeezed together daily by the implacable shaping forces of the Long Bar – improvisation, iconolatry and red light – to make new inhabitants for the city. What if he were part of that cycle too? Later he told himself in surprise: 'Aschemann, I think you're dying!' He felt enlarged – swollen, but not exactly sick. Some time on the third, or perhaps the fourth day, he looked down at himself and saw the lower part of his legs dissolving into thousands of bright, energetic white sparks. He felt no pain. Despite that – and though no sound accompanied the process – he had a lively sense of himself as part of the entertainment. He was fizzing and crackling into the dark like a firework. He wondered what would happen when the fire reached his cock. The sparks blew away uphill on a light breeze, and out over the lip of the cliff, where they rained down, he could only suppose, on to the Café Surf two-piece under its sign *Live Music Nightly*. His legs had plenty in reserve. They went on pouring out the benefit in them as sparks and illuminated smoke. They were certainly good value for money. Then he saw his wife toiling up the slope towards him at last, waving and smiling across the wasteland. She was calling his name. She had on the yellow silk dress he remembered so well. No shoes.

'Aschemann, is that you?' she called. 'Is that you? Aschemann, always something new! You'll never change!'

What if there was no new species after all, only the same old one trapped in its same old circularity of reinvention? Would some fresher version of himself soon be staggering down the Corniche away from the Café Surf, singing, full of appetites, ready to be amazed? Or had that already happened?

What if we're all code?

'Utzie, hurry!' he called. 'Hurry, or I'll be gone before you get here!'

He was glad to have been alive.

TEN

The Nova Swing

In subsequent weeks, better weather came to Saudade. The dogs of April raced up and down Straint Street from the site to the sea, rattling the boarded-up windows. Above, the sky was bluer than usual, wider and emptier than the buildings would seem to permit. You could smell the ocean. People had a feeling of energy and wanting to be outside. In the New Men warrens, they aired the bedding. Even the chopshops opened their doors, giving sidelong views of matt-black internal walls, dusty shoot-up posters, out-of-guarantee proteome tanks crawling with LEDs and smart readouts; while the tailors played Three Dick Hughie on the pavement or showed off their chops to a passing Mona.

Black Cat White Cat was not exempt from this change of habit: Liv Hula declared a holiday. First she went upstairs.

In the tin box she had used to smash the princess sink, among all the other junk of being forty years old, she kept a cheap hologram which related some of her exploits before she arrived in Saudade, the voiceover of which began, 'Liv Hula was mediated Halo-wide after she dived her flimsy dipship, the *Saucy Sal*, five thousand kilometres into the photosphere of France Chance IV.' A long, almost documentary item, it went on in that vein for a full ninety seconds, over images of Liv as a child, Liv as a teenage rocket-sport bum in the bar of the Venice Hotel on France Chance; then a sequence of the ship, if you could call anything that small a ship, the paint job fried right off it, cooling in the parking orbit. They had most of it wrong. *Saucy Sal* wasn't a dip, for instance: she was the first of the true hyperdips, with a lot of subtle magnetic field action and some kind of hot alien sponge-carbon hull. But they had footage of Liv being hugged by Chinese Ed himself, who she beat to that particular achievement, which was nice if only because Ed – tall and undependable, with the usual Halo tan and associated burden of debt – was acknowledged a dipship legend in his own time. The record didn't hold long, she never expected it to; but, 'Go deep!' they had shouted for the cameras, her and Chinese Ed, pilots of the future gurning out at the Halo together, rocket-sport being so fully hot at the time, and all of that made the trip worth it. How do you get rid of a hologram? Liv, who never invested in a gadget patch, didn't even know what they were made of. She decided to throw it in the sea.

She shut the box and then the bar and walked down Straint to the noncorporate port, where she stood for a while in the rim of thick, silky weeds by the chainlink fence in the morning light in her black wraparounds, watching the rockets come and go; then caught a rickshaw the rest of the way to the beach.

'You don't want the Vientiale,' the rickshaw girl warned her. 'It's wall-to-wall. It's crawling.'

'Maybe I want crawling.'

'You don't.'

Monster Beach was wall-to-wall too: after a glance at the rammed fish restaurants and boardwalk amusements, the shoals of beautifully turned-out Monas, the famous sign pointing not to the sand but crazily upwards at the parking orbit, she had the girl take her to the Point end of the bay. There she could get down to her white singlet and black boy-leg underpants and watch children running in and out of the tide. She played the hologram again. You couldn't tell what she was thinking when she watched it. Her haircuts were just as short in those days, only in bad colours. She gazed out to sea. She ate an ice cream. She picked up a man. The way that happened, she was walking back empty-handed from the ocean, feeling suddenly light and needing something to hold her down. He was a lot younger than her, with a sweet, candid smile, bleached-out yellow hair and a neat triangular tuft of beard under the lower lip. Maybe, he suggested, she would like an ice.

'That's such a good idea,' she said. 'But I'll buy.'

While they were walking along eating the ices he said, 'Sun and shade sometimes seem like equal things? Both, in a way, kind of illuminating? And both so ungrudging?'

'I've often thought that,' Liv said.

She took him back to the bar anyway. Late afternoon he said tentatively, 'I've seen you somewhere before. Are you someone?'

'These days we're all someone.'

Up in her room, he stared at the broken sink. She could see him trying to find a way of asking about it. The middle of the night, Liv woke and couldn't get back to sleep. She looked down at his body, the colour of honey and just this side of beautiful. Really, he seemed a lot too young for the sex subtleties he knew. It was probably a chop anyone could get these days. After she thought this over she got up and went down to the bar, where she wrote out a rough sign, FOR SALE, and propped it in the window, low down on the right-hand side. When she got back upstairs, the boy was awake and on his feet. He was worrying about the sink again.

'You didn't try to piss in that, did you?' she said.

'I could get it fixed.'

'Anyone could get it fixed. I don't want it fixed. Fix me instead, I need fixing.'

He gave her a long slow smile, which reminded her of Ed.

'But really,' he insisted, 'are you someone?'

Liv pretended to look around her room. 'Would anyone who was anyone live here? Just come and fuck me.'

'How about I fuck you and come?'

After all, she thought with a certain relief, he was as young as he looked. She laughed. 'So what was all that crap about sunshine and shadows?' she said. 'Down at the beach?' Next morning she felt lots better about herself. She cleaned bar. She cleaned tables. She wrote out a neater version of the FOR SALE sign, on a piece of white card she found behind the bar. Her energy was back. As if in response, her first customer of the day came in and ordered hot mocha with cream and rum. It was none other than Antoyne Messner, out on his own for once. 'I walk past earlier,' he said, 'I see your sign. I'm fascinated.' He was on his way to Carver Field, he informed her, to do business. As if to substantiate that, he had on all new clothes. A short brown leather zip-up pilot jacket; cavalry twill chinos with their own expensive belt. It looked as if he already came into money. 'Irene,' he made sure to say, 'sends her regards. She don't forget how you were kind to her when Joe Leone died.'

'How is Irene?' Liv said.

'Irene's good. We're both good.'

That morning, the world did seem different. Liv felt light, but not so light she would escape gravity and float away. She could convert that into achievements. She cleaned glass. She cleaned the floor. Caught by surprise, her shadow operators furled and clustered round the ceiling fans; then wheeled as one, outdoors into the light and back. Fat Antoyne seemed full of energy too. Out of Vic Serotonin's shadow he had a more relaxed way with him. He engaged you more directly, and seemed liberated. Also, as became clear after a couple of drinks, he had a proposition for her; which when she heard it made her think.

Edith Bonaventure, the accordion case slung with a kind of sexy gallantry over one shoulder, trudged home from her by-now-regular gig at the gates of the corporate port. She loved Globe Town. The lights were on. Later, a mist would rise up in the little streets between the tall houses, but for now the air was soft, full of small winds, cooking smells – bream baked in sea-salt, three-way herring. If Edith had a tired look, she could at least afford a new coat, which she wore open over her costume; it was too warm for the evening, but she wasn't ready to be sensible about something so nice. Edith's walk said something new too. Edith herself wasn't sure what. The talent, she would tell her audience silently as she played one more encore (*Carmen Sylva*, in the version made popular by Olavi Virta, king of the old New Nuevo Tango), is fractious now, and hungry. It is ready to take its money and run. The talent gets tired, but never forget it will always have that good special glow.

It was a short commute. One drink with Curt, the barkeep at The World of Today, and Edith was home. She went up the steps and into the hall. She dropped the accordion on the floor.

'Emil,' she called up the stairs. 'What do you want to eat?'

When he didn't answer, she laughed.

'You are a bad old man,' she called. 'Emil, you don't like me to go to the port you should just say, don't sulk.' She arranged her new coat carefully on a hanger. 'Be nice, Emil. I'm having a bath, we'll eat then.' She lay for half an hour with the hot water up to her chin, up to her pink aureolae and counted from memory the money she made that afternoon. Saw herself at the port gate, as if from the outside, a fixture, an isolated but energetic figure of a woman in a pool of halogen light, rain or shine. It was a living. Emil slept a lot while she was out. He was going down a little faster now. Sometimes he had a relapse to tell her he missed her. He had an accident. Every day she came back, cleaned and fed him, they looked at his diaries together, he had his hallucinations, his syncopes, his periods of absence far into the night when he would say conversationally, 'We're fucked here, Atmo. We should never have tried to follow the map.' Or: 'Where's the fucking gun?' Edith would wait him out, sleep a few hours from dawn, go down to the port to do it all again.

She hauled herself out of the tub.

'Emil, it's time you forgive me now!'

Her father sat propped up in his bed with his emaciated legs stretched out in front of him. The sheets were tangled and yellow with sweat. He had been trying to write something and lost patience with himself. Books lay on the floor where they had fallen. She gathered them up. 'I was looking,' she read, 'at something no one else would ever see.' Emil's face was papery and grey, with an air of being both exhausted and rested at the same time, as if he had just that moment given up and leaned his head back against the wall and closed his eyes.

'Emil?'

He smiled. 'All my dreams rushed back,' he whispered, 'while you were out.' Edith squeezed his hand tight. 'You would have loved them,' he said.

'Emil, you had a sweat, you threw up a little, it's nothing to worry about.'

He opened his eyes. They were a perfect, excited blue she hadn't seen since he was forty; and that was how they stayed, looking at something no one else would ever see. The smart tattoos crawled slowly about in the crust of white hair on his chest for a while, then stopped. She leaned down to examine one of them before it faded – not a map but a line from a poem, perhaps, in simple red letters: *Send me an eon heart.* 'Emil?' She sat there and held his hand for perhaps an hour, perhaps more, waiting for him to wake, or notice her, or whatever would happen next. Nothing did. She was too warm after the bath; then too cold. Streetlight filled the room.

'Emil, that was cruel,' she said.

He was my father, she let herself think eventually. He was my lovely father and I miss him so. After a while she went downstairs and got dressed. She fetched out the money she received for giving up Vic Serotonin and counted it. She took down her new coat and looked at that. When I was little, she thought, I wanted nothing except to stop travelling. I wanted time for each new thing, each new feeling, to be held properly in suspension until it could be joined by the next. Given the chance I could easily hold all those beautiful things together. I could be like a box in which they would be held new forever. Instead, everything aged and changed. People, too. I wanted him to myself, she thought. I wanted him to myself. Edith didn't know quite how to be on her own yet, so she went back upstairs and held his hand again and sat by him all night.

She knew it was dawn when the black and white cats began to pour into the room through the open door behind her. Those cats! she thought. They would come in anywhere if you left the street door open. Silent, fixated, their eyes flat and a curious dry spiciness to their smell, they packed themselves close to her father's bed, flowing around it, rubbing heedlessly against any part of Emil they could find in the tight, cramped space.

He was my lovely, lovely father.

At Carver Field, even the tubbiest of the ships on sale tower a hundred feet high. They stand in rows. They're old. They're used. They leak. They exhibit the gentle patina of being too long on the ground. They have names like *Radio Mary* and *Soft Error*. They have always hauled their guts on behalf of others. They have muled and trafficked and smuggled and led a life. They have been the mainstay of commerce, the prey of outlaws. By day they emit radiation. By night cheap navigational code trickles through their corroded firewalls like a contract between Marburg fever and a trail of sparks. They began their career five hundred lights across the Halo as someone's dream and took fifty years to work their way here, where they will inevitably become someone else's; because even for these tubby little ships there is always someone to exclaim:

'I never saw a thing so beautiful!'

Five-thirty a.m., two or three days after Antoyne Messner called in at Liv Hula's bar. The gates were already unlocked. Buyers were already out, craning their necks, pointing upward, resembling from a distance the little accurate figures inserted to provide scale in an architectural model. Pale strong light bleached the machine sheds and peeling moderne administration block. All that month Carver had sported a crop of alien weeds, silky, poppy-looking copper-coloured blossoms forcing their way up through the concrete, going strong in the light of this to-them distant sun.

Irene the Mona, box-fresh in metallic linen bolero with matching shorts and transparent sidebutton ankle-boots, glanced sideways at her companion. Hints of anxiety touched her little mouth.

'*Is* it beautiful, Antoyne?' she said.

The ship looked no different than a hundred others. Its hull was just as shot. Its three-fin tail and outboard reactor casings were streaked with just as much birdshit and re-entry stains. But Antoyne and Irene had read in the catalogue that it had carried out many years' efficient service under the livery of the famous circus and alien show, Sandra Shen's Observatorium & Native Karma Plant; they were impressed. The story was this, Madame Shen had not been heard of for many years. A man called Renoko now looked after the circus, stripping its assets from an office on some planet light-years down the Beach. So here the ship was, the usual tramp freighter past its best and renamed a dozen times, already warming for take-off in Antoyne Messner's mind. He felt the tremble in the tips of its fins. He felt the mystery of it. The oily preflight roll of the Dynaflow drivers rose up to him from somewhere below deck, causing, for the millionth time, the hair to rise on the back of his neck.

Beautiful, Antoyne didn't know. He had, he said, no remit for beautiful. 'This here looks like a good workaday unit,' he told Irene, 'though for that it is priced a little high.'

Irene saw right through him and out the other side.

If you understood ships like these, Antoyne had often said to her, this was how your CV could be expected to run:

At thirteen you lived on an orbital factory. Or a farm planet with infinite horizons and no room for you anywhere. Or you lived in a port city which stank of the outright bizarreness of things and made you raw all your childhood with … what? Delight. Anticipation. The desire to escape. The desire to know. Thirteen years of age, you looked older. You were a girl, you were a boy, your gender was indeterminate. You were pressganged by EMC. Or you met a salvage expert from Nueva Cardoso. You loved her instantly for the sheer breadth of stuff she knew; also her alien smut tattoos and neat prosthetic arm. She made you an offer and that's how you came to ride the rockets. You flew with Fedy von Gang, you flew with Chinese Ed. You spent five years in a research tub at Radio RX-1 with the Kefahuchi Tract hanging over your shoulder like a huge boiling face, stripped, raw, heaving with some emotion you couldn't recognise. It's been fun. It's been heartbreak all the way. It's never been less than a trip.

Whose story was he telling when he said these things?

Irene thought she knew. 'Antoyne,' she felt bound to remind him now, 'I'm beautiful, and you understood enough to find your way to me through this life.'

'Anyway,' Antoyne said, 'we got to wait to find out more.'

They didn't wait long. Soon enough, Liv Hula threaded her way across the crowded field to find them. She checked out the gathered ships, and had the air of someone in her own world. For a moment they thought she would walk right past, and when Antoyne called her name, she seemed surprised to hear it. A barkeep always looks vulnerable away from the bar. Liv Hula, it was the Mona's opinion, seemed often too defensive in her personal presentation; yet when Liv considered that ship – its ripe-avocado geometry, its hull blackened by tail-down landings from Motel Splendido to the Core – she certainly was business itself.

'It's a dog,' she said.

Antoyne chuckled. 'Go inside,' he invited, 'tell me something I don't know.'

The ship smelled of old food, sweat, Black Heart. It smelled of refugees, contraband, animal shows. It had the air of a place just vacated. Liv Hula wasn't sure how she felt about being there alone. Her footsteps filled the dimly lighted hull, then echoed out past it and into some other kind of space. Shadow operators, clustered round the portholes like tourists, whispered and touched one another as she passed. The air in there was colder than outside. Liv found the dusty pilot seat and sat in it. At the sound of her voice the equipment dialled itself up. Direct connexions made themselves available, in the form of a nanofibre mass.

Liv said, 'Accept.'

She sat back and gaped. The system grew itself deftly through the soft roof of her mouth and into her brain.

This used to be her profession. A sun-diver like the *Saucy Sal* was more mathematics than substance. It didn't really know what to be, and without an active pilot interface would revert instantly to a slurry of nanotech and smart carbon components, a few collapsing magnetic fields. It was in the class of emergent artefacts, a neurosis with an engine. You don't so much fly your hyperdip as nurse it through a programme of dynamic self-reinvention. You have to tell it a story about itself. Long before she went deep at France Chance – which in a sense ended her career because she never matched that achievement but just did the rocket-sport circuit like anyone else – Liv bought the best chops you could get for that kind of work. So now there was a disconnected moment when she wasn't even Liv Hula but some New Venusport code monkey, then she was all over the freighter's mathematics like a life coach.

'So, then. What can you tell me about yourself?'

Navigational holograms, dull. Star charts and fakebooks, dull. Fifty years of cargo manifests, agency fuel purchases and parking orbit stamps, dull, dull, dull. Main dealer service record (none). Infrastructure schematics. Cabins and crew quarters. Holds (empty); fuel tanks, empty, empty. The mathematics could show her a view of Carver Field, on which she easily discerned the little architectural figures she knew as Irene and Antoyne. It could even show her, via proxies and an ageing FTL uplinker, and for reasons unclear, realtime images of selected parking orbits from three to a thousand lights along the Beach.

Liv viewed all this without sympathy.

'I don't know why you're so shy,' she said. 'You've got nothing I haven't seen before.'

She waited a nanosecond, then added:

'What I'm already reading here, just in this short time, you have the most extraordinary qualities if you would only let people know about them. You won't mind me saying this, but somehow you've forgotten that it's all about *you*. And about presenting yourself.'

Twenty minutes later, a little nauseous, a little nostalgic, she was blinking in the sunshine again.

'I need breakfast,' she said, and took her friends back to Straint Street, where she made a relaxing rum no ice for herself and their favourite cocktail drink for Irene and Antoyne. Then she sat across a table and laid out the information Antoyne had paid to hear; also the benefit of her experience for what that was worth. 'You got fifty years of guano in there,' she advised him, 'but what's new? Also they used the code to run something my chops don't get, some type of alien bolt-on. Maybe, and this is weird, I admit, some kind of an outboard motor?' The concept caused her to look perplexed for a moment, after which she made a gesture of *who knows anything, this world we're in*? 'Whatever it was, it's not there right now, so I don't think you need worry about it. Otherwise the ship's clean. Navigation tools don't leak. Good hygiene, given its age. The code itself? Pussy for me, but not for some. Antoyne, you will have to upgrade, or one night wake up with it crawling into your nose.'

At this point Antoyne opened his mouth to confess something. If Liv had let him speak, perhaps that would have changed her mind about the whole deal as Antoyne had put it to her, but she didn't, only went on, 'By the way, I dialled up hardware reports too. Jesus, don't even talk about them. Those engines it has? With the *power cable*, and big flywheels? What kind of physics is that about? Antoyne, don't look like that, I'm teasing you. Anyway, they'll last two, maybe three trips.' She finished her drink and said aside to Irene, 'Be sure and make him wear his lead pants; the hull's ablated to a wafer.'

The Mona, who had been looking out the window and thinking about poor Joe Leone, repeated, 'Lead pants,' and laughed.

'I'll fix all that,' Antoyne said.

'Rather you than me.'

If you understand ships like the one Antoyne wanted to buy, you can always make a connexion. You can walk into a bar on Motel Splendido or New Venusport and always see someone you know. They owe you money. They owe you a drink. They owe you an explanation. And it's true that you owe them all or most of those things too; in fact it's the only reason you can do business at all. Perhaps Liv was thinking about this when she nodded judiciously and said:

'At least change the name, Antoyne.'

Antoyne took Irene's arm. They smiled at each other.

'We plan on that,' the Mona said.

Thirty thousand miles above Liv Hula's bar, Paulie DeRaad had recently arrived in the quarantine orbit.

He was not the Paulie they had known. Gone were the sharp nose, the lively blue eyes, the shock of white-blond hair in its signature widow's peak, the fragile radiation-thinned skin which in some lights gave you the illusion you could see right down into the musculature of his face. Like everyone on the ship that brought him in, Paulie was by now more of a notion than a person you could actually describe. Individual voices might still be heard in the human quarters. But while, in a sense, Paulie was still being Paulie – that is, someone who never closed, who still liked and wanted everything – and you had the clear feeling that someone was still genuinely alive in there, you knew it would be hard now to separate Paulie from the members of the vacuum commando that had brought him in. What these connexions – volunteers to a man – said oftenest about Paulie was:

'You fucking fuck, DeRaad. You fucking tourist.'

Most of the quarantine ships were huge; pocked and used-looking; alive with the dim crawling lights of beacons and particle dogs. Typically you found old pipeliners that had worked the Carling line, obsolete Alcubiere warps the size of planetisimals even with their relativity drivers torn off, anything with a thick strong hull, especially if it was easy to reinforce further. Other things they had in common: they were mined, with high-yield, top-shelf assets from the EMC catalogue; and their hatches were welded tight. No one was sure what kind of atmosphere they now contained, if any. Inside, whatever their age or origin or state of outer preservation, they had only two qualities: pitch dark or light too bright to bear. Hundreds of them, as far as you could see, rolling around forever in gluey braided orbits, drifting together and then apart. Once in six months, complex resonance effects put them on collision courses. Alarms went off. An engine fired for a millisecond or two in the dark. For a day or two afterwards the vacuum between the hulks took on an ionised look, as phase-changes rippled through a smart gas of nanodevices designed to monitor hull thickness, skin temperature, core temperature, and emissions in all regimes including, curiously, soundwaves, generated by so-far undescribed events inside.

How many human beings were stored in the quarantine orbit? How many escapes did they represent?

No one knew.

Any number of smaller vessels could be found drifting between the hulks. They were still volatile. Their trajectories were impossible to map. They were a danger to everything with their fragile contemporary hulls and lively contents. They still had windows and hatches. One of them was the K-ship *Poule de Luxe*, originally on grey ops out of Radio Bay, but lately seconded to Quarantine.

Poule de Luxe, everyone's favourite survivor of the Nastic Wars, tumbled aimlessly end over end, her armaments extending and retracting meaninglessly, her riding lights off. She had come a long way since exfiltrating Paulie DeRaad from the Saudade Lots. When they understood it was too late to find DeRaad a place in a hygiene facility – too late not just for Paulie but for themselves – the vacuum commando had tried to steal her. To their credit they got halfway across the Halo before her K-captain regained control. It had been a long flight back. There had been some problems. There had been shrieks and screams from the human complement as they realised fully what Paulie had brought them. Now, its mission completed, the mathematics had switched itself off. The K-captain had switched herself off too, in case she could be extracted at a later date. Power was down.

Aft, in the crew quarters, it was cold but not dark. Charred and buckled bulkheads contained the escape, which presented, like the majority of escapes, as a loose, luminous fluid medium sometimes the consistency of rice pudding or lentil soup, sometimes having the visual qualities of a pool full of chlorinated water agitated gently in powerful sunlight; often too bright to look at, and developing intricate internal flows independent of input. If there was code in there, no one knew what it was doing. No one knew how it bound to the substrate of proteins and nanomech. It looked beautiful, but stank like rendered fat. It would absorb you in seconds. Was it an end-state? Was it a new medium? No one knew. The hulks were full of it. No one knew what to do with it. No one knew what it was: except that, in this case, in a previous life, some of it had been a Saudade gangster and some of it had been his friends from EMC. Shock fronts raced through it. Random state changes were precipitated. Every so often a shape assembled itself with difficulty and made its way to the porthole, and a barely audible voice whispered:

'Wow. Fuck. See that? Alcubiere, right off the port bow! See?'

Hard to know if the shape was Paulie; if he was able to retain that much of a sense of himself. But perhaps nothing is hopeless, and perhaps he had found a way to enjoy life again. Meanwhile the remainder of the mass boiled resentfully and said:

'De Raad, you cunt.'

Edith Bonaventure, in the aftermath of Emil's death, found it hard to know what to do with herself. She worked the port gate and the tourist traps. She visited a new bar every night, after which she went home determined to throw out Emil's things, and couldn't, and couldn't sleep either, and in her state only ended up sitting on the floor as if he was still alive, reading his journals aloud.

'The site,' he had written, 'behaves just like a child with a secret. No one must know, but everyone has to try and guess.'

Edith had other needs than working her father through her life and into his proper place, if ever that turned out to be possible. These needs were less readily defined. They sent her to the fights in the soft early darkness of summer evenings, but at Preter Coeur the smells of fried food, alcopops and haemoglobin held less goodness than before. (You can claim, and people do, that every fighter is different: but it is a difference, Edith had begun to feel, that works itself out within sameness: so that when you've seen one monster cock you've truly seen them all.) They sent her to stand in the pool of light outside the Uncle Zip and Nueva Cut franchises, but though she wanted to be new, she couldn't believe in newness; though she wanted to travel, she was reluctant to leave. Window-shopping Straint Street one early evening, for a cheap deal on a different self, she passed the Black Cat White Cat bar, where she saw the notice in the window and inside found the barkeep standing in the usual trance behind the zinc counter.

'Do you really want to sell this place?'

Liv Hula, who had spent the morning wiping arcs in a decade's dirt and the afternoon in bed, yawned and said, 'It isn't much.'

'I see that.'

'For instance, that wall was white when I came here.'

Edith tuned out. She closed her eyes, so that when she opened them again they would be adjusted to the gloom. The first thing she saw was the light running like water over black floorboards, reflecting off the bottles behind the bar, seeping into the plastered wall, which remained yellow despite the barkeep's efforts. She saw the mismatched tables of different heights with their chrome legs and chipped marble tops; and above them, up in the ceiling corners, the cobwebby mass of shadow operators. She saw the wet cloth on the zinc bar. There were two or three customers at tables but she could tune them out too – she could see that there were times of day when almost no one came into Black Cat White Cat because it was too late to eat and too early to get bagged. She went to the window and looked up and down Straint Street, which for a moment she visualised as a new Globe Town: after Edith started her business people would come home at night to live there, or at least visit for more than just a makeover. That wasn't quite it, though. That wasn't what you wanted from a bar. Nevertheless she said:

'You know what I see here?'

'What.'

'Nothing yet. But I hear music. That's the thing I hear.'

'Can I get you a drink?' Liv asked.

Edith said she could. She could make it rum. 'You can make it rocks.' She put half the drink down her in one brisk move, then leaned on the bar. 'At any time,' she felt bound to point out, 'you could have had the shadow operators clean the walls for you.'

'It wouldn't seem authentic.'

'I'll never be sentimental that way,' promised Edith.

Between them they contemplated the implications of this form of words. Eventually, Liv said, 'Maybe you don't remember me. You were here before.' This received no response. 'I was sorry,' she pressed, 'about what happened with you and Vic.'

'I don't think about him,' warned Edith.

They talked another five minutes in the same fashion, during which Liv's beach bunny came downstairs and smiled shyly at Edith. 'Hey,' he said. He poured himself a glass of tapwater, put his arm round Liv's waist while he drank it thirstily, and wandered off to stand in the doorway where the illumination slanting in from the street could show off his legs through the calf-length un-bleached linen pants he wore. Liv made more drinks. Then Edith asked what Liv wanted for the bar, and Liv told her, adding, 'There is accommodation upstairs. Though the plumbing is not complete at the moment.'

'This is a good deal for me,' Edith said, after some thought.

'You could move in as soon as you liked.'

'One thing,' asked Edith, 'does he come with it?'

They laughed, and Edith counted out money on the zinc counter, and she left, and that was how it was done. Ten minutes later, without thinking once, Emil Bonaventure's daughter, a property developer with no coherent plans to limit her increasing sense of vision, had made her way to the site end of Straint. There she stood for a long time, watching the sunlight shift towards red – which everyone knows is a measure of the speed at which things get away from you – and thinking about Emil. It was the first time she had ever been there. She was jealous, but puzzled too. This was what he had enjoyed all those years: adventures in broken houses and factories, heaps of rubble like streets bombed in a war; rusty road signs like signals from your own unconscious; acres of empty con-crete reaching away to standing waves of fog, atmospheric lensing and other forms of optical confusion. A lot seemed to be going on there, but it was hard to make out. She could hear music, as of a fairground. Then a second sunset appeared, great wheeling bars of light flashing alternately purple and green like a cartoon drawing.

'Do you expect me to believe that?' Edith said.

After Edith Bonaventure left, Liv felt too light for comfort. She washed glasses, just to have her hands in warm water. She stared at the money on the bar. Then she counted it again. She sheafed it up into two piles, carried the larger pile over to one of the corner tables and placed it carefully on the tabletop.

'So now I am all the way in,' she told Antoyne Messner.

Antoyne took his turn at counting the money. When he had finished, he didn't look as pleased as she expected.

'Hey, it's real,' she assured him.

He knew it was real, he said.

'Then is something the matter, Antoyne?'

He'd come around every afternoon since they looked at the ship together, sometimes with the Mona on his arm, sometimes without; but it wasn't like the old days when he caned it night after night with Vic Serotonin. Antoyne said less than he used to; and if his mood was generally more stable and energetic, his lows arrived lower. He drank more. His leather flight jacket grew shabby, his chinos oil-stained. He was always on dial-up, saying something like, 'Jesus Christ, Andrei, this was supposed to be a favour.' Now he turned sideways on his chair and looked away from Liv for a few moments to compose himself. He looked back, and toyed with his glass, which had a quarter of an inch of his cocktail left in it. However low that drink got in a glass, however often you swirled it around, smart molecules built into the mixer ensured it was still made up of precise pink and yellow layers. The planets where Antoyne had spent his time, that was the height of sophistication. He drank it and made a face.

'I can't fly no more,' he admitted. 'I was going to tell you all along.'

He thought about when he rode the Dynaflow ships, and all the places he saw then, and the things he saw on them. Gay Lung, Ambo Danse, Waitrose Two and the Thousand Suns: he had scattered himself like easy money across the Beach stars and down into Radio Bay. He had gone deep in those days. Surfed the Alcubiere warp. Owned one rocket after another; for want of imagination he called them all the *Kino Chicken*. Smuggled this and that. Kept one step ahead of both EMC and the rogue code from his own navigational systems. But in the end he failed at looking after himself, which men like Antoyne often do, and on Santa Muerte inhaled something that deviated both his septum and his sense of where things were. That was it for being a sky pilot. That was it for believing yourself indestructible. What the hell, he had always tried to think, until he wound up in Saudade as Vic Serotonin's gopher: nothing keeps. He was surprised to find himself blinking when he tried to think it now.

'I lost the feel for it.'

Liv Hula studied Antoyne for a minute or two. Then she got up from the table and made him put his pilot jacket on.

'Come with me,' she said.

Ten minutes later they stood on Carver Field, in a mild wind and gathering greenish twilight, with the Halo stars coming out, sharp actinic points at the top of the sky, where their ship, the tubby curves of which now gave back a bargain brass glitter to the scattered halogen lights of the port, stood almost ready to fly. Antoyne put his hands in his pockets. He shrugged.

'So why are we here?' he said.

'To enjoy this heap of shit you had us buy.'

Liv took his hands between both of hers. She made him look in her eyes and understand what she meant. 'Antoyne,' she said, 'I dialled up Irene to meet us here. Later we can get a drink, the three of us, we can celebrate how our lives will soon move on from what they were. You can explain these stupid old-fashioned engines to me one more time. But for now, look up in the sky. See that red giant there? That's McKie, fifteen lights out. We can go there. Or we can go there, to American Polaroid. Or there, You're Worth It. We've got a ship. We can go anywhere now in these million stars!'

'Do you think I don't know places,' he replied, 'or the names of them?'

'The first time you came into my bar I saw that though you had been a pilot all your life, piloting was over for you.' Antoyne tried to pull away from her, angry that she should express such an intuition, even in the middle of an empty field where no one but Antoyne could hear; even though it was only what everyone knew about him already. 'I always understood that,' she said. She kept his hands between hers a moment more. Then she let go, because it came to her that they had already left Saudade a hundred light-years behind them anyway. When she looked up at the ship again, it was black and comforting against the afterglow. 'In the end, Antoyne, what does it matter to you?' she said.

'Because it means I am not anyone any more.'

'None of us is anyone any more. We all lost who we were. But we can all be something else, and I will be so happy to fly this rocket anywhere you suggest, even though you and Irene called it *Nova Swing*, which is the cheapest name I ever heard.'

Antoyne stared at her, and then past her. His eyes lit up.

'Hey,' he said, 'here is Irene now.'

Site Crime accountants had followed the money from the back office of the Club Semiramide to a room off Voigt Street, one of the many DeRaad bolt-holes they were finding and closing daily.

Voigt was full of vehicles and flashing lights. Fire-teams had been deployed. Code jockeys worked on the locked, reinforced door. Quarantine and Hygiene were also in attendance, represented mainly by mid-rank uniforms, exchanging precedence issues by dial-up while they waited with simulated patience for the action to begin. It was the usual scene, except that a tall, heavily tailored young woman with a forearm datableed had overall charge of the operation. They all knew who she was, but no one trusted her, or understood how she had advanced herself so far so quickly. Since the débâcle out on the Lots, they were uneasy working with Site Crime anyway, but their body language and hers confirmed they had no choice.

The lock proved to be mechanical, which no one knew how to finesse. They blew the door off instead.

The teams went in looking confident but feeling nervous. No one wanted to be first at the scene of a big escape. In the event, they were too late. Something weird had happened here, but now it was over. How you would describe it was this: the room stank. It was the same smell, rank and fatty, you got in a quarantine facility, but reduced because it had settled into the fabric – the bare floor, the bed and its foul grey sheets like a disordered shroud, the white walls with their freight of dried human secretions and undecodable graffiti. The room was vacant, but only just. The Site Crime people all understood this. It was a category of fact they were familiar with. Something had lived here until very recently, but how you described that something – or what you understood by the term 'lived' – was very much up to you. If you had been able to stand there twenty-four hours ago, they knew, you might have seen the composite entity formerly known as 'the Weather' leave its hiding place for the last time. The door would have unlocked itself without agency, then closed and locked itself again. There would have been silence outside, except perhaps for the strong, calming sound of summer rain, children laughing and running for shelter, the bang of a door further down Voigt. Those sounds would have had, for a second, too sharp an edge. The woman with the datableed checked out the graffiti. She consulted the discreet codeflows rippling up the inside of her forearm. She shook her head thoughtfully.

'You can finish up here,' she told Hygiene.

She drove herself back to the uptown bureau at the intersection of Uniment and Poe. There she ran nanocam footage of the other big unsolved mystery in her career.

This impeccable record, assembled by the vanished detective himself and projected across the walls by his shadow operators, left no one the wiser. In the year after the death of his wife, Aschemann had continued his investigation of the Neon Heart murders. All the details were there. They summed to zero. He watched, he asked questions and took names, he went by the gates of the noncorporate port and smelled the money and the violence in the air. He went from bar to bar. ('At one time or another,' he told the cameras, with the impish, inturned smile his co-workers had begun to recognise, 'all brave men have seen the sky through bars.') He had himself driven to and from the Bureau every morning and afternoon in a pink Cadillac roadster, 1952. He sat in his office with his feet on the green tin desk, and wrote letters to women, and to Prima. Had he killed her? Was he the Tattoo Murderer? The fact was, the assistant thought, he didn't know, any more than she did. All he knew was what Saudade wanted from him: that he be a detective, and have some plan for how that worked. That year, and every year after, he was like a man reassembling himself – not as something new, but not entirely in his own image either. His sense of guilt dated from Prima's death. But his sense of discontinuity dated from marrying her in the first place.

'All crimes,' she remembered him advising, 'are crimes against continuity – continuity of life, continuity of ownership, systems continuity.'

She sighed.

'Switch this off,' she ordered.

Not yet midnight. It was too soon to visit the tank farm on C-

Street. The office blinds were down, admitting erratically pulsed strips of neon light, rose-pink and a lively poisonous blue. The furniture smelled of authentic furniture polish. Every so often the assistant said something into her dial-up. Or the shadow operators fluttered close, murmuring, 'If you could just sign this, dear.' Or they pulled themselves about on the desk in front of her like grounded bats, through the jumbled papers and stripes of neon, hoping that she would notice them. Data ran down the inside of her arm. It was her office now. She had a major escape to deal with. She had operations of her own. She could wait another hour before she made her next move. She could wait another hour after that. But she was restless and didn't know what to do this minute. Damp winds chased wastepaper across the intersection outside, to where a lost blonde stood in her short white dinner frock, smiling vaguely at the deserted pavement and holding both her shoes in one hand.

Another month passed, the *Nova Swing* completed her refit. They had port authority approval. They had a new paint job. They had a company name, Bulk Haulage, thought up after hours of numb effort by Antoyne; and a corporate mission statement which Irene discovered written on her heart, 'Aim to the Future'. They had hot new upgrades in the drive train. Early one wet autumn day, with rain lashing across Carver Field, Liv Hula heated up the rocket engines, swallowed the pilot interface with the usual combination of optimism and self-disgust, and with Antoyne strapped in the second chair, went all-out for the parking orbit.

'Shit,' she was saying five minutes later, her voice issuing eerily from the ship's speakers. 'It works.'

'Isn't that something,' agreed Antoyne.

They stared out at space a moment, then at each other in wild surmise. Space! Tests on the infrastructure showed what they already knew. 'It's a tub but it actually works!' Scared and elated, anxious, yet somehow secure in their professionalism, they scuttled for home, where they found Irene the Mona looking pale but happy in rose-pink pedal-pushers, refreshing her make-up from her little shiny red urethane vanity case Antoyne remembered so well. 'So, does it work?' she wanted to know. During the take-off, she admitted, she sat in the administration building bar with a White Light sundae and didn't even dare watch. 'But I saw the flash went over everything. You lit up the rain, I got to say that. I had my legs crossed for you.'

'I can't believe it works,' Liv Hula said.

After that, they lived in the ship, all three of them, and made frequent baby steps like this, little journeys into space. Though they had their differences of viewpoint, Liv and Irene got on well together, as long as they could manage Antoyne in their different styles. Antoyne was content to be managed. In the end, it was what he was used to, although he wouldn't admit that to the Mona. There was always something to talk about. Antoyne and Irene talked about their personal development and aspirational goals. Irene and Liv talked about the importance of self-presentation. Liv and Antoyne talked about Vic Serotonin, who had in so many senses brought about their present business venture.

'I always got involved with people stronger than me,' Antoyne told Liv. 'In the end you would have to say it was a pattern. But it can work out well.'

Liv shuddered.

'People like Vic are too strong for everyone around them.'

But when she repeated this opinion to Irene, it received only a sniff. 'Vic Serotonin was as weak a man as I ever saw,' the Mona stated firmly. 'Trust me, I seen a few of them.' She laughed. 'And fucked them all,' she added, 'disincluding Vic himself.'

This conversation occurred about thirty thousand miles off-planet. Without they took her off the beach, Antoyne said, and into the surf, everything was known about the *Nova Swing* that could be known. So now they were going to switch on the Dynaflow drivers for a nanosecond or two and see if she survived that blatant challenge to physics. But before they could do that, they had to fly through this huge secret-looking region of derelict ships they found themselves in. Cutting arcs flared as bright as pSi engines, through a smart fog of nanotech like ionised gas. Tugs were pushing and pulling the enormous rusty hulks about. It was a region of activity stretching away like a shell round the whole planet, an expanding wavefront a thousand, two thousand miles deep. Irene stared out the porthole. She knew human beings a little, she said, and that was hard enough because there were so many of them to know; but she would never cease to be surprised about the endless wonders you saw up here in space.

'What are those things?' she whispered to herself.

'The quarantine orbit,' Liv Hula told her, 'gets bigger every day.'

Straint Street: Edith Bonaventure knocked out Liv Hula's old zinc bar and had a small stage built where it used to be. The floor was ripped up and replaced with black and white tiles. A contractor fixed her some wall panels of faux mahogany in a warm burnt-orange shade. Edith dispensed with the ceiling fans and fitted chandeliers in their place. She had a new bar manufactured from one long block of artfully melted glass, backlit glass shelves behind.

With the change of theme she wanted light. The theme was Edith. It was all of Edith's memorabilia, with which she could now experience a different, much more certain, much more creative relationship. Light was everywhere, gilding the keyboard ivory of fifty or sixty accordions in their deluxe presentation cases lined with every shade of pink from salmon to neotony; glittering as off shallow water from clear resins over maroon and ginger metal-flake finishes; spiking the corner of your eye with reflections and interference patterns of otherworldly weirdness. There were silver buckles on every strap to catch it, and brass-plate rocket ships craftsman-tacked to silky alien wood finishes: but chrome shooting star emblems predominated.

'Because,' Edith would explain, 'that's what I was, in my day.'

Twice a week she got up on stage and played tango standards to a packed house, adding curios and marginal items for variety and to demonstrate the strength in depth of her technique. Some of these – *Lindie's Alcine Rein*, for instance, which was really a polka written for a five-million-year-old instrument no one was sure how to play – grew popular in their own right. Despite the fading ads recovered from venues all over the Halo, which she set to fluttering round the room with news of gigs she had played twenty years before, no one remembered her. Instead, they received her act as something novel and surprising. This hardly mattered to Edith, to whom it seemed enough that she should rediscover herself. She stood dazzled in the spotlight in her straps and taps, her pipeclayed face, her too-tight little costume, perhaps with a cowboy theme that night, and she could hardly tell herself from the thirteen-year-old Accordion Kid in the hologram. She had begun to feel awkward again without the burden of the instrument, as if perpetually released to lean backwards from the waist. She practised new tunes in the afternoon.

Edith was always on the premises, but she didn't keep bar. For that, she had hired Liv's ex-beach bunny, who, it turned out, called himself Nicky Rivera because he liked that upscale brand of luggage. Nicky was a successful choice. He lived quietly above the business. He fixed the sink. His people skills proved pivotal in attracting trade. He helped out with new acts, too: Edith was picking up musicians from all over the city. Within months they were crammed every night.

The crowd was new to the tango, pleased with itself because it learned so quickly when to cheer and when to be rapt. Its signature was high-end cocktails, honey-coloured fur; its underwear, Nicky could confirm, was from Uoest. It was a slumming crowd, and if she hoped to gentrify the street by her efforts, Edith could only be disappointed. But as a result of her investment in herself, the reputation of her venture grew out beyond Straint, and even Saudade itself, out into the Beach Stars and across the Halo, and she had to be content with that. Not many people get two chances to be new. She stopped playing the gates of the corporate port. Instead, she placed her own ads with the rickshaw companies, and later with the tourist lines themselves.

Sometimes the applause at the end of the evening caused her some tears. Then she would whisper, 'This encore I would like to dedicate to the one who meant most to me in this life, Emil, my father: *Le Tango du Chat*, which he particularly enjoyed,' which was how Liv Hula's bar came by its new name.

One afternoon near Christmas, Liv herself could be found sitting at a table with the Accordion Kid, drinking vodka and Brilliantine, no ice. Out on Straint the chopshops were closed early. Little hard gusts of wind ran up and down the street driving the flurries of snow before them; while inside, on the dusty unlit stage, three teen sisters in sequinned one-pieces cast sidelong glances at Nicky the barkeep, who sat on the edge of the stage in conversation with their manager. 'Sun and shade sometimes seem like equal things,' Liv heard him say. 'Both, in a way, kind of illuminating?'

At this the Accordion Kid, her sensibilities honed by thirty years in bars, smiled and closely watched Liv Hula's face.

'So now how do you like what I did?' she said.

Liv wasn't sure. It was Christmas. It was coming dark. Next day she would be out on the cusp of a new life, a rocket jockey delivering unwaybilled cargoes to ports she didn't know on planets she was the last to hear of; some of those cargoes would be more clandestine than others. The first time Liv came back to the Tango of the Cat, some weeks before, she had been ready for change, but also nervous what she would find. When she went inside, ten years of her life tucked themselves away in an instant, like the theoretical dimensions of long-ago cosmology. This was how life went. A single moment seemed to extend forever, then suddenly you were snapped out of it. The forward motion of time stretched whatever rubbery glue-like substance had fixed you there until it failed catastrophically. You weren't the person you were before you got trapped; you weren't the person you were while you were trapped: the merciless thing about it, Liv discovered, was that you weren't someone entirely different either. Pondering these notions, she heard herself say:

'It seems very successful.'

'I promised you I wouldn't be sentimental,' Edith said, and fetched Liv another drink.

They were joined by Irene and Fat Antoyne, whose first time it was at Le Tango. A person could have mixed feelings, was Irene's belief, about returning to a previous stamping ground. She had forgotten, she had to own, what Black Cat White Cat looked like in those past days; though it would always stay mixed up in a part of her life she could not find it in her heart to reject. The fat man, meanwhile, rubbernecked around, then fell into a game of Three Dick Hughie with Nicky the barkeep, so no one knew what he thought. Night drew on. After a few more drinks they left for Carver as a threesome. It was a pity, Edith said as she walked Liv Hula to the door, that it had been too early in the day to get an idea of what a good trade she did.

'Though I never knew it so slow, even at this time.'

When they had gone, calling to one another, 'Hey, this snow!' in receding voices down the street, she picked up her instrument of choice at that time – a worn old three-row diatonic in pearlescent mint-blue, with a contrasting bellows which revealed in its open phase the ace of hearts, or perhaps a welcoming vulva – and played a few notes. That didn't seem to suit her. She refused another drink. She picked up one of Emil's notebooks she always kept by her, and leafed through it. Five o' clock, a tall woman entered the bar and sat down at a table by the door.

This woman had blonde hair cropped down to nothing much, and a fuck-off way of moving only the heavily tailored can achieve. Some kind of datableed ran oriental-looking ideograms down her arm. She parked a pink 1952 Cadillac roadster at the kerb outside. Known to everyone as a police detective operating out of what used to be called Site Crime, she was a frequent visitor at Le Tango. You also saw her at the fights. She knew the talent, she knew their chops. She knew Straint. She would come by early and stay late. Her order: double Black Heart rocks. She would stare around at the clientele as if they puzzled and amused her in equal parts. This evening she sent Nicky the barkeep away with a smile which said she would probably see him again soon; then nodded over at Edith Bonaventure.

'Good book?' she said. 'You're always reading it.'

It was a busy night in the end. They had a guest two-piece over from some surf bar down on the Corniche, an old man who'd had himself Zipped to look like Samuel Beckett, a young man in a suit a size too big, keyboards and saxophone, bebop jazz, complicit, clever deconstructions of simple popular tunes, stuff Edith didn't get, but a clear winner with the corporate clientele who came in once a week to hold shouted conversations and spill Giraffe Beer. Three a.m. it was all over. The two-piece packed itself away, took its money, melted into the night. Dry snow continued to blow up and down the street outside. It didn't settle. After the barkeep said goodnight and went upstairs, only Edith and the police detective remained. It worked out like that most nights. They sat at their separate tables. Every so often one of them might look up and smile at the other, or go to the door and stare along Straint Street towards the event site. A rocket from the noncorporate port cut the sky like scissors.

Acknowledgements

A version of Chapter One was published at Amazon.com under the title 'Tourism'; a few paragraphs of Chapter Ten appeared in *Locus* as part of an essay. I'm indebted to Luis Rodrigues, who made me think about *saudade*; Jukka Halme for the Finnish tango; Zali Krishna, not just a webmaster, but an eye across the manuscript; and Philippa McEwan, who loaned me her house to write in. The Phillips family proved as kind and supportive as ever.

Turn the page for a preview of
M. John Harrison's final part of the
Kefahuchi Tract sequence, *Empty Space*

ONE

Organs

Anna Waterman heard two cats fighting all evening. At ten o'clock she went out into the garden and called in the family tom. A decade or so ago, her daughter Marnie, age thirteen and already unfathomable, had named this animal 'James'. Late summer displayed a greenish afterglow at the bottom of a sky full of stars. Anna's was a long garden, perhaps fifty yards by twenty, with lichenous apple trees in unmown grass and a leaning summerhouse which looked like something from a 1970s Russian film – falling apart, surrounded by overgrown flowerbeds, filled with those things you discard but don't throw away. The flowerbeds had an unhealthy vitality. Every year, tended or not, they produced dense mixtures of indigenous weeds, wild flowers and – since the warming of the mid-2000s – exotics with large petals and fleshy leaves, blown in as seeds from who knew where.

'James!' Anna called.

James didn't respond, but neither were there sounds of him killing or being killed. Anna was encouraged.

She found him in the base of the hedge at the end of the garden, where he had something cornered among the roots and dry earth. He was nosing it about, tapping at it with a front paw, purring to himself. She stroked him and he ignored her.

'You old fool,' she said. 'What have you found now?'

Some gelid bits and pieces loosely scattered with soil. Except for the size and colour, they looked like internal organs. They had the swelling curve of pig's kidney. There was a faint glow to them. Anna picked one up and dropped it immediately – it was warm to the touch. The cat, delighted, sprang upon it and knocked it about.

'How disgusting you are, James,' Anna told him.

Later she put on Marigold gloves, slid two or three of the objects into a plastic bag and carried them back to the house. There, she emptied them into a glass dish. Slumped on the worktop they looked like any offal, unused to supporting themselves in the world. Their colours resembled the flasks of liquid you could still see in the windows of pharmacies when Anna was young – blues, greens and a rich permanganate – now faded and a touch acidic under the halogen lights. Anna removed her best Wusthof knife from the block and then, nerve failing her, put it back again. She stared at the contents of the dish from different angles, then went to telephone Marnie.

'Why are you calling?' Marnie said, after five minutes.

'I suppose I just wanted to tell you how lucky I'd been. In all sorts of things.'

At a glance, Anna knew, this seemed absurd. She had been anorexic throughout her twenties; twice a failed suicide. Her first husband, Michael, who wasn't much better, had walked into the sea one night off Mann Hill Beach south of Boston. They never found his body. He had been a brilliant man but unbalanced. 'He was a brilliant man,' she would tell people, 'who took things too much to heart.' But since then she had remarried, borne Marnie, lived a life. She had made quite a nice life with Marnie's father, first in London and then in this quiet, expensive house near the river. It wouldn't have suited Michael. Living had to be an effort for him; a kind of punishment.

'Neither of us knew how to live,' she said now.

'Anna—'

'He had some difficulties.'

Marnie received this in silence.

'You know,' Anna said. 'Sex difficulties. Your father was much better at that side of things.'

'Anna, that's more information than I need.'

Marnie had been conceived out of both guilt and relief at losing Michael – literally, misplacing him – that night on Mann Hill Beach. Confused, Anna had flown home to London and fucked the first kind person she found. That was the only way to put it, especially from this distance. She had no regrets, although at times the memory made her feel she ought to be especially nice to Marnie. Now she had a sudden surprised recollection of Michael leaning over her in the dark, and one of them saying something like, 'Sparks! Sparks in everything!'

'Anna? Anna, I have to go now. It's late. It's midnight.'

'Is it, dear?'

'You've got Dr Alpert tomorrow,' Marnie reminded her.

'I'm afraid I've lost the details of that appointment,' said Anna in a vague but mutinous way.

'Good job I kept a note of them, then.'

Anna, suddenly overwhelmed with anxiety and love, said, 'Oh, Marnie, I do hope you enjoy sex. I'd hate to think of you missing out on something so lovely.'

'I'll drive you to the station in the morning. Goodnight, Anna.'

Why *was* I phoning? Anna asked herself. When no answer came, she went to the kitchen door and looked out. Mist had pooled two or three feet deep in the rough pasture between the garden and the river. Above it, she could just make out a line of willows. She called the cat; offered him rabbit-flavoured food; took herself to bed, where her dream woke her as usual at ten past four in the morning, soaked to the skin and with a kind of leaden buzzing in her ears. It was less a sound, as she often tried to explain to Dr Alpert, than a feeling. 'It's a feeling from the dream,' she would say. It was a physical sensation. 'I'm not even sure it's me who's feeling it.'

She struggled out of bed, weary and ill, and went downstairs to get water. Grey light was creeping in round the edges of the kitchen blinds. She thought she might have another look at the organs – or whatever they were – in the dish, but they'd gone. James could easily have jumped up on the counter and eaten them, but Anna felt they'd simply melted away. There was a drop of liquid left. It looked enough like ordinary water to be tipped down the sink. She decided not to use the dish for food again.

Every night since Michael walked into the sea, Anna had gone out to call in a cat, fetch a chair from the lawn to save it from the damp, look up at the stars. Wherever she lived it was the same. Each night it had been the same dream.

She thought: I was phoning for someone to talk to.

Next morning she truanted on Dr Alpert, changed trains at London Victoria and made her way down through the postal codes until, the other side of Balham, she thought she recognised the way the streets curled and dovetailed across the swell of a hill. 'Orchid Nails', read the signs outside the station: 'Minty Pearls Dental Clinic'. Anna descended from the train and wandered thoughtfully along staring into the windows of empty houses. She had no plan. She favoured quiet residential avenues and a particular kind of four-bedroom mock-Tudor, with laurels and a slip of driveway to one side of its front garden. The shabbier a place looked, the more likely it was to hold her attention. By mid afternoon she thought she might be in Sydenham Hill. She had covered miles under the enamel light, trespassed on the hard standings of a dozen middle class homes. She was exhausted. Her ankles hurt. She was lost. It wasn't the first time she had done this.

Sydenham Hill turned out, in point of fact, to be Norbiton, a place named after an imaginary suburb in an Edwardian novel. Anna sat down with a cup of tea in the station café and emptied her bag on to the table. It was full of the usual silt – ends of make-up, a single glove, an address book bloated with the names of people she never saw anymore, her phone with its flat battery. There were receipts folded into very small squares, foreign coins and coins no longer in circulation. There was an old outboard computer drive: this, she took up.

It was perhaps two inches by three, with curved, organic-looking edges, its smooth dull surface interrupted at one end by a line of firewire ports – one of those objects which, new and exciting in its day, now looked as dated as a cigarette case. Michael had left it with her, along with some instructions, putting his warm hand over Anna's – they were in a railway café just like this one – and urging her:

'You will remember, won't you?'

All she could remember now was being afraid. When you're afraid of everything, especially each other, you have to walk away; consign each other to the world.

Anna had arrived in Norbiton between trains. She drank a second cup of tea and stared out with vague good will at the empty platform, where everything had a thick fresh coat of paint. After about twenty minutes an old man was helped into the café by some railway staff. He had outlived himself. His bald brown head seemed too big for his neck; his underlip, the colour of uncooked liver, drooped in exhausted surprise at finding himself still there. They sat him at Anna's table, where he banged her feet and legs about with his stick, shoved the contents of her bag carelessly across the table towards her, and, as soon as he was settled, began eating salmon sandwiches directly from a paper bag. His hands were ropy with veins, the skin over them shiny and slack. He ate greedily but at the same time with a curious lack of interest, as if his body remembered food but he didn't. As he ate he whispered to himself. After some minutes he put the bag down, leaned across the table and tapped Anna's hand sharply.

'Ow,' said Anna.

'Nothing is real,' he said.

'I'm sorry?'

'Nothing is real. Do you understand? There are only contexts. And what do they context?' He gave Anna an intent look; breathed heavily a few times through his mouth. 'More contexts, of course!' Anna, who had no idea how to respond, stared angrily out of the window. After a moment he said, as if he hadn't already spoken to her, 'I have to get on the next train. I wonder if you would be kind enough to help me?'

'I wouldn't, no,' Anna said, collecting up her things.

It was almost dark when she arrived home. Marnie had left irritable messages on the answerphone. 'Pick up, Anna. I'm really very cross with you. It's not the first time you've done this.' Anna made herself an omelette and ate it in the kitchen standing up, while she rehearsed what she would say to Marnie. The last of the daylight was fading out of the sky. James the cat jumped up on to the kitchen top and begged. Absent-minded with guilt, Anna gave him more of the omelette than she had intended to.

'I forgot to go,' she repeated stubbornly to herself. 'Marnie, I simply forgot.'

Later, she thought she saw a glimmer of light in the summer-house. Thin river mist had lapped up past the garden hedge and now hung between the apple trees. The grass was damp. Everything smelled sharply of itself, including the cat who – his faith in the generosity of the world confirmed – ran ahead of Anna with his tail up until he found something to interest him in the hedge. Anna pulled at the summerhouse door. Junk lay about in the dark: two leather chairs, Marnie's old Pashley bicycle, a carpet someone had brought back from India. Rooting about under the window, she burst a cardboard box, from which spilled a quantity of orna-ments, photograph frames, bits of china and silk, shellac records – family stuff of Tim's going all the way back to the 1920s, stuff she had been meaning to clear out since he died. Each generation, she thought, leaves itself scattered in a kind of alluvial fan across post-codes and sideboards, inside wardrobes, jukeboxes, secondhand shops and places like this.

'Titanium,' Michael had said as he closed her hands round the computer drive: 'Today's popular metal.'

All those years ago she had promised to return it to a colleague of his in South London. She remembered the man's name: Brian Tate; but though she remembered what his house looked like, she couldn't really remember where it was. If she saw it she would recognise it. Something awful had happened, or was about to happen, the last time she was there. We never went back, she told herself. I know that. We were too afraid.